SHIRLEY TEMPLE IS MISSING

Also by Kelly Durham

The War Widow

Berlin Calling

Wade's War

The Reluctant Copilot

The Movie Star and Me

Hollywood Starlet

Temporary Alliance

Unforeseen Complications

Also by Kathryn Smith

*The Gatekeeper: Missy LeHand, FDR and
the Untold Story of the
Partnership That Defined a Presidency*

*A Necessary War: Anderson County
Residents Remember World War II*

SHIRLEY TEMPLE IS MISSING

A Missy LeHand Mystery

To Molly

**Kelly Durham and
Kathryn Smith**

Kathryn Smith

ISBN-13: 978-1983873904

ISBN-10: 198387390X

First Edition

March 2018

In memory of Missy and Shirley,

two phenomenal women who did their
jobs with grace and style!

PROLOGUE

May 1934
Washington, D.C.

"Mrs. Nesbitt outdid herself tonight," President Roosevelt said as he pushed his wheelchair away from the table in the private dining room of the White House. "I didn't think it was possible to ruin a meat loaf, but she did it. Assuming there was any meat in that loaf."

"Now, Franklin, she does her best," admonished the First Lady, coming to the defense of Henrietta Nesbitt, the supervisor of the White House kitchens. "We've got to demonstrate to the American people how to stretch their nickels and dimes, and sometimes that means supplementing the meat with a bit of bread."

"I don't mind supplementing the meat," the President protested. "But that tasted like beef-flavored bread!"

"You need to be watching your weight anyway," Mrs. Roosevelt said, eyeing his waistline. "Well, I'm off to my study. I've got a stack of letters to answer before I can get to sleep, and then I leave tomorrow for West Virginia to tour the women's prison. I'll give you a full report when I return."

"I have no doubt, Babs," FDR said. "You are the best eyes and ears a president could ask for." His own eyes twinkled behind his pince-nez glasses. "When anyone asks where you are, I can say, 'She's in prison.' Of course, the next question will be, 'What for?'"

The exchange had been watched with quiet amusement by the only other person at the table that night, Franklin Roosevelt's long-time private secretary, Marguerite Alice LeHand, known to all as "Missy." A pretty woman in her late 30s with striking blue-gray eyes and silver-streaked dark hair, she had worked for FDR for more than a dozen years and was considered a member of the Roosevelt family. Marguerite had a small suite of rooms on the third floor of the White House and took most of her evening meals in the private dining room with the Roosevelts and whoever had been invited to join them. The guest list could include any of their five children and members of their extended families, New Deal officials, members of Congress, or someone Mrs. Roosevelt had met during the day and impulsively invited to join them. On one occasion, the guests had included a hitch-hiker she picked up while driving her convertible home from a speech. The Secret Service had a fit.

Once Mrs. Roosevelt had bustled off, Missy turned her wide blue eyes and wider smile to her boss. "I've got a surprise for you, F.D.," she said in her throaty voice. "The new Shirley Temple movie everyone is talking about is ready to go in the movie projector in your study, and Ambassador Bullitt sent a large jar of caviar in the diplomatic pouch from Russia. I even found time today to run out and buy us a box of real Ritz crackers!"

A huge smile lit up the President's face. "Missy, what would I do without you?"

Half an hour later, they were settled in the President's oval study, which adjoined his bedroom on the second floor. It was a cozy room, for all its size. The walls were decorated with the naval prints FDR collected, and there were stacks of books, papers, and other clutter covering every surface. A portable screen had been set up against one wall, and the President was happily ensconced in his favorite chair, a martini garnished with olives in his hand and a plate of caviar and Ritz crackers at his elbow. Mrs. Nesbitt had sent up a bowl of popcorn when she got wind they were watching a movie, but half the popcorn was too blackened to eat, and the rest of the kernels were un-popped.

"Incredible," FDR muttered, examining the dismal contents of the bowl. "She's managed to both undercook and overcook popcorn. Popcorn!"

"Ready?" asked Missy.

"Perfectly ready, Missy," FDR said. "Let's see what all the fuss is about this little Shirley Temple."

Missy turned off the lights and expertly flipped the projector switch. Soon they were watching the credits for the new Fox Film *Stand Up and Cheer*. The first scene opened in the White House, where several female secretaries were excitedly anticipating the arrival of Broadway producer Lawrence Cromwell.

"Hmmm," Missy whispered. "Doesn't look like anyone on my staff."

Next, a small plane landed on the grounds of the Capitol and a handsome man emerged, the much-anticipated producer. In short order, he was being ushered into the Oval Office.

"Not very realistic," the President chuckled. "My desk is much more cluttered than his. And where are all my little donkeys?"

The camera was shooting behind the "president," so Missy and FDR couldn't see his face, but his remarks sounded oddly familiar. Outlining the problems facing the nation due to the Great Depression, he told Cromwell, "We are endeavoring to pilot the ship past that most threatening of all rocks—fear! The government now proposes to dissolve that destructive rock in a gale of laughter. To that end, it has created a new cabinet office—Secretary of Amusement."

"I wish I'd thought of that!" FDR said. "That would have been a nice cap to the Hundred Days."

"You did plenty in the Hundred Days!" Missy chided him. "Even God rested now and then."

In the next scene, Cromwell was meeting with his twelve assistant secretaries, including the one female appointee, Mary Adams.

"I'm glad he has a woman on his team," Missy said.

"And she doesn't wear those funny hats like Frances Perkins," observed the President, who had been known to pass Missy notes making fun of the labor secretary's hats during Cabinet meetings

When Cromwell told his staff that Congress had appropriated $100 million for the Department of Amusement's first year, FDR let out a low whistle.

Shirley Temple Is Missing

"Missy!" he said. "That's ten times what we got from Congress for the Civilian Conservation Corps!" The program that sent unemployed young men into the national forests to plant trees and make park improvements was one of the President's favorites. He liked to hear the CCC referred to as "Roosevelt's Tree Army."

But the plot thickened. A coterie of bearish Wall Street speculators vowed to undermine the new program with "a campaign of ridicule" on the radio. "We'll put up millions in cash to back our scheme," declared their leader. Meanwhile, on Capitol Hill, grumpy senators railed against the Department of Amusement for "squandering millions of the taxpayers' money."

"Sounds familiar," FDR said, inserting another cigarette into his ivory holder. "Republicans."

"And some southern Democrats," Missy added.

And then, Shirley Temple appeared. She was sitting in Mary Adams's waiting room with her film father, the actor James Dunn, a dark sailor cap perched on her blonde curls.

"Oh," breathed Missy, "she's adorable! Have you ever seen such a cute little girl?"

"Look at that smile," the President said. "And those dimples!"

The pair sat transfixed as Shirley and her screen father tap-danced together, backed by a bevy of chorus girls, to the song "Baby, Take a Bow." Shirley wore a short polka dot dress, stiffened with petticoats. Her tiny feet flew, her curls bounced, and her incandescent smile never faltered.

The movie continued, a mish-mash of musical and comedy acts interspersed with dramatic scenes involving Cromwell, but concluded with the welcome news that the country's mood had been lifted, the Great Depression had ended, and full employment had been reached. Gleeful farmers with pitchforks, miners in helmets with head lamps, Pullman porters balancing trays, and uniformed nurses sang, "The worst is over, here comes the clover." Little Shirley led a contingent of girl drummers, flashing her bright smile.

"Wow," FDR said, exhaling a stream of smoke as the credits rolled. "You know, Missy, during this Depression, when the spirit of the people is lower than at any other time, it is a splendid thing that for just fifteen cents an American can go to a movie and look at the smiling face of a baby and forget his troubles."

Missy rose from her chair, stretching her arms as she walked over to the projector and then turned on the lights. She grinned at him over her shoulder. "That sounds like a line you can use at your next press conference," she said.

"You know me too well, Missy," he laughed. "Why not? Movies work their magic for very little money."

"Well, I know I've had a lot of fun with my home movie camera," Missy said. "Maybe I'll get a chance to go out to Hollywood and tour some studios, see how it's done. I'd love to meet that little girl!"

FDR ground out his cigarette. "That would be grand, Missy. I've always wanted to take a fishing cruise departing from the West Coast, through the Panama Canal.

Shirley Temple Is Missing

If I can work that out, you can come along on the train and then stay in California and do those tours."

"F.D.," she said, "what would I do without you?"

CHAPTER 1

September 25, 1935

Los Angeles

The pebble sailed wide of the target.

"You're moving your arm," Andy Archie said, squatting next to the curly-haired little girl with the slingshot. She was wearing a nineteenth-century period costume for her current role in *The Littlest Rebel*. She played Virgie, the pampered daughter of a plantation owner during the Civil War, and today was wearing a beribboned pink dress with a hoop skirt, lace pantalets, and white stockings and shoes for a birthday party scene. Andy knew to be careful during these breaks between scenes. If he allowed her to get dirty, it could mean trouble, maybe even getting him kicked off the set.

"If you want to hit that bottle, you've got to keep your arm still. Watch how I do it." Andy knelt, took the slingshot in his right hand, picked up another pebble, and positioned it in the leather pouch. He held his right arm straight out from his shoulder. "See? Now watch that can." Andy nodded toward a dented baked beans can he'd set next to an empty Coca-Cola bottle on top of the fence. He pulled back on the pouch, tightening the bands, his red hair glinting in the morning sunlight. Holding his arm steady, he let go of the pouch. The projectile zipped toward the can, striking it with a satisfying "plink" and knocking it off the fence post.

"The trick is to keep everything still until you let go." He handed the slingshot back. "Try it again, Shirley."

"I bet I hit it this time!" Shirley exclaimed, pursing her lips in determination. Andy would have bet so too. He'd seen the little girl work—who on the Twentieth Century-Fox lot had not?—and knew she was a quick study. She always knew her lines and she was always ready to perform, unusual for many of the adult actors he'd worked with around the Fox lot. The fact that she was only six years old made her all the more remarkable.

"Here," Andy said, sitting back on his heel and handing her another pebble. "Nice and steady, now."

Shirley held the Y-shaped weapon in her left hand, her arm extended straight out. She released the pouch and the small pebble streaked toward the bottle. A near miss.

She pouted, her arms falling to her sides. "I'm never going to hit that ol' bottle!"

"Sure, you will. You've just got to practice, that's all. It's like when I have to fall off a horse or pretend I'm in a fight. We practice those things until we can do them right every time—just like you practice your tap dances. Let's try again." Andy handed her another pebble.

Shirley spread her stocky legs and flexed her shoulders. She straightened her arm and locked her elbow.

"Nice and smooth now," Andy coached. "Let it go easy."

Shirley pulled the pouch back slowly and then released it. The pebble flew toward the bottle and glanced off its neck, causing it to wobble.

"You hit it!" Andy chuckled.

Shirley laughed out loud. "I hit it!" She threw her arms around Andy's neck. "You're the best slingshot teacher in the whole world!"

"I think I'll call you 'Sure Shot' for short!"

"Shirley!" Donald, the assistant director was approaching, a clipboard held in one hand. It was Donald's job to make sure cast members—featured players, extras, stuntmen--were all in their places when the director was ready to roll the camera. "Time for the next scene. This is the one in which Sally Ann gives you your birthday present. Ready?"

"Aw, I was just getting good, wasn't I, Andy?"

"You certainly were, Shirley."

"'Sure Shot,' remember?" she said, giving him a wink and her famous smile with the unusual dimples between her lower lips and chin.

"You certainly were, Sure Shot!" Andy laughed.

The assistant director took Shirley Temple's small hand in his and walked with her back over to the set, the broad front porch of a plantation mansion. Andy dusted off his Union-blue cavalry trousers and headed toward the horse corral.

CHAPTER 2

September 26, 1935

Los Angeles

Joan Roswell took a deep breath, straightened the feather on her green felt hat and pushed through the doors to the city room of the Los Angeles *Standard*. Her senses were overwhelmed by the staccato clacking of a dozen typewriters and the stagnant layer of cigarette, cigar, and pipe smoke floating at eye level. Long rows of desks stretched from the door she'd just entered all the way to the water cooler by the window overlooking First Street.

"Hey, Joanie! What's cookin'?" Al Lister asked as she strode by. "Any leads on the Lindbergh kidnapping?" Al laughed at his joke, drawing chuckles from a few of the nearby reporters and editors—all of them men.

Joan stopped, smiled, and leaned over the corner of Lister's desk. "It was Hauptmann. He was sentenced eight months ago. Don't you read the papers? Is Billy in his office?" Al's gaze had drifted down from Joan's green eyes to her attractive figure, lingering on her bust. "Up here, big boy," Joan said with a patronizing smile. "Is he?"

17

Al focused on her emerald green eyes and smiled. "Yeah. I think so. But be careful. He's in a real mood today. Jacky fell over drunk right after lunch, so Billy's got to finish the last two-thirds of his column plus lay out the city section and—" Al looked up at the large wall clock at the far end of the room, "—he's got to get that done by four-thirty. Probably not the best time to go barging in. Why don't you sit down and tell me your troubles? Maybe I can help you."

"That's so sweet of you, dear," Joan said, still smiling and dragging an empty chair over from the next desk. She sat down and leaned forward, as if to share a confidence. Al leaned in closer, enjoying Joan's pleasant orange and jasmine scent as well as her appealing looks. "You see, dear," Joan said in a soft voice, looking down at her gloved hands, "I've been dealing with this nasty yeast infection and I need some advice on just how to handle it."

Al pulled back as though he'd been stuck with a cattle prod. "Well, uh, I think, maybe Billy's your best bet after all. He's got three daughters, you know." Al exaggerated a look toward the back corner of the city room. "Yeah, there. He's just hanging up the phone."

Joan stood and smoothed the wrinkles from her light grey skirt. "Maybe next time, darling." She smiled and winked and then resumed her march between the desks until she came to the glass-walled office of city editor William Bryce. Billy had been the paper's city editor for ten years, having worked his way up the ladder from stringer to reporter to assistant editor. He knew most of the city's precinct captains, clergymen, elected officials, movers and shakers—and all of the bartenders. He could write copy that would tear your heart out or make you laugh out loud. And he could be a real son-of-a-bitch.

Joan tugged on the sleeves of her gray suit jacket, frowning at the worn cuff on the right one, knocked twice, and then entered as though she'd been invited. Contrary to what Al had told her, Billy was still on the phone, his office filled with stacks of old newspapers, piles of story drafts, and at least three overflowing ash trays that Joan could see among the clutter.

"...I know you want it by four o'clock," Billy was saying into the phone. "I wanted it by three o'clock. I didn't get my wish and you aren't going to get yours either and the longer you keep me on this damned phone the later it's going to be before you get it at all. Are you following me, Luther?" Joan stood silently, wishing that her timing was better, but a working girl had to do what she had to do. "Luther? Hello? Damn it!" Billy slammed the earpiece back on its cradle.

He looked up at Joan with tired brown eyes and growled, "What do you want? Make it fast. I'm already out of time."

"Sorry to bother you, Billy, but I need a little favor."

"Favors are considered between 9 and 10 a.m."

"You don't come in until eleven."

"Exactly. What do you want?"

"I'm following a lead over at Pacific Pictures. One of Abe Baum's stars apparently got caught with his pants down over at the mayor's big fundraiser last week."

"Great. So, bring me a story." Billy turned back to the sheet of paper in the center of his desk and picked up a blue pencil. "Until then, beat it."

"Billy," Joan said, crossing the small office and perching on the corner of his desk where he could get a nice view of her legs. "I need a little advance."

Billy snorted without looking up and made a mark on the paper. "What's the matter, Joan? Reporting a little tougher than actress-ing? Aren't you still doing some work for Zanuck over at Fox?"

"I haven't gotten any work over there—or anywhere else except here—in two months. I'm down to my last two nickels, Billy. Can you advance me ten bucks? Please."

Billy slapped the pencil on the desk and looked up. "I told you when you came here that you'd have to earn your way in. You've got to bring me stories, kid. This isn't a charity and it isn't an internship. I don't have time to train you. Neither do the rest of the boys." Billy tipped his head toward the rows of desks outside his office.

"I can do this, Billy. I know I can. I'm good. You've just got to give me a little time."

"Take all the time you need, kid, just don't expect handouts. Go out there and get me a good story. That's the currency in this business. Find out who's hiding what. Who's sleeping where he shouldn't? Who's taking what doesn't belong to her? What public employee is driving a nice new Cadillac? C'mon, Joan. Give me something to work with! Go stake out the train station or something. Find out who's going to Tijuana for a quickie divorce or discreet medical help. You told me you were the hardest working actress in Hollywood. Show me some of that gumption!"

"Billy," Joan hesitated. "I haven't eaten since yesterday morning."

Billy frowned, then shook his head and reached into his pants pocket. "I'm getting soft in my old age," he muttered. "Here, here's two dollars."

Joan took the silver coins and squeezed them in her hand. "Thanks, Billy," she said, standing. "You won't regret this."

"I already regret it! Now get out of here. I got work to do." Joan smiled and blew him a kiss as she slipped back through his office door. "And bring me a story!"

CHAPTER 3

September 28, 1935

Los Angeles

"What happened to your leg, Andy?" Shirley asked, staring at the ice-filled towel the stunt man was holding on his ankle. He was sitting in the shade of an oak tree, his pink, swollen ankle resting across a cavalry saddle. She was wearing a short-sleeved dress with a hoop skirt today, her curly blonde hair framing chubby cheeks and a smile known to millions of movie-goers the world over.

"I turned it, Shirley, in that last scene where we chased you and John down in the wagon. I was getting off my horse, but just as I was about to hit the ground, she shied off to the side and I lost my balance. My foot got caught up in the stirrup."

"Gee! Does it hurt?"

"A little. I can't walk on it right now, that's for sure."

Shirley put her hands on her hips and in her most authoritative voice said, "Well, you've just got to be more careful next time, Andy!"

"That's what Donald said." Andy grimaced, shifting his weight and glancing over to his right. "Speak of the devil." Shirley followed his gaze and giggled as the assistant director approached with his clipboard by his side.

"We're ready for the next scene, Shirley," he said, squatting down to address his star at eye level. "Why don't you head back over to your mother and let Andy rest up, huh?"

"Sure thing! See ya, Andy!" Shirley smiled, winked, and skipped back toward the camera set-up where her ever-present mother, Gertrude Temple, and the director were standing watching her.

"How is it?" Donald asked, pointing toward Andy's ankle.

"Tender. I don't think it's busted, but it won't support my weight, that's for sure."

"Hard luck."

A lot harder for me than for you, Andy thought. *When I don't work, I don't get paid. When I don't get paid, my kids don't eat.* "Listen, Donald, I can't ride for a few days, but I could take any part where I could be still, you know, sitting or leaning. I can't afford not to work."

"You can't afford to do any more damage to that ankle either." Donald flipped over a couple of sheets on his clipboard. "The only extras we need for the next couple of days have to stand on the boardwalk and watch the dance number. Not sure that'd work for you right now." He let the clipboard fall back to his side. "Tell you what. You take a couple of days to rest up and when you can stand for more than a few minutes, come back and I'll put you in the prison scenes as one of the Union guards."

"When you filming those?"

Another quick look at the clipboard and Donald replied, "Next Thursday."

"Donald!" the director shouted, waving toward his assistant.

"Gotta go. Take it easy and let that thing heal." Donald patted Andy on the shoulder and trotted back toward the camera and the next sequence of shots.

Great. Andy thought. *Just great!*

"What happened?" Iris asked as Andy limped through the door of their garage apartment carrying his left shoe in his hand. His freckled face was paler than normal. He slumped into the worn, upholstered chair and sighed.

"I sprained my ankle. My horse started just as I was dismounting. The studio doctor said to keep it iced and elevated. We got any ice?"

Iris stepped over to the small icebox and chipped off a shard of ice. She wrapped it in a thin dish towel and handed it to Andy. "Here. Did you get paid?"

"Yeah," Andy grimaced as he placed the towel on his swollen ankle and then propped it on a stack of old film magazines. He reached into his pocket and pulled out six dollars. "I only got credit for half a day. We've got to make that last 'cause I won't be able to work again until next week at the soonest."

Iris eyed the greenbacks. "Dennis needs shoes."

"He needs to eat worse than he needs new shoes," Andy said, glaring at his wife.

"He can't go to school barefoot!"

"He can wear my shoes. I won't be needing them. He can stuff newspaper into the toes to make them fit. Listen, Iris, we've got to make that last." Andy nodded toward the money. "I begged a part in another scene, but it doesn't shoot until next week—and it'll only be at extras wages, not stunt wages. We're going to have to be tight to get us through the next couple of weeks. All right?"

"Half of this gets swallowed up by rent on Monday. That doesn't leave us much to eat on."

"Can you take in any washing or sewing?"

"If I can find some needs doing." Iris perched next to Andy on the arm of the chair. She sniffed. "But you had enough to stop at Harmon's and get a beer?"

"Medicinal purposes."

"Does it hurt?" she asked, combing her fingers through his red hair.

"It throbs." But it wasn't the physical pain causing Andy the most discomfort.

CHAPTER 4

October 1, 1935

San Diego

Missy LeHand and her assistant, Grace Tully, stood at the rail of the USS *Dewey* waving their handkerchiefs at their departing boss until the USS *Houston* was a speck on the horizon in San Diego harbor. Then they turned, linked arms, and simultaneously laughed.

"Here's to a well-earned vacation!" said Grace, grinning and showing her deep dimples.

"For the Boss, or us?" Missy asked mischievously, arching a dark eyebrow.

"Both!" said Grace. "I love the man, but, gosh, it's good to get some time away."

It was indeed a well-earned vacation. Besides putting in long days at the White House as the chief secretaries of President Franklin Delano Roosevelt, the two women had just spent a long week on a cross-country train with their boss. They had boarded the presidential train at Washington's Union Station on September 26, joining President Roosevelt, his wife Eleanor, and seventy-five other staff and dignitaries for what amounted to a campaign trip thinly disguised as an inspection tour. After traveling from Washington to Chicago, they had been greeted by huge, adoring crowds and brass bands in Nebraska, Utah, and Wyoming. On September 30, the President had dedicated the new Boulder Dam in Nevada, declaring, "This morning I came, I saw, and I was conquered as anyone would be who sees for the first time this great feat of mankind."

FDR was impressed by engineering, but his first love was the water. Their arrival at San Diego had been an occasion for a ceremonial review of the Pacific Fleet, complete with a mock battle that the President and a few close aides had watched from the USS *Houston*. Mrs. Roosevelt, Missy, and Grace, with a large contingent of guests, had watched from aboard the *Dewey*. From there, FDR and a small coterie of men had departed for a long fishing cruise that would take them through the Panama Canal. The plan was for an arrival at the port of Charleston, South Carolina in late October.

Until then, Missy and Grace were largely on their own. The two secretaries, bound by their common Irish Catholic background, adoration of their boss, and an innate mutual liking that, in Grace's words, made them like "two sisters who never quarreled," had big plans. They were scheduled for a week in Los Angeles, where they planned to visit several movie studios, and then take the luxurious new *Coast Daylight* train to San Francisco for a long weekend of fine dining, theatre nights, and socializing.

"I was a little worried he was going to cancel the trip, because of that business with Ethiopia and Mussolini,"

Missy said, referencing the Italian dictator's mobilization to invade an independent African country he coveted. "I'm beginning to wonder who is worse, Mussolini or Hitler! I hope he backs down."

"Oh, let's not worry about that ol' Mussolini," Grace chided her. "We can't do anything about him anyway. Our train to Los Angeles doesn't leave for a few hours. How shall we fill the time?"

"Children's Hour?" Missy asked, using the name for the daily ritual they enjoyed in the President's private study at the end of the White House work day.

"Sounds good to me," Grace replied with a giggle, "and we don't even have to pretend we like the Boss's martinis!"

CHAPTER 5

October 3, 1935

Los Angeles

Shirley was in a fine mood. She liked being on the set, enjoyed her interaction with the rest of the cast and the crew. She particularly liked dancing with Bill "Bojangles" Robinson, who was playing the plantation's chief house servant, Uncle Billy. Robinson was generally considered the best tap-dancer on Broadway before coming out to Hollywood to make movies. He and Shirley had made their debut together performing his signature stair dance in *The Little Colonel* earlier in the year under the direction of David Butler, who was also directing *The Littlest Rebel*.

On this particular Thursday, Shirley had an additional reason to be happy: her pal Andy was back on the set after almost a week's absence—even though his left ankle still looked a lot fatter than his right. She had concealed a special gift for him in the pocket of her dress.

"I'm just glad I didn't break it," Andy said with a smile as he sat at the small wooden table beside the entrance to the stockade. Today's scenes centered on the imprisonment of Shirley's Confederate father, played by John Boles, and the sympathetic Union colonel, played by Jack Holt.

"Me too! Why that would have been dreadful!" Shirley agreed with her most serious expression. "You look smaller, Andy. Do you feel all right?"

"I feel fine, Sure Shot. I was on a diet last week."

"I wish you'd been here last week. Mr. Burke wrote in a special scene, just so I could use my slingshot." Edwin Burke was the screenwriter on *The Littlest Rebel*. "I got to shoot Jack with the slingshot! I hit him first try! I kept my arm straight!" She smiled, and Andy couldn't help but chuckle at the pride she was taking in her marksmanship.

"I am sorry I missed that. I bet Jack was glad when that scene was over!"

"I'll bet he was too!" Shirley said and laughed. "Hey, Andy, I have a gift to thank you for teaching me to use a slingshot." She reached into her pocket and pulled out a shiny badge. "You are now officially a member of the Shirley Temple Police Force! You should wear this badge at all times when you are on the set—unless we're filming, that is."

"Hey, that's pretty special, Sure Shot!" Andy said, admiring the tin badge. "My ankle feels better already!"

"All right, everyone," Donald, the assistant director called out. "Places, please, for scene seventy-six."

"Better get going, Sure Shot," Andy said, smiling and pinning the badge to the inside of his shirt.

Shirley leaned over toward Andy and stage-whispered, "Don't break your other leg!" Giggling, she skipped across the set and climbed on to a stool behind the camera.

"Hey, Donald!" Andy waved the assistant director over. "What other work can I get on this picture? I'd like to think that you'd look out for me since I got hurt helping you make this masterpiece." The smile on his face masked the desperation in his voice.

"Sorry, Andy. After today, we're pretty much done. The only other scenes are with Shirley and Bill and 'President Lincoln.' There're two more pictures shooting on the lot, though. I'd be happy to put in a good word for you. Check with me later."

Donald turned back toward the jail set and addressed the actors participating in the scene. "This is the scene when Colonel Morrison and Captain Cary receive news of their sentencing."

Director David Butler had set up the camera inside the jail, looking from its back wall past the two cells on the right out to the front door where Andy sat at his table. Receiving a nod from Donald that everyone was set, Butler called out, "Lights. Sound. Camera."

"Speed," the camera operator announced.

"Mark it," Butler ordered.

Donald stepped in front of the now-filming camera and held up the chalked clapper board. "*The Littlest Rebel*, scene seventy-six, shot one, take one." He brought the two sides of the board together with a loud *clack!*

A Union captain passed by Andy's table and into the jail, approaching the two cells with a mournful expression on his face. He stopped in front of Captain Cary, who was peering through his cell's bars.

"I'm afraid I've got bad news, Captain."

The loud and sudden cooing of doves interrupted the take.

"Cut!" David Butler turned to Donald. "Where's that racket coming from?"

"Those are the doves we used in the plantation scene."

"What are they doing here? Doves don't belong in a prison! Get 'em out of here."

"Yes sir!" Donald scurried off to remove the offending birds.

"Why can't they stay?" Shirley asked, climbing down from her stool and leaning against the director's leg. "They make a pretty sound!"

"Doves don't belong in a military prison, Shirley," Butler explained. "Doves go with peace, not war like...well, like down in Africa, for instance."

"Africa?"

Butler squatted down so he could face Shirley at eye level. "Sure. It's been on the radio and in the newspapers that Mussolini and the Italians have invaded Ethiopia. That's in Africa."

"Why doesn't somebody tell Mussolini to stop?"

Donald reappeared. "We've moved the doves out of sound range."

"All right. Let's get back to work. From the top of the scene," Butler directed.

Nobody paid any attention to Shirley's question. Almost nobody.

CHAPTER 6

Hollywood, October 4—Out of the mouths of babes... Little Shirley Temple, who leads the nation in box office appeal, is now taking the lead in response to Signore Mussolini's ill-advised Ethiopian adventure. On the set of her next picture, The Littlest Rebel, *Miss Temple yesterday urged "somebody" to "tell Mussolini to stop!" Shirley, with that appealing combination of spunk and sweetness movie audiences have come to love, summed up the national mood better than any of our elected politicians. No wonder she's so popular!*

I'd love to see the look on F.D.'s face when he reads this, Missy LeHand thought with a chuckle as she reviewed Louella Parsons's column in the Los Angeles *Times.* Missy would make sure the column was included with the official communications being sent to the President aboard the USS *Houston.* The pretty woman sighed. *Poor F.D. He was so looking forward to a restful vacation.*

The President was in a ticklish position. Because of the Neutrality Act passed by the isolationist Congress, which FDR had signed just a few weeks before, he had to avoid any action which might involve the U.S. in war. *One thing's for sure,* Missy thought, smiling, *that child doesn't have a future as a diplomat. She's much too honest! I'll have to remember to compliment Shirley on her insight into world affairs if the visit to the Twentieth Century-Fox Studio comes through.*

"How is it that I read about this in in our competitor's newspaper?" Billy asked quietly, the spent stub of a cold cigar clamped in the corner of his mouth.

Joan squirmed in the hard, wooden chair in front of her boss's desk. Billy intentionally kept two such chairs in front of his desk because he didn't want visitors to get comfortable. Comfortable visitors tended to linger. But it wasn't just the chair that was making Joan uneasy. She knew that a quiet Billy was often a prelude to an eruption of volcanic proportions.

"You told me you had connections, Joan; that you could freely come and go at several studios, including—specifically—Zanuck's. So here we have America's most popular film star sounding off about international events which have graced the front page of our paper—not to mention our competitors'—for a week and we, I should say 'you,' get scooped! And by Parsons! Parsons who is fifty-something-years-old if she's a day! You're letting her outhustle you!" Billy's volume was growing, his face getting redder. "And after I bought your sob story about not having anything to eat." He shook his head, plucked the cigar from his mouth and threw it into the overflowing trash can by his desk.

Shirley Temple Is Missing

Joan felt herself shrinking under Billy's brown-eyed stare.

"I'm sorry, Billy. I guess I just wasn't in the right place at the right time. It won't happen again."

"Of course it will, knucklehead." Billy shook his head and looked out the window. When he resumed speaking, his voice had returned to a level that for Billy passed as normal conversation. "You're never going to be where a story breaks, Joan. Reporters aren't successful because they happen to be at the right place at just the right time. Reporters are successful because they build networks of people who call them when *they* are at the right places at the right times. You think Parsons was on that set? Of course not! Somebody in her network heard the Golden Child utter her now-famous remark and that somebody passed it along to Parsons, who probably embellished it and who no doubt compensated that somebody for his efforts. Do you get how this works, Joan?"

"Yes sir."

"If you're counting on being present when the story breaks, you better switch to the sports beat. Game times are published in advance. Otherwise, you better build yourself a network." Billy paused and opened one of his desk drawers. He pulled out a fresh cigar and tore off the wrapper. "You said you could cover Hollywood." He bit off the end of the cigar and spat it into the trash can. "You said you had contacts at MGM, Fox, and Paramount and that you knew people at the other studios as well." He stuck the stogie in his mouth and struck a long match, carefully lighting the cigar.

"If I have to read show biz news in somebody else's paper, I don't need my own Hollywood reporter. You understand?"

"Yes sir."

Billy nodded and Joan stood, the interview—if that's what you'd call it—over. She walked to Billy's office door and reached for the knob.

"Build a network, Joan. And build it fast, because you're only one person and you're never going to stumble onto a story as it's breaking."

CHAPTER 7

October 5, 1935

San Francisco

Cosimo Palladino ran his fingers through his thinning gray hair as he sat hunched over the cable on his desk. It looked harmless enough, a small yellow rectangle of paper taped to a letter-sized piece of Italian consulate stationery upon which the message had been decoded.

URGENT XMIT RESPONSE SHIRLEY TEMPLE COMMENTS SOONEST STOP DUCE CONSIDERS PRIORITY STOP

The League of Nations had branded Italy an outlaw nation over its invasion of Ethiopia and Il Duce's focus is on a six-year-old? Cosimo couldn't understand. Didn't the leader of the Italian Empire have more important matters with which to contend? After all, he had an army in the field in Africa and world opinion mounting against him—and he was worried about a six-year-old child? *Well*, Cosimo thought, *not just any six-year-old!* She was the most popular child in America—which made her the most popular child in the world. Her pictures were filling movie houses everywhere, from Rome, New York to Rome, Italy. And Il Duce wants to pick a fight with her?

Cosimo flipped the switch on his desk top intercom. "Send Fausto in here, please."

He leaned back in his comfortable leather chair. Cosimo liked America. He liked living in San Francisco. He hoped to stay at least until his daughter Renata finished high school. Getting into a public fracas with Shirley Temple seemed a poor way to advance Italian-American relations—not to mention his diplomatic career—especially at a time like this. There was a confident knock on his office door.

"Come in."

Fausto Trevisano, the assistant consul for cultural affairs, closed the door behind him, walked across the plush blue and gold carpet and came to a stop, three feet in front of Cosimo's desk. He struck a dignified pose, his chin up, back straight. Even from that distance, Cosimo detected a strong whiff of men's cologne.

"You asked to see me, Excellency."

Cosimo picked up the decoded message and thrust it across his desk. "Read this and pray offer your best advice."

Fausto took the paper and read it, his brow furrowed beneath his thick, black hair. He was tall and handsome, like the movie star he had once aspired to be. Fausto had been hired at the consulate only two months before Cosimo had assumed his present post. Fausto had failed to find steady work in Hollywood and had, somewhat reluctantly, applied for the vacant post of assistant consul for cultural affairs. The younger man had so far compiled an undistinguished record, spending more of his time traveling to film premieres in Los Angeles and attending parties and receptions with California's beautiful people than promoting Italian cultural heritage. Still, Cosimo believed, here was a problem tailored to Fausto's talents and contacts.

"This is very serious, Excellency."

"Your analysis is most insightful, Fausto. What response would you propose if in fact Il Duce called you into his office at this very minute?"

"I would counsel a vigorous response, signore, one in keeping with Il Duce's dynamic leadership of our heroic armies in Italian East Africa."

"And what form would this 'vigorous response' take, Fausto?"

"This impudent child should stand before Your Excellency and recant her ill-formed criticisms. She should then be compelled to apologize not only to Il Duce but to the historically great Italian people. Following this, she should receive instruction in diplomatic protocol!"

"She's only six, Fausto."

"I have, signore, many contacts within the American film industry. I shall be happy to travel to Hollywood personally to deal with this most serious crisis."

Cosimo leaned back in his chair, his eyes registering the sincerity—and utter naiveté—of his young colleague. "Very well, Fausto. Thank you for your advice. I will give it every consideration."

"Grazie, Excellency. Know that I remain at your command, eager to erase this stain from the honor of the Kingdom of Italy."

"Of course, of course. I would expect no less from you. Thank you, Fausto."

Fausto bowed, turned, and left the office, the heavy oak door closing behind him.

Cosimo sighed. *Mio Dio! What an idiot!*

He was already late for dinner. In another twenty minutes, he'd be very late. Cosimo hated to miss dinner with Renata. Except when official consular functions intervened, Cosimo made it a point to always take his evening meal with his 11-year-old daughter. That he had to endure her mother, the shrew, was a burden he was willing to bear. Ironically, Renata favored her mother, a classic beauty with dark lustrous hair and almond-shaped eyes. Fortunately, Renata's happy, compassionate, and friendly personality distinguished her from her mother. Also, fortunately, she doted on her father to almost the same extravagant extent that he doted upon her.

But on this evening, the blank page on Cosimo's desk top had effectively chained him to his duties. His cable from Rome had included the word "soonest" and this instruction could be ignored only at his own peril.

The intercom on his desk squawked and he reached to answer it.

"Si."

"Excellency, would you like the kitchen to send up a plate?"

Cosimo looked at the round face of the clock on his desk. "Yes, and please convey my regrets to Signora and Signorina Palladino. I expect to be here yet a good while."

Shirley Temple Is Missing

He snapped off the intercom and returned his attention to his task.

The smart thing, Cosimo knew, was to do nothing; to let this Temple tempest blow over. Within a day, two at the most, the American press would be onto another titillating, but not terribly important story, and the little girl's innocent comments would be forgotten.

But doing nothing was not an option. Il Duce's messenger had made that clear. Cosimo snorted. How had Italy's grab for glory in east Africa become his problem half a world away?

Cosimo unscrewed the cap to his fountain pen and set it aside. He pulled the sheet of paper closer and began to write:

1—Provide friendly reporters with background on Ethiopian aggressiveness in east Africa

2—Develop joint Italian-American cultural festival in San Francisco to include cinema exhibits

3—Invite American movie stars to attend, possibly including Miss Temple

4—Do not directly address Miss Temple's remarks

Why would Il Duce Benito Mussolini, Head of Government, Leader of Fascism and Founder of the Empire concern himself with the off-hand comment of a six-year-old child? Il Duce clearly did not understand the Americans. Yes, they loved their movie stars, particularly the cute little girl, but they rarely looked to their celebrities for political direction. Yes, the best thing to do was to let the matter fade away.

Cosimo's response to Rome would include this advice. Unfortunately for Cosimo, Fausto Trevisano had his own plans.

CHAPTER 8

October 6, 1935

Los Angeles

Tony Oliveri made a good living doing odd jobs. His client list—well it wasn't actually a list because Tony was too smart to commit names to paper—included many famous and a few infamous members of the elite of Los Angeles. Tony's acquaintances--for that's what they were really, acquaintances who knew how to express their appreciation for certain favors—included lawyers, politicians, the powerful, the rich, the good, the bad, and, occasionally, the desperate. Tony wasn't sure into which category his lunch appointment fit.

Tony was seated in his favorite back-corner booth in the dining room at Perino's. Leave the front tables for Gable and Flynn and all those swells who needed to be seen. Tony much preferred to dine—and labor—anonymously.

He was wearing an olive-colored, double-breasted suit from Hamburger & Sons. Nice, but not flashy, just right for a friendly, exploratory lunch. Business-like. The right attire helped set the proper tone for business dealings. Tony adjusted the polka-dotted navy-blue silk handkerchief in his breast pocket. Important to make a good impression. He'd never met this guy before but knew who he was, of course. The guy had bounced around some of the studios on Poverty Row doing some bit parts, but his repertoire was limited. He had a distinctive look—and the accent to go with it—that pigeonholed him into a very narrow range of parts. Hard to make it in the picture business if you weren't versatile. Hell, hard to make it in the picture business if you *were* versatile.

That's one thing Tony Oliveri was: versatile. His job was to know just a little about everything: who was getting ready to build; who was getting ready to buy; to wed; to divorce; to produce; to steal; to donate; to hire; to fire… Tony's business was information and connections. Without the one, the other was useless. And vice versa.

The front door opened, briefly letting in the noise and light from the street and attracting Tony's attention. Silhouetted against the brighter light from outside was Tony's lunch appointment, a tall, good-looking man wearing a stylish navy sport coat with wide lapels over cream-colored slacks. His tie was patterned with light blue and silver diamonds, a matching light blue handkerchief in the pocket of his jacket. Tony stood as the maître d' escorted the younger man toward his booth, noting that his guest hadn't been able to resist checking himself out in a mirror he passed.

"Tony Oliveri," he said, extending his hand.

"Fausto Trevisano. It pleases me to make your acquaintance." He exuded a strong scent of men's cologne.

Tony gestured toward the other side of the booth with a sweep of his arm. "Please sit down." Fausto slid onto the bench seat opposite Tony. "Shall we start with a drink?"

"Please."

Tony looked up at the waiter standing by the table. "*Due prosecchi, per favore.*" The waiter bowed his head and withdrew.

"Thank you for making the time to meet with me, Signore Oliveri," Fausto began. "One hears that you are the man who gets things done in Los Angeles."

Tony spread his hands apart. "I simply bring people together, my friend. You need a bath, I find a man with soap." Tony chuckled.

Fausto smiled. "The need is more than soap. And in truth, the need is not my own."

"No?"

"No, signore. The request I make comes directly from Rome." Fausto paused portentously. "From the highest offices in Rome, signore. It is a matter of national pride. This is why I have come to you for help." He fell silent as the waiter returned and set their drinks on the white tablecloth.

"Are you ready to order, gentlemen?"

"The filet of sole is excellent, if I may recommend it?" Tony said, opening his hands toward Fausto.

"As you say," Fausto nodded with a smile.

Tony shifted his attention back to the waiter. "Filet of sole for both of us and a bottle of Franciacorta, please." The waiter again nodded his head and withdrew.

"So," Tony resumed, turning back to Fausto and raising his eyebrows, "how can I be of service to Rome?"

Two days later, Tony Oliveri and Fausto Trevisano met again, not in a restaurant, but in front of the display window of Larsen's Hardware Emporium at the corner of Parnell Avenue and Santa Monica Boulevard. Neither was in the market for garden tools, but the large window offered a fairly clear reflection of the store fronts on the opposite side of the street. That was where Fausto's attention was focused, after he gave his personal appearance a quick assessment.

"I believe," Tony Oliveri said, speaking in a quiet voice, "that is your man right there."

Fausto peered into the window to see the reflection of a man wearing a flat work cap as he limped to the doorway of Harmon's Bar and disappeared inside.

"Grazie, Signore Oliveri! I will never forget your assistance. I will make sure that it is well known in Rome." He leaned closer to the older, shorter man and added in a whisper, "Including Il Duce."

"I seek no attention, my friend. Your gratitude is reward enough." Tony put his hand on his heart, which, coincidentally, was next to the pocket that held the envelope full of cash Fausto had given him. "You had better go. Good luck." Tony offered his hand. Fausto shook it vigorously and then trotted across the street, dodging a Ford work truck. Tony watched him go, then headed off to his next "odd job."

Fausto pushed open the door of Harmon's and stepped inside. The long, L-shaped bar was to his right. A juke box at the back of the room was blaring "She's a Latin from Manhattan." Fausto glanced around the room, giving his eyes a chance to adjust to the bar's dimness. At this hour of the afternoon there were few patrons in the establishment. It didn't matter. His quarry's red hair would have made him easy to spot even in a crowd. The man was seated at the near end of the bar, his back to the street, his cap resting on the bar next to his beer. Fausto slipped onto the stool next to him.

"I have a friend who says you might be able to help me." Fausto nodded to the bartender and held up his thumb.

"Is that right?" the man beside him answered without looking at him.

"I understand you are friends with someone I would very much like to meet."

"So I've been told. Why don't you just call the studio and come see her?"

"I'd like to meet her under more confidential conditions."

Andy Archie glanced at the stranger as the bartender set a foaming glass in front of him. "Why?"

"The reasons are my own."

Andy hesitated for a moment. "She's a friend of mine. If I set up a meeting, it has to be on the up-and-up. No monkey business."

"Of course, my friend. I assure you that although my reasons must remain confidential, my purposes are purely educational. Your friend would not be exploited in any way and I would personally vouch for her safety at all times."

47

"I don't know, Mr.—"

"We won't use names."

"I'll have to think about it," Andy said, taking a swig from his beer.

"Perhaps this will help you consider my request." Fausto placed his hand on the bar between his glass and Andy's. When he removed it, a twenty-dollar bill remained. "This, of course, is just a small deposit to encourage you to consider my request."

Andy's eyes widened. "I said I'll think about it." He took another sip, trying to remain nonchalant. "How do I contact you?"

Fausto smiled. "You don't contact me, and I don't contact you. I'll meet you here. Same time tomorrow. If you're not here by four o'clock, I'll find someone else to pay so handsomely for this small favor." He turned his head to look at the red-haired man. "Think it over carefully, my friend. I'm offering a large sum for a very small favor." Fausto drank from his glass and set it back on the bar. He put two bits on the bar. "Your beer is on me." He slipped off the stool, exited through the front door and turned right.

When he reached the end of the block, Fausto ducked behind the corner of a bank building and watched. After a few minutes, Andy Archie left the bar, turning left and heading toward Santa Monica Boulevard.

THURSDAY, OCTOBER 10, 1935

CHAPTER 9

Los Angeles

There were certain advantages to working for the President, Missy decided as she looked into the mirror, adjusted her black velvet beret, and admired her new dress. It was an unusual choice for her, brown silk printed all over with colorful dog bones. At the White House, she dressed much more conservatively, but she was on vacation, after all. Of course, there were the long hours, half the pay of her male counterparts in the West Wing, public scrutiny, and the pressure of pleasing the right people at the right time, but occasionally there were also trips like this one which found Missy and Grace in sunny California while the Boss was out at sea. And, on this day in particular, Missy's status as Franklin Roosevelt's personal secretary was opening the door to a visit with America's most popular movie star.

Missy reckoned that Clark Gable might be a little more exciting; Grace would certainly think so. But Shirley Temple would be more fun. And besides, F.D. adored the little girl. Here was one celebrity Missy would have met that the Boss hadn't!

Shirley Temple Is Missing

Missy picked up her black alligator clutch purse monogrammed "MALeH" and stepped out into the corridor of Los Angeles's glamorous Biltmore Hotel. She knocked on Grace's door and waited impatiently for her assistant to open the door. The brass knob turned and the door swung open, but Grace, instead of coming out into the hallway, was retreating toward the bathroom.

"I'm almost ready! I was reading this dreadful account in the paper of the accident John and James got into yesterday in Boston. It's a wonder they weren't killed."

"I know! It made me quite ill to read it," Missy said. James Roosevelt, the President's 27-year-old son, had been in a car driven by his 19-year-old brother, John, headed to the airport to catch a flight to New York. John had unsuccessfully tried to beat a train at a crossing and at the last second turned his car parallel to the tracks. The car was crushed between the train and the crossing gate, but neither brother was injured.

"Can you believe James is in the insurance business?" Missy asked. "I hope he doesn't insure John's cars. That's at least the third one he has wrecked since he started driving. C'mon, we're supposed to meet Marvin in the lobby in three minutes." Marvin McIntyre was the President's genial appointments secretary, who was also enjoying a few days of vacation. Missy leaned against the bathroom door while her colleague dabbed on her red lipstick.

Grace turned toward Missy and asked, "How do I look?"

"Like you're ready for Hollywood. Now come on!"

51

CHAPTER 10

"I'll make it up to you," Joan Roswell had pleaded with Harry Brand, the chief of publicity at Twentieth Century-Fox Studios. "I'll give your pictures excellent coverage. I'll use your press releases. I'll be your friend in the press. You've just got to help me get a scoop!"

Brand had chuckled. It wasn't every day a beauty like Joan Roswell was begging *him* for favors. He had ended the conversation with a non-committal, "I'll see what I can do," but had called her back that same afternoon with a tip. It wasn't a big deal, really. Nothing that would make or break a picture. He wasn't even sure Joan could build a story around it. But he was sure it would put Joan in his debt and the irony of a reporter owing *him* a favor pleased Harry Brand to no end.

"Can't you go any faster, dear?" Joan Roswell leaned over the cab driver's shoulder. "I need to be there before ten-thirty."

"Lady, if you needed to be there at ten-thirty you shoulda left before ten-fifteen. What is it with you dames?"

"You're not being very chivalrous." Joan slumped back into her seat with a pout.

"Look-it, I'm sorry, OK, but this is a red cab, not a white horse. I'll get you there as quick as I can." The cab driver turned left onto West Pico Boulevard and Joan felt the taxi accelerate. "What's the big rush anyway? You got a screen test or something?"

Joan cocked her head, making eye contact with the driver in his rear-view mirror. "Do you recognize me?" she asked with a smile.

"Sure! I've seen you in the pictures. You're…" He hesitated as though searching for her name.

"Joan Roswell, dear."

"No, that's not it," the driver said, shaking his head. "It'll come to me in a minute."

Before "it" came to him, they arrived at the gate to Twentieth Century-Fox Studios. Joan paid the tab, neglecting to tip due to the cabbie's gaffe and her own paucity of funds. She checked in at the gate and was cleared to Soundstage 8.

The Twentieth Century-Fox lot was composed of ninety-six acres of soundstages, backlots, administration buildings, warehouses, shops, and physical plant just west of Beverly Hills. Five miles of roadway wound through this small city within a city. Darryl Zanuck, the thirty-three-year-old head of production at the studio, planned to produce thirty-five pictures in 1935, a task complicated by the recent death in an airplane crash of the studio's top male star, Will Rogers.

Joan hiked briskly toward her destination, hoping she was ahead of the White House party coming to pay a morning call on the set of Shirley Temple's current picture, *The Littlest Rebel*. Joan was sure Harry Brand would provide a photograph of the Washington entourage with little Shirley which she could use to build a story around the visit. Government officials always liked to have their pictures taken with movie stars. After all, the movie stars in general, and Shirley Temple, in particular, were far more popular than most politicians. A little mutual admiration was good publicity for both parties—and would be good for Joan as well.

"Hey, good-looking!" Joan turned to see the smiling face of a handsome man. He was leaning against the trunk of a pepper tree smoking a cigarette.

"Why, Bruce Cabot!" Joan purred, stepping off the sidewalk and approaching the actor who was famous for his role as the hero in the 1933 hit *King Kong*. "What a pleasant surprise!"

"What are you doing here? I don't think Zanuck's on the lot today. Besides, I heard you packed it in for the newspaper business."

"I'm certainly not looking for Mr. Darryl Zanuck!" Joan said, annoyed that her appearance had triggered that association in Cabot's mind. "I might ask you the same question. What are you doing outside on such a pleasant morning? I would have thought you'd be in some dark old soundstage wooing some beautiful starlet or fighting a giant ape and recording for all posterity another performance guaranteed to make the females of America swoon over their popcorn."

Cabot laughed and crushed out his cigarette. He was wearing a navy double-breasted suit, his tie loosened, and his collar unbuttoned. "Nothing so glamorous today. I'm working with Caesar Romero on a picture. You ever met him? Hollywood's newest Latin lover."

"Heard of him, but haven't met him."

"If you're going to be around for a while, I'll introduce you."

"That would be lovely, dear. But right now, I'm following up on a story for my paper. Some big shot politicians are visiting Shirley Temple's set on Stage 8."

"That's it, right there." Cabot pointed to the soundstage to his right. "The door's on the other side. You just go around that corner there."

"Thank you, dear. Always so helpful." Joan patted Cabot on his arm and stepped toward her objective. "Hope to catch up with you later," she called over her shoulder.

CHAPTER 11

Joan rounded the corner of the soundstage and saw Harry Brand standing out front looking at his watch. Harry had friendly eyes, wavy dark hair, and was wearing a double-breasted gray suit with a red and white striped tie.

"You made it," he said with a smile as Joan's movement caught his eye. "I thought maybe you were chasing a bigger story."

"They're not already here, are they?" Joan asked, her brow wrinkled.

"No. Just got a call from the gate. Their cars were passed through a minute ago. Your timing couldn't be better. There," Harry said, looking over her shoulder. "I bet that's them."

A large, black Cadillac limousine pulled up in front of the building. Its uniformed driver came around to the back door and held it open. A woman in a patterned dress and velvet beret climbed out, followed by a younger, shorter woman in a dark suit and matching felt hat, and then a cadaverous-looking man wearing a chalk-striped suit with a white carnation in the buttonhole.

"Here's our group," Harry said, stepping past Joan and flashing a broad smile. Joan stayed where she was and watched as Harry approached the visitors. "Welcome to

Twentieth Century-Fox Studios. I'm Harry Brand, chief of publicity, and I'll be your escort this morning."

"I'm Marguerite LeHand, the President's private secretary," Joan heard the taller woman say. "This is my assistant, Miss Grace Tully, and the President's appointments secretary, Mr. Marvin McIntyre. Thank you for taking time out of your schedule to show us around. We are so thrilled to be here!"

"It's our pleasure. I thought we'd look around the studio a bit, show you some of the sets inside the soundstage here and then ride around the backlot. But before we do any of that, there's someone inside who's eager to meet you. Follow me!" Brand led the group into the warehouse-like soundstage, winking at Joan as he passed. She hesitated a moment and then tagged along.

Once inside the building, Harry stopped and turned toward his visitors. "You're now inside a working soundstage. Most of our motion picture work is done indoors when possible. Of course, that makes perfect sense for interior sets, but we actually film a lot of our 'outside' scenes inside as well. That gives us almost full control of lighting, which is so important, plus we don't have to worry about weather or ambient noise."

Joan knew all this from her intermittent career in front of the camera. She stayed several feet behind the official guests, realizing that while Harry's introduction was designed to tell them a little bit about movie-making, it was also intended to give their eyes time to adjust to the relative darkness of the inside of the soundstage—and to alert them to hazards.

"Of course, since we're controlling the lighting, we have to use a lot of lights of various sizes and purposes to achieve the director's desired look for each scene. Plus, we have cameras, sound gear, the occasional wind machine and other devices and nearly every one of those pieces of equipment has a power cable or cord attached to it, so make sure you watch your step.

"Now today, you're in for a treat, because we're filming Shirley Temple's newest picture, a Civil War drama called *The Littlest Rebel*. And since you all are special guests of Mr. Zanuck's," Harry's eyes strayed to Joan for the briefest moment, "we've arranged for you to meet Shirley during one of the breaks between scenes."

"How delightful!" Missy exclaimed. "I have enjoyed all her movies, and the President is a big fan."

"First, let's take a walk over to the set, which you probably won't recognize, even though it's a replica of the President's office—President Lincoln, that is! Watch your step now."

Harry led the party through a stack of flats leaning against a wall, past some sawhorses, over some cables winding off into the darkness, and toward a lighted area in front of which sat a large motion picture camera on a dolly. Several people were standing around while a man in a suit looked up toward a catwalk where a worker in overalls was positioning a small spot light.

"A little more to the left," the suited man said, alternating his gaze between the set and the man above. "Right there. Good. Tighten it down."

"David?" Harry said, approaching the man in the suit. "I'd like you to meet some friends of Darryl's from the White House."

"Wonderful," the director David Butler said with a smile. He stepped around a gaggle of chairs, consoles, and technicians. "And you've come all this way to see us? How flattering."

Joan watched and listened as Harry repeated the introductions she'd already heard. She thought about taking out her note pad and writing things down, but she figured the less obtrusive she was, the more likely she would be to catch candid moments. Hollywood people were in the business of pretend, after all. Imagine how fantastical things could get with these Washington people added to the mix. *No*, she considered, *the less conspicuous I am, the better*.

"Now, come right over here," the director said. "I want you all to take a turn sitting behind this desk."

"Why isn't there a ceiling?" Grace asked.

The director launched into a tedious explanation about the importance of lighting. Joan's eyes began to wander around the set, her ears attuned to something more interesting than candlepower. To her left, on the periphery of the set, a young man with headphones hanging around his neck was flirting with a petite young woman in a flowered dress. A red-headed man in dungarees was leaning in close to a young man in shirtsleeves and a tie. The younger man was shaking his head and shrugging his shoulders. Joan crept cat-like in their direction.

"I already tried *Show Them No Mercy!*" the red-haired man was saying. "No dice."

The young man consulted his clipboard. "You could try *Navy Wife*, over on six. Dwan is directing."

"Never worked with him. You got any pull?"

"Me? No. I'll give you a good reference, though."

"All right, everyone," the director called out, diverting Joan's attention. "Let's take our places, please. Donald." He nodded toward the man with the clipboard. Joan noticed an actor costumed and made up to resemble Abraham Lincoln had taken a seat behind the desk. A shiny red apple and a pocket knife were sitting on the desk top, props to be used when Lincoln and the "littlest rebel" shared a snack as they talked.

While Harry guided his visitors to a spot behind the camera, Donald moved out front. "Places, please!" He picked up a marker board and quickly wrote on it with a piece of chalk he removed from his pocket. He held the board up in front of the camera.

"Lights, please," the director called out and the set brightened, flooded with artificial illumination. "Sound. Camera."

"Speed," responded the camera operator.

"Mark the scene."

Donald held up the marker board and said, "This is scene eighty-one, shot one, take one." He slapped the two sides of the board together and stepped off the set.

"Action!"

The office door opened, and an aide ushered in Shirley Temple and Bill Robinson, both dressed for travel. Shirley was wearing a plaid jumper with matching jacket and hat, while Bill wore a frock coat and string tie and carried a battered felt hat in his hand. Movement off the set caught Joan's attention. Her eyes followed the redhead as he quietly limped away from the brightly lit action and faded into the darkness.

Joan turned back toward the White House contingent. Grace, the younger woman, and Marvin both had smiles on their faces. The other woman, Miss LeHand, the one who seemed to be in charge, was watching the filming with studied concentration.

For Joan, the action on the set was old hat. She'd been around the studios for a dozen years, enduring the daily casting calls for extras and working—if that's what you'd call it—her way up to a few featured player roles. Zanuck had helped with the latter, of course, but once he'd moved on to the next starlet in the Fox heavens, the once-steady stream of parts had dwindled to a trickle and then to nothing at all. Once the merger with Twentieth Century Pictures had been announced earlier that year, Joan couldn't even get Zanuck's secretary to take a phone message. *Water over the dam.*

"Cut!"

Joan turned her attention back to the action on the set, where Shirley was sitting on the corner of President Lincoln's desk. Joan knew the actor playing the part; she'd worked with him on a Fox picture once, but she couldn't recall his name. Not that it mattered. As the shoot ended, Harry Brand walked onto the set, helping Shirley off the desk and leading her over to his guests.

"Shirley, I want you to meet some friends of mine. They've come all the way from the White House in Washington to see you. This is Miss LeHand, Miss Tully, and Mr. McIntyre."

Shirley smiled and said, "Pleased to meet you!" She shook hands with the three White House staff members. "You must work for the big boss, President Roosevelt."

The Washington trio chuckled. "That's right," Missy replied. "But while the President is at sea with the Navy, we're having a little vacation of our own here in California."

"And these are Shirley's parents, Mr. and Mrs. Temple," Brand said, presenting a fashionably dressed middle-aged couple. Mrs. Temple wore an expensive-looking tweed suit with wide lapels and a stylish slouch hat. Mr. Temple, a tall, slim man with thinning hair, wore an impeccable three-piece suit, befitting his profession as a banker. "Please, call us Gertrude and George," Mrs. Temple said.

"Everyone calls me Missy," replied Miss LeHand, shaking hands.

"All right, everybody," Harry said, "step right this way and let's get a few pictures with Shirley." With the knack of someone who'd managed hundreds of publicity photos, Brand quickly arranged the group, including the Temples and handsome actor John Boles, Shirley's on-screen father in *The Littlest Rebel*.

"Look this way and say 'box office,'" directed the studio photographer. His bulb flashed.

"What do you think of Shirley?" a deep voice asked from over Joan's shoulder. She turned to find the familiar face of burly John Griffith.

"What are you doing here?" Joan asked. "Zanuck give you the morning off?"

Shirley Temple Is Missing

"I'm not his bodyguard any more. I'm Shirley's."

"A six-year-old needs a bodyguard?"

"That one does. And she's seven—though keep that under your hat; even Shirley thinks she's six. More to the point, what are you doing here? Darryl's not on the lot today."

"Like he'd see me even if he was."

"He always liked you, Joan."

"Liked." Joan reached into her clutch and pulled out a Chesterfield. Griffith offered her a light. "I'm taking a shot at a new career—one where the work is steadier." *The work, but not necessarily the pay.* "So why does a seven-year-old need security more than the head of the studio?"

Griffith snorted. "You read the trades? That little girl there," he dipped his head toward Shirley, who was mugging for the VIPs and the camera, "has single-handedly turned the financial fortunes of the newly merged Fox and Twentieth Century film studios."

"You sound like a press release."

Griffith chuckled. "Maybe so, but just because you read it in the papers doesn't mean it ain't true. She's Zanuck's top box office star. Put Shirley in the picture and it makes money. Zanuck knows that. Why else would he buy a $795,000 insurance policy on her?"

Joan stared into Griffith's face, her green eyes widening. "Seven hundred ninety-five thousand dollars?"

"Yeah. Hey, you're working for the newspaper now, right?"

"Right."

"Well, do me a favor for old time's sake and don't quote me about that life insurance business—or her age."

"Well, all right," Joan said reluctantly. She looked up at Griff with her cat's eyes. "But, remember, you owe me one."

The picture-taking session had ended. Shirley had her autograph book out and was passing it to Missy. "Look at that," Griffith said, nodding his head toward Shirley. "The biggest star in pictures is asking visitors for *their* autographs. No wonder people love her."

"Do you, dear?" Joan asked, raising an eyebrow.

"Hard not to. Want to meet her?" Griffith began walking toward Shirley's group.

"No thank you, dear. I'll just admire her from afar." Joan wanted a story, not a six-year-old pal. She didn't want to sign the autograph book either. Still, she followed behind Griffith. She needed a story in the worst way—even if it was about a photo op.

CHAPTER 12

"Do you like dogs?" Shirley asked Missy, pointing to the unusual dog-bone print on her silk dress.

"I love dogs!" Missy said. "I especially like cocker spaniels. Do you have a dog?"

"I have a little dog named Sniff," Shirley said, puffing out her chest importantly. "He's a Scottie. I take care of him myself!"

"I know the President would love to meet Sniff," Missy said. "His cousin Daisy Suckley breeds, er, raises Scotties, and he loves to play with them when he is at home in Hyde Park."

"The President plays?" Shirley asked, widening her brown eyes in astonishment. "I didn't know presidents ever had time to play!"

Missy laughed. "He loves to have a good time, Shirley. He especially likes to watch your movies! But his favorite thing to do is fish, and that's what he's doing on his vacation."

"Mother," Shirley said, turning to the hovering Mrs. Temple, "can we take Miss LeHand and Miss Tully to my cottage? I want to show them some pictures of Sniff."

"I don't see why not, Shirley," Mrs. Temple said. "You've got a break until two o'clock. You'll have to eat your lunch and lie down for a nap, though, so they can only stay a few minutes. You've got to finish that scene with President Lincoln this afternoon."

"I would love that," Missy said. "Just let me go powder my nose first. Go ahead, and I'll get Mr. Brand to take me to your cottage."

"Why don't you and I get a bite to eat at the commissary?" Mr. Temple said to Marvin McIntyre.

"That would be grand!" Marvin said, and began explaining how his favorite bartender at the Mayflower Hotel in Washington used a cobalt milk pitcher emblazoned with Shirley's face to mix a martini. "He pours in gin to the chin and vermouth to the tooth, says it's foolproof," Marvin said.

Mr. Temple chuckled. "I've not heard that one before," he said. Missy rolled her eyes. *Marvin and his bar stories! I hope Mrs. Temple wasn't listening!*

As Shirley skipped away with Mrs. Temple and Grace, Missy slipped into the ladies' room. When she emerged from her stall a few minutes later, the attractive blonde who had been standing in the shadows during the tour was seated on a small floral-upholstered love seat opposite the sinks, smoking a cigarette.

"Oh, hello," Missy said, removing her onyx pinky ring and washing her hands. She looked at Joan in the mirror. "You were part of our tour, weren't you? I'm Marguerite LeHand."

The woman exhaled a stream of blue smoke. "Joan Roswell," she said. "Delighted to meet you. Are you enjoying your tour?"

Shirley Temple Is Missing

"Oh, yes," Missy said, drying her hands on a towel hanging from a dispenser on the wall, and replacing her ring. "It's been a long-time dream of mine to come to Hollywood and tour the studios. I hope to pick up some tips to make my home movies better. Do you work here?"

"I used to act in the movies," Joan said, smiling. "You might have seen me in *You Can't Beat the House*. I played the hat check girl in the casino scene."

"I'm afraid I missed that one," Missy said. "Well, I guess I need to get going. Nice to have—"

"Miss LeHand," Joan said, rising to her feet, "to be honest, I haven't done so well in the movies, and I'm trying to build a new career for myself, as a newspaper reporter. I'd be so grateful if you would let me ask you a few questions about your work at the White House."

"Oh, I don't know about that," Missy said. "I really don't like to give interviews unless President Roosevelt's press secretary is with me."

To Missy's surprise, tears pooled in the woman's green eyes, and her chin trembled as she said huskily, "Miss LeHand, I'm a little desperate. If I don't come back to the office with some kind of story today, I'm afraid I will lose my job. Please, just a few questions, one career woman to another?"

Missy's face softened. "Of course, Miss Roswell. But just a few. I'm expected at Shirley Temple's cottage."

The reporter quickly opened her purse and withdrew her pad and pen and the two women sat down on the love seat. "First, how long have you worked for President Roosevelt?"

"Since 1920," Missy said promptly. "I joined his campaign staff when he was running for vice president, and after the election, when he was rather badly defeated, I went to work for him in New York at his law office."

"Is that a New England accent I detect?" Joan asked.

Missy laughed. "Yes, you can say I'm a Boston girl all right," she replied. "I grew up there, though I was born in Potsdam, New York."

The reporter smiled back, then looking down at her pad, said nonchalantly, "So you were working for Mr. Roosevelt when he contracted infantile paralysis. That must have been hard."

Missy stiffened, thinking, *I don't like where the interview is going.* "Yes," she said simply. "But as you can see, he has overcome that hardship completely."

Missy's interrogator smiled widely, changing the subject. "Little Shirley was quite interested to learn the President likes to play," she said. "What do *you* do to play?"

Missy relaxed. *That's better.* "Well, I love reading. I read myself to sleep almost every night. Biographies, mostly, though I share the President's love for a good detective story. And I enjoy our weekends on the *Sequoia*, the President's yacht. I'm a pretty good fisherman! I go to the theatre every chance I get, especially in New York. And I love to dance."

"Ever dance with the President?" the reporter asked, all wide-eyed innocence.

Shirley Temple Is Missing

Missy's smile disappeared. "He isn't much for dancing," she said. "Look, Miss Roswell, can we go off the record here?"

"Of course, dear," the woman said, laying down her pen.

"There is a gentlemen's agreement among the members of the press that no mention is made of the President's disability. No photos are ever taken of him in a wheelchair or being lifted from a car. You've never seen one, have you?"

"No," she admitted. "I was unaware of that gentlemen's agreement... Of course, I understand women are not allowed in the President's press conferences, so I guess a gentleman's agreement doesn't apply to me."

Missy eyed her warily. "I'm not sure you're a lady, either, Miss Roswell. This interview is over." She stood, smoothing her dress, and walked out of the room without a backward glance.

When Missy finally arrived at Shirley Temple's cottage, her face was still white with rage. Grace pulled her aside and whispered, "Missy, what happened? Are you alright?"

"Ambushed in the ladies' room by a barracuda disguised as a reporter," Missy hissed. "I'll fill you in later."

Just then, Shirley ran forward, grabbing Missy's hand and leading her around her cottage, with its murals of Humpty Dumpty and other Mother Goose rhymes on the walls and its child-sized furniture. It was an airy, happy place, with pleated chintz curtains in the windows.

Glancing outside, Missy noted a sand box that looked like it had seen regular use.

"Would you like to see my Oscar?" Shirley asked.

"Yes, indeed," Missy said. "Grace and I listened to the awards ceremony on the radio in February. In fact, we're staying at the Biltmore Hotel, where the dinner was held."

Shirley walked over to a bookshelf and picked up a miniature version of the famed Academy Awards statuette. "My mommy said it's because I made the most movies last year," she explained, "but not the best. That's why it's small."

"Oh, I don't know about that!" Grace said. "I thought all your movies were pretty darn good! We've watched many of them at the White House. Mr. Roosevelt thinks you're the best dancer he's ever seen, and he loves it when you say, 'Oh, my goodness.' He laughs every time."

Shirley beamed. "Maybe I'll get to meet him some day," she said.

"He would love to meet you, Shirley," Missy said. "Maybe you can visit us at the White House!"

"So, what are your plans during the rest of your stay in California?" Mrs. Temple asked. "I hope you'll see more of our beautiful Golden State."

"Yes," Missy said. "Grace and I leave tomorrow on the new *Coast Daylight* train for San Francisco—I hear it's the most beautiful train in the world, and we have seats in the observation car, so we'll have the best views of the scenery—and we'll spend a few days there. I'm really looking forward to riding the cable cars and seeing Fisherman's Wharf."

"Oh, Mother," Shirley piped up. "Can't we go too?"

"Now, Shirley," Mrs. Temple said. "You know you start rehearsals for *Captain January* next week. You need to rest this weekend."

"Oh, please, Mother," Shirley said. "I want to ride the most beautiful train in the world!"

"We'll discuss this later, Shirley," Mrs. Temple said firmly. "It's time for your lunch. They sent baked chicken today."

Shirley pouted. "Again?" she whined.

"Now, Shirley. There are children starving in China who would be glad to eat your baked chicken. Be a good girl and say good-bye to your guests."

Before their eyes, Shirley transformed from a pleading child into the perfect pint-sized hostess. She curtsied to Missy and Grace, an act enhanced by her wide plaid hoop skirt, and said, "Thank you so much for visiting me. I hope I will see you again. And tell the President hello!"

CHAPTER 13

Joan was lingering outside Shirley's studio cottage, standing in the shade of a pin oak while the White House secretaries visited inside. She had kept her distance from the group following her clumsy attempt to interview Missy LeHand in the ladies' room. *What did you expect? She handles the Washington press corps all the time. Did you think she'd open up for you just because you're another woman?* Harry Brand ducked out of the cottage's door.

"She's quite a little actress, isn't she?" Joan said.

"You still here?" Harry said, his broad smile suggesting his satisfaction with the way the VIP tour was going. "If you want to wait around, I'll get Charlie to get you prints of a couple of the shots he took. You can decide the best one to share with your readers. Or, I can have them messengered over if you've got over things to do."

"I'll wait."

"I'll let Charlie know so he can hurry things along." While Harry was happy to get free publicity for the picture and the studio, there were no percentages in a member of the press hanging around the lot any longer than usual. "Quid pro quo, Joan." Harry smiled again.

"Huh?"

"You owe me." Brand's smile grew even wider. "I'll let Charlie know you're waiting." He strolled off toward the photography shop, whistling.

Joan combed through her purse and dug out the last cigarette from her pack of Chesterfields. She stuck the smoke between her lips and pulled out her lighter. She spun the flint, but couldn't get it to light. She looked around, but Harry had already disappeared around the corner of the cottage. The only other person nearby was sitting at the base of a cottonwood tree smoking, his legs stretched out in front of him, his work cap askew.

Joan approached the man and asked, "Can I trouble you for a light?"

The red-headed man looked up. "Sure. Here." He held his cigarette up and Joan used it to light hers. She took a long pull on her cigarette and exhaled before handing the fag back to the man.

"Thank you, dear."

"Don't mention it."

The exit from the cottage of Mrs. Temple and the two White House secretaries attracted Joan's attention. She nodded to the seated man and slunk back toward the cottage. Joan remained at a discreet distance, far enough away so she wouldn't have to apologize for her earlier brashness in the women's room, but close enough that she could eavesdrop on the conversation.

"I hope we didn't cause a problem by mentioning our trip to San Francisco in front of Shirley," Missy was saying. "Although it really would be a pleasure to have both of you join us. Shirley is delightful. And so well behaved!" Missy lowered her voice and inclined her head toward Mrs. Temple. "Far more so than the President's own grandchildren. Sistie and Buzzie lived on my floor of the White House for a year. They could have used some lessons in good manners from Shirley!"

Gertrude Temple chuckled. "To tell the truth," she said with a smile, "a little break between pictures would probably do Shirley—and her mother—some good. It might be fun at that. Let me speak with my husband and Mr. Zanuck. Where can I reach you?"

Joan listened as Missy gave Mrs. Temple her room number at the Biltmore Hotel.

"And what time is your train?"

"Eight-fifteen in the morning," Missy replied. "It arrives in San Francisco at 6 p.m. Do let us know if you can join us."

Harry Brand rounded the corner, a large manila envelope in his hand. As he drew nearer, Joan could make out the bright red stamp on the envelope: PHOTOS DO NOT BEND.

"Here you are, Joan. As promised." Harry handed over the envelope. "Quid pro quo, Joan," he said, smiling again.

"I don't speak French, Harry."

Brand laughed. Joan took the envelope and turned to head back toward the gate. She noticed the red-headed fellow standing up, dusting off his dungarees, and limping slowly in the other direction.

CHAPTER 14

"Whose payroll are you on?" Billy Bryce asked, tossing the glossy photograph on his desk. "Sit down!" When Joan had slid into the uncomfortable wooden chair, Billy stood up, took a deep breath and perched himself on the front corner of his desk. "I don't think you've figured out how all this is supposed to work yet, Joan." His voice was calm, paternal even, as though seeking to educate a child.

"The objective of a reporter is to report the news. It doesn't really matter what beat you're on—city, crime, sports, entertainment—your job is to find out what's going on."

"And that's just what I've done, Billy." Joan held her head up, her chin thrust out.

Billy folded his arms across his chest, the unlit cigar wiggled in the corner of his mouth. "What you've done is act as a conduit for free publicity for Darryl Zanuck, the same Mr. Zanuck that I thought you were trying to get away from. Does he still have his hooks in you, Joan? If he does, I need to know right now. Right. Now."

Joan's pride in bringing in the picture of Shirley Temple and her White House visitors was fading fast. "There is nothing between Darryl Zanuck and me. Nothing.

75

I have not even laid eyes on him in three months, not since before I asked you for a job."

Billy stared at her as he considered her statement. He dropped his hands back to his sides and stood. "Two bucks," he said, moving back behind his desk and sitting down. He pulled a notepad toward him and began scribbling. When he finished, he tore the page from the pad and held it out to Joan. She rose and took it, but Billy held on for a moment. "This is the last time I pay you to rewrite a studio press release, Joan. Understand?"

"Understood."

"Beat it."

"Thanks, Billy."

"Git!"

CHAPTER 15

Fausto stood at the corner and checked his watch. It had been fifteen minutes since he'd watched Andy Archie enter the bar. *Let him wait,* he thought. *Let him become anxious. Let him worry that there will be no more money and then, at the last moment, show up and make his dreams of good fortune come true.*

At seven minutes after four, Fausto left the shade at the side of the hardware store and crossed the street. He entered the bar, caught the eye of the bartender, and held up his thumb and forefinger, nodding toward the red-haired man who sat at the end of the bar with his back to the door.

The bartender nodded and turned back toward the taps, taking two mostly clean glasses from the shelf behind the bar.

"So, my friend," Fausto began with a smile, as he slid on to the stool next to his contact, "here we are again. And what news do you have for me? Were you able to set up a meeting?"

"Not exactly," the red-haired man replied, shaking a Lucky from his pack. Fausto pulled a gold lighter from his pocket and spun the flint. "Thanks," Andy said, taking a drag. The bartender set two glasses in front of them and turned away toward the other end of the bar. "I don't think a private meeting is going to be possible. What I hear is she's leaving town tomorrow."

"Going where?"

"San Francisco maybe."

Fausto tried to control his excitement. "San Francisco? Is she shooting a picture there?"

Andy snorted. "No. Her pictures don't have budgets like that. No, some big shots from the White House visited the lot today and I heard them invite her to join them on a short vacation."

"And she's going?"

"That's all I know. I figure that's worth another twenty."

Fausto smiled and sipped his beer. "Not so fast, friend. How will she travel? When will she leave? Who's traveling with her? I need more details before your information is of value. And if she is leaving tomorrow, I need it fast."

Fausto watched their reflections in the mirror behind the bar as Andy's brow wrinkled and he stared down at his cigarette pack. "Not sure I can get any more information for you. They finished filming her picture this afternoon. She doesn't start her next one for a week or so. She won't be back on the lot and I won't have any more contact with her until then."

"Surely there must be some way to find out." Fausto pulled a twenty-dollar bill from his pocket and slid it under Andy's pack of Luckys. "There is more money to be earned, friend. You know already that I am a serious man. Help me and I will help you. Once the job is complete, there will be a generous payment for you."

Shirley Temple Is Missing

Andy looked up then, his worried blue eyes staring into Fausto's guileless brown ones. "This isn't a kidnapping or anything, right?"

"Of course not. I have no need to hold someone for ransom. Do you think I need money?"

Andy's eyes shifted down to Fausto's hand-made shoes and slowly worked their way up past his immaculately tailored suit and back to Fausto's eyes. "I guess not."

"You, on the other hand..." Fausto left the statement unfinished.

Andy hesitated, staring at the twenty on the bar. "I'll see what I can find out. How do I reach you?"

"We meet here at 8 p.m." Fausto said. "I buy you a nice dinner." Andy rolled his eyes.

"OK." Fausto laughed and held up his hands. "I buy you a hamburger!"

CHAPTER 16

Missy was giving herself one last critical look in the mirror in her hotel room prior to meeting Grace and Marvin for a drink in the Gold Room downstairs when the phone rang. "This is Miss LeHand," she said, glancing at her watch; Marvin had only half an hour before he had to leave for the station to catch his cross-country train to Washington.

"Miss LeHand? Oh, I'm so glad I caught you in. This is Gertrude Temple."

"Oh, how nice to hear from you," Missy said, the warmth of her smile transferring itself into her throaty voice. "I hope this is good news about the trip to San Francisco."

"As a matter of fact, it is," Mrs. Temple said. "I talked it over with my husband and got Mr. Zanuck's OK to travel with you tomorrow. There are a couple of conditions Mr. Zanuck insisted on, for Shirley's safety and security, but they shouldn't pose a problem."

As a regular member of President Roosevelt's traveling entourage, Missy knew a good deal about such "conditions." "Tell me," she said.

"Well, since Shirley has become so popular, she simply creates mob scenes everywhere we go," Mrs.

Temple said. "When we went to Hawaii this past summer, we only got her off the boat by putting her on the shoulders of Duke Kaha—, Kaha—oh, you know, that famous surfing fellow--and surrounding them with police officers. What Mr. Zanuck wants to do this time is disguise her as a boy and have her board the train separately from me, with Mr. Griffith, her bodyguard. He's got someone in costuming at the studio working on the clothes, and they may even do a little makeup. Shirley thinks it's a great adventure. She's practicing lowering her voice to sound like a little boy and wants us all to call her Tommy!"

Missy chuckled appreciatively, then asked, "What will you do once she's on the train?"

"We'll keep her in costume at least until we arrive at the hotel in San Francisco," Mrs. Temple said, "then Griff and I will decide how to handle things during our visit. Which reminds me, where are you and Miss Tully staying? We'll want to book rooms at the same hotel."

"The St. Francis, on Union Square," Missy said. "Why don't I handle it for you? I can request rooms for you and Mr. Griffith on the same floor as ours. A double for you and Shirley and a single for Mr. Griffith?"

"Oh, yes, thank you," Mrs. Temple said. "The studio has already made the arrangements for the train tickets. We'll all be in the observation car together, at the end of the train. Griff and Shirley will travel in his personal car to the station, and my husband offered to pick you girls up at the Biltmore on our way to the station. That way it can appear I'm just having a little weekend getaway with some friends."

"Which is exactly what you're doing," Missy assured her. "What time can we expect you in the morning?"

CHAPTER 17

Andy Archie passed through the studio gates at ten minutes after five o'clock, the cargo in his back pocket pressing against his hip. He hoped he wasn't too late. Once filming was completed, there'd be no reason for Shirley to stick around. He figured his chance of finding out about Shirley's trip—if in fact she was going at all—was diminishing quickly.

He fingered the small badge he'd pinned to the front of his shirt and headed toward Shirley's cottage. Only when he saw John Griffith sitting on the cottage's small porch did he begin to relax. If Griff was still around, then Shirley was too.

"Hiya, Griff," Andy called out as he opened the gate in the white picket fence surrounding the cottage.

Griff looked up from the newspaper he was reading. "Andy. How's the ankle?"

"A lot better. Another week or so and it'll be good as new. Say, I was wondering if Shirley was still around." Andy reached for his back pocket and pulled out a store-bought slingshot. "I've been coaching her a little on how to use one of these and I thought she'd enjoy a real one, not one of those cheap things made from a y-shaped stick."

Griff chuckled. "So, you're the guy! She couldn't stop jabbering about that scene where she thumped Jack. Hang on. I'll tell her you're here." Griff ducked into the cottage. Andy shifted his weight to his good leg and felt the sweat sliding down the back of his neck. He was more nervous right now than when he had to fall off a horse.

"Hi, Andy!" Shirley exclaimed as she bounded across the porch, coming to a stop in front of the stunt man. Griff was still inside. "Hey, you're wearing your police force badge. Lucky for you! I would fine you if you didn't!"

Andy dropped to his knee. "You bet, Sure Shot! I'm hoping to get promoted to sergeant. Say, I thought maybe you'd need a real slingshot for your trip. I picked this one out especially for you. Here, try it out." Shirley gripped the tapered wooden handle and stuck her arm out straight. "That's it," Andy said. He picked up a pebble from the pathway leading to the cottage and held it out to her. "I hear you're going to San Francisco."

"That's right," Shirley said, squeezing one eye shut and pulling the slingshot's pouch back. "Watch this." She let the pebble fly and watched it carom off the top of a fence post.

"Nice shot!"

"You should come with us!" Shirley smiled and turned toward Andy.

"What time should I meet you?" Andy asked with a laugh.

"We're taking the morning train, the really fancy one."

"The *Daylight*?"

Shirley Temple Is Missing

"I don't know what it's called, just that it's the best train there is. Missy and Grace work for the President so they always go first class! Mother said we'd get to sit with them in the observation car on the trip. That's the last one on the train, with all the swivel seats. And guess what, Andy?"

"What?"

"It takes all day to go from here to San Francisco. We'll get to eat on the train and everything! Mother said I can order anything I want. I can even have ice cream!"

"That sounds pretty exciting. I expect you to tell me all about it when you get back, all right?"

"Aw, why don't you go with us? We could have some target practice." Shirley winked.

"Well, I know that would be fun, but somebody's got to keep things running around here while you're gone, Shirley."

"Sure Shot!"

"That's what I meant," Andy said, laughing. Griff emerged from the cottage, followed by Mrs. Temple. "Well, look, you have a fun time and I'll see you soon."

"OK, Andy. See you soon!" Shirley skipped over to her mother, holding out her new slingshot for inspection. Andy waved goodbye and turned back toward the gate.

"The *Daylight*," Andy said, taking a bite of his hamburger. "Tomorrow morning." He was seated in the back booth of Harmon's Bar, away from the street and away from any prying eyes. The well-dressed stranger with the funny accent was seated across from him, nursing a beer. Andy had returned to the bar confident that the information gleaned from his visit with Shirley would earn him another payment from his nameless benefactor.

"Very good, my friend. If you ever decide to give up stunt work, perhaps you could become a private eye like Sam Spade or Nick Charles." The stranger chuckled, then took a sip from his beer.

"So 'friend,'" Andy said, looking up from his hamburger and making eye contact with the stranger, "I figure that information is worth another hundred bucks at least."

"A relative fortune to you, yes?"

"Yes."

"But perhaps you'd like to make even more?"

The question caught Andy by surprise. He took a long drink from his beer to gain time to consider his response. "You know I've done right by you, mister. I've found out what you wanted to know. I've told you stuff that you couldn't find out on your own and I've kept my mouth shut. But I still don't know what you're up to."

"And you never will, my friend. But, as I've already assured you, no harm will come to your young friend."

Andy wiped the grease from his mouth with a thin paper napkin and looked hard at his companion. "I don't even know your name."

The stranger paused, then he smiled. "Call me Juan."

"All right, Juan."

"But you haven't answered my question: you'd like to make more money, yes?"

"What would you want me to do?" Andy asked.

CHAPTER 18

San Francisco

"Excellency?"

"Yes?" answered Cosimo Palladino, leaning across his newspaper toward the intercom on his desk.

"The assistant consul for cultural affairs for you."

"Send him in."

"He is on the telephone, signore."

Cosimo snatched the handset to his ear, thinking that at least he wouldn't have to smell Fausto's cloying cologne. "Fausto! Where are you?"

Fausto Trevisano's voice echoed through the static-filled long-distance phone line. "Excellency, I am still in Los Angeles attending to the matter we discussed in your office."

"Excellent, excellent," Cosimo responded automatically, his eyes straying back toward the headlines on his desk. "And are you having success?" Cosimo wasn't sure what Fausto was doing in Los Angeles. Whatever it was, it wasn't at the top of Cosimo's priority list just now. The American newspapers were continuing to portray Italy in a poor light, continuing to castigate Il Duce for his Ethiopian aggression. Longshoremen working the Oakland docks had refused to unload two Italian-flagged cargo ships in protest. Several Italian businesses with offices in the city had reported that customers were upset, and orders were down. It was only a matter of time, Cosimo felt, before Italian tourists would feel the displeasure of their hosts. *I shouldn't have taken this call*, he thought as Fausto rambled on. *I've got important work to do.*

"Signore? Are you still there?" Fausto's question snapped Cosimo's attention back to his subordinate.

"Yes, Fausto."

"I asked if you can work us in on Saturday. I know you must be very busy."

"Yes, Fausto. That will be fine. Set an appointment for Saturday afternoon with my secretary. Thank you for your report."

"Thank you, Excellency! We will see you Saturday!"

Cosimo hung up the phone, wondering, *Who's "we?"*

FRIDAY, OCTOBER 11, 1935

CHAPTER 19

Los Angeles

Joan Roswell scanned Friday's headlines in the *Standard's* morning edition as she loitered between the lobby of Los Angeles's Central Terminal and the platforms serving the departing trains. Joan was desperate for a real story, one that would give her some credibility with her boss, so she'd taken his advice and was staking out the city's railroad station. Her stomach growled as she glanced over the top of the paper, searching the steady flow of passengers for a newsworthy face. She'd settled on a five-cent cup of coffee and a cigarette for breakfast. She knew she'd get hungry later and had reserved her last dollar and thirty cents for real food.

According to the paper, fifty members of the League of Nations were now demanding that Italy pull its troops out of Ethiopia or face sanctions, whatever those might be. Of course, the nations that were braying the loudest were Great Britain and France, both of which already ruled colonies on the African continent. *Those that have, get.*

Shirley Temple Is Missing

Joan looked up in time to see a large, expensively-dressed man swagger past, a much smaller woman on his arm. Not only was he nattily attired, but beneath his gray fedora, he wore a famous face that was a favorite of western fans. Joan folded her newspaper and fell into step behind the couple, struggling to catch up with them in the crowd jostling toward the trains.

"Mr. Thorpe!" Joan called out. The big man turned his head even as he kept walking. He flashed a white smile and waved. Joan jogged to catch up, barely avoiding a collision with a red cap pushing a cart of luggage toward the terminal's taxi stand.

"Mr. Thorpe!" Joan shouted again. This time the big man stopped and turned. Joan smiled, putting on her friendliest face. As she reached the man and woman, Joan stuck out her hand. "Joan Roswell with the *Standard*. So nice to see you again so soon!"

A puzzled look crossed Thorpe's face as he tried to place Joan's. "We were together at the mayor's charity ball last week," Joan continued, working to coax a response from the reticent movie star.

"I'm sorry," Thorpe replied, a blank look on his tanned, handsome face, "I was only there for a few minutes and the publicity boys were telling me what to do. You know, pose for this picture, sign this autograph."

Joan glanced from Thorpe to the woman clinging to his arm. "Hello, dear," she said, extending her gloved hand. "I'm Joan Roswell."

"Forgive me," Thorpe said, blushing. "This is Mavis Hunnicutt." Turning toward the smaller woman, Thorpe said, "This is Miss Rostron."

"Roswell, dear," Joan corrected without taking her eyes off the petite young woman's pretty face. "Delighted to meet you. Tell me, where is Kit Justice, the king of Saturday morning serials, off to on such a beautiful day?"

"Terry and I are going up to San Francisco. We're going to see the sights, aren't we, Terry?" Mavis said in a squeaky voice with a strong Brooklyn accent.

"That's right," Thorpe replied with a nod.

"It must be quite thrilling to be seen on the arm of one of Hollywood's leading men, a star who movie-goers pay to see on the big screen. Have you two been together long?"

"Listen, Miss Rostron—"

"Roswell."

"Right. Well, listen, this is a private trip. If you want any kind of statement, call Larry Gosnell at Pacific Pictures." Thorpe touched the brim of his hat and said, "C'mon Mavis. We'll miss our train."

Joan watched as Thorpe and Mavis resumed their brisk walk toward the distinctive orange, red, and black liveried carriages of the Southern Pacific's new *Daylight* train. She smiled, watching Mavis taking two steps to keep pace with every stride of Thorpe's.

She followed at a distance, but doubted that she'd get anything more from Thorpe. Besides, Terry Thorpe spending the weekend with some cute little strumpet was hardly news, not the kind that would satisfy Billy Bryce anyway. Joan stopped and listened as the loudspeaker blared the pending departure of the *Daylight*, its locomotive already belching white steam toward the glass skylights of the station. She watched as Thorpe helped Mavis onto the step stool at the bottom of the first-class carriage. *Probably going into a private drawing room,* she thought. *Wonder what it's like to ride first class on that train. And wonder what stories those cars could tell.*

Thorpe disappeared up the steps and Joan turned back toward the late arriving passengers. Several small groups stood here and there along the platform waving to friends or loved ones already on board the train. One man in a gray three-piece suit was trotting toward the train, a sweating porter with two suitcases struggling to keep up. Joan leaned against a support column and unfolded her newspaper. It would be nice to travel first class, just once.

"Last call, all aboard the *Coast Daylight*, express service to San Francisco!" came the disembodied voice over the loudspeakers. As the message echoed off the concrete platform and heavy iron of the locomotive, Joan glanced up. A man and a boy were jogging toward the train. The man carried a single tan leather suitcase and held the boy's small hand in his. Joan glanced back down at her paper. Then she looked back up in time to see John Griffith hand the boy up the steps to the extended hands of a conductor. Next Griffith boarded, clutching the suitcase handle. A whistle blew, and a white-jacketed attendant reached down and picked up the step stool and handed it up to waiting hands on the railway car's steps. Joan took a tentative step toward the train, tossing her newspaper into a trash basket. Her mind was clicking now, keeping time with her quickened steps across the platform.

"Hold on!" she called to the attendant at the next car toward the engine as he bent to pick up the stool at the base of the car's stairs. The uniformed man flashed a broad smile and stood up, offering his hand to Joan as she stepped up on the stool and grabbed the iron railing of the carriage's steps.

"You just made it, miss!" He lifted the stool and set it up on the stairs and then swung himself aboard. "The passenger cars are this way," he pointed, holding open the door at the end of the carriage. "Just go right on through the tavern car and show your ticket to the conductor. He'll help you to your seat. Any bags?"

"What?"

"Do you have any luggage I can help you with?" the man clarified with a smile.

"I… no, they're already aboard. Thank you so much." Joan turned and headed through the doorway. As she moved between the art deco-style bar to her left and the half-moon-shaped window-side tables on her right, the train began to move. She grabbed a seat back for balance. Joan's mind was racing, trying to make sense of what she'd seen, of what had moved her to jump on this train without a bag, without a plan and, worst of all, without a ticket or the money to purchase one. As the platform fell away behind them, Joan was sure of only two things: she'd seen John Griffith climb on board and she'd bet her remaining dollar and thirty cents that he wasn't traveling with a little boy.

CHAPTER 20

On the *Daylight*

Andy Archie sat staring out the window as the train gathered speed on its way north. His starched collar and necktie felt tight as a noose around a neck unaccustomed to business attire. Juan had insisted he dress the part of a traveling businessman.

"You'll blend right in," he'd said.

Sure, Andy thought, *as long as nobody looks too closely*. He'd worn his dark gray funeral suit and shined his black, high-top shoes. His one good hat, a gray fedora, sat on the narrow luggage rack above his head. Wardrobe was the least of his worries. He still had to find Shirley, avoid her armed bodyguard, convince her to get off the train with him in San José, and then rendezvous with Juan outside the station.

Andy had hoped to be done with the whole business once he had reported Shirley's travel plans, but Juan—and the promise of another five hundred bucks—had persuaded him to remain a part of the conspiracy. *What could go wrong*? Andy asked himself, then pictured the .38 John Griffith carried in his shoulder holster.

When he'd taken the new slingshot to her the previous afternoon, Shirley had said something about an observation car. Andy figured the observation car was the one with the rounded back end at the rear of the train. According to the timetable printed in a colored pamphlet at his seat, the train wouldn't reach San José for more than eight hours, but Andy felt the sooner he learned the layout of the train and the sooner he figured out where Shirley was, the better. Once in possession of that information, he'd have to come up with a plan to get her off the train—a good plan that would earn him the rest of the money.

As the car swayed gently and the click-clack of the rails increased in frequency, Andy grasped the back of the seat in front of him and stood. He had been seated in the passenger section of the baggage car, right behind the locomotive and its tender. He stepped into the aisle and began the long walk toward the rear of the train.

Without a ticket—and therefore without an assigned seat—Joan Roswell calculated her best option was the coffee shop. One of the articulated cars on the train, the coffee shop shared a truck—the heavy set of iron wheels that kept the car running smoothly along the rails—with the kitchen car where food for both the coffee shop and dining car was prepared.

Joan navigated the narrow passenger corridor that ran along the outer wall of the kitchen car and pushed through the tightly sealed door into the coffee shop. She claimed a rear-facing window seat at a table along the right side of the car and ordered a ten-cent cup of coffee.

Now what?

She needed to find Griff, but she needed to find him when he was alone, not with Mrs. Temple or that brassy woman from the White House. Alone, Griff would talk to her, maybe even give her a quote around which she could build a good story.

Griff and his companion had boarded the train toward the rear, same as Terry Thorpe and the little tramp traveling with him. *That must be where the rich folks ride*, Joan thought. *So that's where I need to be looking.*

It's a nice train, Andy thought as he passed from one car into the next. The colorful seats lent an almost festive air to the interior, the scenery outside the windows was pleasant, and the passengers appeared excited to be traveling in such fine style.

His mood was more anxious than excited. He'd passed by a small cubicle at the end of one of the chair cars in which sat three blue-coated men, members of the train's crew. They represented, at least in part, the authority aboard the train. These were the conductor, the ticket taker, and the Southern Pacific passenger agent, whose formidable task it was to see no rider left the train unhappy.

As a stunt man, Andy was no stranger to moving conveyances. He'd been shot, punched, and roped from a number of trains in the course of his six-year career. This train he hoped to ride all the way to the station and exit via the stairs—and not alone, either.

Andy pushed open the door to the coffee shop car and felt it close behind him, locking out the noise of the rails and sealing in the cool conditioned air. He took a moment to steady himself, glancing at the few customers seated at the tables. There was an older couple on his right sharing a Danish and coffee, a woman with two young children, both of whom were sporting chocolate milk mustaches, and another woman sitting by herself facing away from him.

He passed through the seating area and by the service counter and proceeded along the hallway running the length of the kitchen car. Next, he entered the dining car, where attendants wearing white mess jackets, snappy bow ties, and long, spotless white aprons over their black trousers were setting the tables for breakfast service.

"Good morning, sir," a man in a three-piece suit with brass buttons said, shifting his attention from the waiters to his passenger. "We aren't quite ready to serve yet," he said looking at a large pocket watch, "but if you'd like, I can go ahead and seat you."

"No, thank you. I'm just looking for my wife," Andy said. "She was headed in this direction when I saw her last."

"Ah. I haven't seen any ladies heading in this direction. Perhaps she's visiting one of the ladies' lounges."

"Where would those be?"

"There's one in each carriage, on the locomotive end of the car. Any porter would be happy to assist you."

"Thanks," Andy said with a nod. "If I don't find her between here and the end of the train, I'll know where to look next."

"Very good, sir. When you find her, come and have breakfast with us." The man smiled and nodded.

Andy exited the dining car and crossed the walkway connecting it to the next carriage. Once inside, he immediately noticed the ladies' lounge the crew member had referred to. He scanned the faces of the passengers in the car as he made his way along the aisle. No familiar faces so far. He passed through two more cars and then found himself in the tavern car. Although it was still fairly early, Andy was surprised to find a few people, mostly men in business suits, already drinking at the bar. He licked his lips, thinking how good a beer would taste right then.

When he opened the door to the parlor car, Andy felt as though he'd stumbled onto a whole different train. Gone were the twin side-by-side chairs flanking a center aisle. Instead, wide, comfortably upholstered swivel chairs were arrayed along both sides of the car, their inhabitants reading newspapers and magazines and being served by a uniformed waitress.

"Help you, sir?" a man in a blue blazer bearing the *Coast Daylight* logo asked. Andy recognized the uniform of one of the passenger agents; he was probably assigned to that car.

"I'm looking for my wife," Andy said. It was at that moment that he saw Griff seated two-thirds of the way toward the rounded end of the car. Griff's chair was turned to look out the back window, toward where the train had already been.

"Only passengers holding parlor-observation tickets are permitted in this car, sir."

"No," Andy said. "I don't see her. She's given me the slip, I guess." He smiled, making a joke of it.

The railroad man leaned in and gave Andy a conspiratorial smile. "Happens to me all the time." He winked.

Andy turned and made his way back into the tavern car, but he'd seen what he needed. A few seats past Griff, kneeling in a backward-turned seat looking out one of the rear-facing windows, was a young child—with a slingshot hanging out of her back pocket.

CHAPTER 21

As the *Daylight* gained steam outside Glendale, Missy, Grace, and Gertrude Temple were comfortably ensconced in upholstered swivel chairs in the parlor car. Mrs. Temple had relaxed visibly when Griff boarded with Shirley. Or Tommy, as she was now calling herself. The child had bounded into the car, to the amusement of the other passengers, and said in a deep voice, "Hello, ladies! Mind if I join you?" Shirley's signature curls were completely hidden under a plain wool newsboy cap. She was wearing a pair of brown corduroy coveralls and a denim jacket, with simple black boots on her feet. A make-up artist from the studio had given her face a darker skin tone and penciled in her eyebrows a bit. No one would recognize America's little blonde sweetheart.

"Why, certainly, young man," Mrs. Temple had smiled. "In fact, I think I have a seat for you and your 'father' right here." She looked up at Griff and arched an eyebrow. "Any problems?"

"None at all," he assured her, settling into a seat near his young charge's. Shirley had immediately begun testing her seat's 350-degree swivel capacity. After a warning look from her mother, she knelt in the backward-turned seat, looking over the seat back out the window.

The *Coast Daylight*, which had made its debut in March with tremendous fanfare, was known for its speed, luxury, and service. It also passed through some of the most spectacular scenery in California: the San Luis and Santa Lucia mountain ranges, acres of orange groves, and more than a hundred miles of Pacific shoreline. Announcements over the public-address system kept passengers apprised of upcoming sights, as well as the availability of food, drink, and other amenities in the train's dining car, coffee shop and, especially, its tavern car.

"Good morning, Ladies and Gentlemen!" boomed a voice over the PA. "Breakfast is now being served in the coffee shop and dining car located in the center of the train. Thank you!"

A waitress in a black dress and spotless white apron, a pleated white cap covering most of her hair, approached them with a broad smile. "Can I get you anything to drink?" she asked. "Coffee, tea?" She winked at the child. "Hot cocoa?"

"I'd love some cocoa!" Shirley said, forgetting to use her Tommy voice. "Oops! I'd love some cocoa," she said, repeating herself in the lower register.

The waitress gave her a curious look, but turned her attention to the adults. Missy asked for black coffee. "You know, all I ever have for breakfast at the White House is a cup of black coffee and maybe a glass of orange juice," said Missy. "I gain weight so easily."

"You!" said Grace, patting a well-padded hip. "You never seem to gain weight. What I wouldn't give for your figure." She turned to Mrs. Temple. "What do you say? Feel like getting something to eat?"

"I wouldn't mind a little something," said Mrs. Temple. "Sh—er, Tommy, do you want some breakfast, or do you want to stay here with Griff and Miss LeHand and enjoy your cocoa?"

"I'll stay here," the child replied. "I just want to look out the windows for a while. I might even see some wild Indians, or a gang of outlaws attacking the train for the payroll. But don't worry, I can defend us with my slingshot."

"Well, that's a relief," Mrs. Temple said playfully. "I feel much safer knowing you are on the job." Several other passengers in the parlor car smiled or chuckled over the child's remarks, but none seemed to recognize her. They returned to their newspapers, card games, and cigarettes, settling in for a long day on the most beautiful train in the world.

Missy smiled at her young friend. "I'm so glad you got to come on the trip with us today," she said, patting Shirley's knee.

"Me too," Shirley said. "That's a pretty bracelet."

"Thank you!" Missy said, jingling her gold charm bracelet. "It's my favorite one. See, each of these charms stands for a special memory in my life."

"I know that one," Shirley said. "That's the White House, right?"

"Right!" Missy replied. "And this little mailbox was given to me because I handle so much of the President's mail. See? The door opens, and the flag goes up and down, just like a real mailbox."

"Ooh!" said Shirley. "What about this one?" She touched the tiny airplane on the bracelet.

"Well, that reminds me of the first airplane trip I took," said Missy. "I flew to the Democratic National Convention in 1932 with Mr. Roosevelt. That's when he was nominated for president."

"I haven't been on a plane yet," Shirley confided. "But I pretended to be on one in *Bright Eyes*."

"I saw that movie," Missy said. "You had to parachute out of the plane when it got in an awful storm. When I was on my first plane, we got in a storm, too, but I didn't have to parachute out. I just got airsick!"

"Yuck," said Shirley. "I think we're much safer on a train, don't you?"

"Much, much safer," said Missy. "What can go wrong on a train?"

CHAPTER 22

Joan had seen the red-headed man before. She was sure of it, but she couldn't place him. He had walked through the coffee shop car headed in the same direction she needed to go: toward the back of the train.

She opened her clutch purse and took out her compact, flipping it open and checking her lipstick. Using the small mirror, she was able to observe the area behind her, the pathway towards the front of the train. Satisfied that no ticket-taker was approaching from behind, Joan snapped the compact shut and tossed it back in her purse.

The reporter stood and straightened her gray skirt, stepping into the center aisle. She felt the swaying of the train and widened her stance to account for it. Joan entered the passenger hallway through the kitchen car as the train leaned into a curve. She placed a hand on the wall to steady herself and passed through the corridor into the dining car. More than half the cloth-covered tables were already filled with breakfasting passengers, the white-uniformed waiters, accustomed to the constant swaying of the train, moving gracefully through the car balancing trays laden with fresh fruit, scrambled eggs, crispy bacon, and fried potatoes. Silver pots of coffee and glasses of brightly-colored juices adorned most tables.

Joan walked slowly through the car, her gaze flitting from side to side as she searched for the red-haired man. She reached the end of the dining car and turned around, double-checking to ensure that she hadn't overlooked him. She was also looking out for a conductor, mindful that she was riding the rails without a ticket.

Joan continued her walk, her mind racing through images of faces and places. As she reached the doorway separating the dining car from the adjoining passenger carriage, it hit her. Of course! He had been at the studio! He'd lit her cigarette!

The reporter resumed her search, entering the last of the double, articulated cars of the train. She paused at the front of the car next to the ladies' lounge, her eyes sweeping the riders in front of her. Several were reading morning papers, though to her chagrin, more were holding the *Times* than the *Standard*. In the middle of the car, a conductor in a blue uniform with a matching billed cap was leaning over a couple and punching their tickets. Joan slid behind him while he was occupied and made her way to the end of the car.

She glanced over her shoulder to see the conductor working his way through the car in the opposite direction. From here, all she could see were the backs of the heads of the taller passengers. Unless "Red" had somehow given her the slip, unlikely on a train with a single aisle, he had to be either in the tavern car or back with the Temple party in the observation car.

Joan exited onto the narrow catwalk bridging the chair car and the tavern car and opened the door. Immediately inside the door on her left were some lockers, on her right a refrigerator. Beyond a glass partition, she could see the half-moon tables and benches lining both sides of the car, interrupted by a matching semi-circular bar in the center of the carriage.

And just inside the partition, seated at the first booth, his back to her, was the red-haired man. *You're going to give me a story, friend.* Joan took a deep breath, stepped forward, and slid into the booth across from the man, startling him.

Before he could speak, Joan said, "Buy me a drink."

"It's not five o'clock yet." He recovered his composure quickly.

Joan smiled. She was a beautiful woman; she knew that. Darryl Zanuck didn't consort with ugly women. Now was the time to turn on her considerable charm. "It's five o'clock somewhere."

The man looked out the window to his right. "You're on the wrong ocean."

"Maybe so," Joan replied, holding her smile, "but I'm on the right track. I know what you're up to and now I want to know why."

Andy had been surprised when the attractive reporter suddenly interrupted his solitude. He'd been one of only half a dozen patrons in the tavern car. It was still early, not even 10 a.m., well before drinking hours for all but the die-hard.

For a moment, he cursed himself for leaving his fedora in the luggage rack over his seat; his red hair was a dead giveaway. But he recovered quickly, realizing that her arrival was an opportunity rather than an obstacle.

"All right," Andy said, signaling to a waiter, "what is it you want to know, Mrs…?"

"Joan. Joan Roswell with the Los Angeles *Standard*."

"How can I help you, Joan?"

"Start by telling me your name and how long you've been one of Shirley Temple's bodyguards."

Andy paused. "Bottoms," he said.

Joan reached in her clutch for her pen and small notepad. "And your first name, dear?"

"That's it, Bottoms. As in Bottoms Up."

Joan looked up. "Oh, how very clever. Really, now, what's your name?"

"No names right now, Mrs. Roswell."

"It's Miss."

A waiter arrived and took Joan's order, a Bloody Mary. "I'll have another tonic water," Andy said.

"Working, are we?"

"Something like that."

"So, tell me: why another bodyguard? Is Shirley in danger?"

"Put your pad away," Andy said. "I'll tell you what I can, but you'll have to agree to help me and you can't use any of it for now."

"You can't muzzle the press, dear. First Amendment, you know."

"You're right, I can't muzzle the press, but I can muzzle me. I can stand right up and walk back to my seat. That'd make a pretty good story, wouldn't it? Land you right on the front page. Now, you want a story on my terms, or you want to have to pay for your own drink?"

Shirley Temple Is Missing

The reporter frowned and stuffed her pen and pad back in her purse. The waiter returned and set their drinks on the table. Once he had withdrawn, she narrowed her eyes at Andy and said, "All right, buster, spill it!"

"You've pegged me right, I am additional security. Neither Mrs. Temple nor Mr. Griffith are aware of my assignment and I need your word that you'll help keep it that way until I tell you otherwise. Deal?" Andy said.

"How do I know you'll keep your word?"

"Same way I know you'll keep yours," Andy replied, maintaining eye contact with Joan. "Deal or no deal?"

"Deal," the reporter replied after a moment's hesitation.

"Zanuck brought me in after the studio received a couple of unrelated—at least we think they're unrelated—kidnapping threats against Shirley."

"Why not alert the FBI? Kidnapping's federal since the Lindbergh case."

She's smarter than she looks. "Zanuck's working that angle. My job isn't investigations, it's security; an extra level of protection, if you will." Andy reached out and placed his hand lightly on Joan's forearm. "We don't want to alarm the Temples, so I watch from a discreet distance."

"Why not tell Griff? Surely he's trustworthy."

"Of course he is. But who exactly isn't? That's what we don't know. Could be somebody the family trusts. Maybe somebody Griff knows. Most kidnappings start with at least some inside knowledge. Somebody gets close to the family and collects information on habits and routines. Could take several months." Andy took a sip. "Any way, that's what's going on here."

"What's the nature of the threats?"

"I'm not in the loop on that. Like I said, my job is security, not investigation. You help me and once the danger has passed, I'll tell you all I know and point you in the right direction for the rest of the story."

"As long as I don't have to go to Zanuck to get it," she said with a shake of her head.

"I'll point, Joan. It'll be up to you to track it down. But until then, you don't say a word, right?"

"I never betray a confidence. What do you need me to do?"

CHAPTER 23

Los Angeles

Fausto loved to fly. He loved the sun in his eyes and the wind on his face. Most of all, he loved looking down on the beauty of God's creation, the sparkling blue waters of the Pacific to the left and the brown-tinged San Rafael Mountains rising to the right. Travel by air hadn't caught on with the public yet, but it would. As it did, it would become less expensive too. Why, someday, Fausto believed, everyone would travel by air, attracted by the speed and freedom of being able to go in any direction, not just along a set of rails running in only two directions.

Fausto had had no trouble obtaining a plane and pilot to ferry him north. All he had had to do was make his need known to Tony Oliveri. Tony had handled the arrangements with characteristic discretion. The small aerodrome north of Hollywood was home to several small aircraft and, more importantly, quite a few hungry pilots. For just fifty dollars, the pilot of the small, two-seat bi-plane had agreed to fly Fausto to San José and had ensured his arrival by 3 p.m. *More than enough time*, Fausto reflected as he sat in the rear cockpit and watched California drift past below.

Marcello would meet him at the airfield at three and they would drive to the train station. That part was easy. The only part of the plan that Fausto worried about was getting the girl off the train. That he had had to leave up to the stunt man. *Well, no use worrying now*, Fausto thought, leaning back in the open cockpit. *God's mighty hand will guide events for the glory of the Italian Empire and Il Duce. And if some of that glory reflects on me, then it must surely be the will of the Almighty.*

CHAPTER 24

On the *Daylight*

Joan unfolded the note and read it again:

Sure Shot—let's get some ice cream at 3:30. Bring your slingshot. It's a secret, so don't tell your mother or Griff.

All "Bottoms" expected her to do was get the note into the little girl's hand without her mother or her professional bodyguard noticing. *Piece of cake*. At least it should be a piece of cake if she could avoid having to present a ticket. So far, she'd had success going in the other direction whenever she'd seen a conductor, but sooner or later, Joan feared, that strategy would fail.

At present, she was hiding out in the ladies' restroom in the passenger carriage just north of the tavern car. While the restroom provided good concealment, it also prevented her from keeping an eye on the Temple party two carriages away in the observation car. As a result, she couldn't remain there long before coming out and having another look around—a look that might expose her ticket-less status.

113

The train was now on the ocean front section of its route, the one hundred thirty-five miles between Ventura and Pismo that gave the *Coast Daylight* its name. The train's second stop, Santa Barbara, was twenty minutes or so behind them.

Joan calculated that her best play was to linger in the tavern car, waiting for the Temples to come out of the observation car and pass through on their way to lunch. Depending on how hungry they got, or how bored, that would probably happen no sooner than thirty minutes and no later than an hour and a half. *Patient. Just be patient.*

A short while later, Joan was strategically positioned in the rear corner of the tavern car facing forward. From there, she would be able to see the conductor entering the far end of the car before he would see her. She figured that by this halfway point of the journey, all the first-class passengers seated in the parlor-observation cars would already have had their tickets punched.

Joan looked at her watch. It was five minutes to one and her stomach, running on a cup of coffee and a Bloody Mary, was growling almost loud enough to be heard above the clacking of the train over the rails.

A pop of static sounded overhead as the train's loudspeakers were activated. "Attention please! Our next station is San Luis Obispo, the half-way point between Los Angeles and San Francisco. Our stop here will be very brief, so passengers going beyond San Luis Obispo, please remain on the train. Passengers detraining, please claim your hand baggage on the station platform as you step off the train. Thank you!"

Joan felt the train begin to slow. According to the timetable card at her booth, an extra locomotive would be added to the train at this stop to assist its passage through the mountainous portion of the journey northward.

Wanting to stretch her legs, Joan joined the trickle of passengers moving toward the exits at the end of each car. Porters were busy moving bags with the help of the new baggage elevators built into the ends of each chair car. The elevator was essentially a set of rotating shelves on which smaller bags were placed and lifted into the car. When the train arrived at one of its stops, like San Luis Obispo, the process was reversed and a porter standing on the station platform opened the elevator's outer door and unloaded bags tagged for that stop. *Very clever and very modern*, Joan thought approvingly.

As the train began its sixteen-mile climb toward Santa Margarita, the steepest portion of the journey, Joan headed back to the tavern car.

"Ladies and gentlemen," the loudspeakers came back to life, "we will appreciate it if all passengers who boarded at San Luis Obispo will have their tickets out and ready to hand to the conductors as they pass through your car. Please be sure to tell the conductor and your porter how far you are going so that your baggage can be put off at the right station."

Joan had just settled back into her seat when the door behind her pushed open. She glanced up quickly to see the two women from the White House enter the car, talking and laughing. Directly behind them was Gertrude

Temple and following her, dressed as a boy, was the world's most famous six-year-old. Joan let the women pass by before sliding to the end of the booth and holding out a page from her note pad and a pen.

"Could I please have your autograph?" she said, smiling at the surprised child.

"How'd you know it was me?" Shirley asked as her mother turned around.

"Oh, I'm a big fan!" Joan exclaimed in her most star-struck voice. Mrs. Temple eyed Joan carefully and watched as Shirley took the pen and signed the page. "This is just so exciting! Thank you so much!"

"You're welcome!" Shirley said, tilting her head toward Joan and winking. She leaned in close and said, "I'm traveling in disguise, so don't tell anybody that you've seen me. It's supposed to be a secret!"

"Come along, Tommy," Mrs. Temple said, turning to follow her companions.

"Well, here's your pen," Shirley said.

"And this is for you," Joan whispered, handing over "Bottoms's" note. "It's a secret too." She winked.

Shirley raised her eyebrows and whispered back, "Oh! I love secrets!" The child turned and skipped to catch up with her mother. Sticking the autograph in the pocket of her jacket. Joan exhaled and sank back into her seat.

"Ladies and gentlemen," the voice on the loudspeaker began, "if you look to your right, you will see the southbound *Daylight* heading toward Los Angeles."

An orange, red, and black blur flashed by the right-hand windows, the cushion of air being pushed along in front of the southbound train buffeting its northbound sister.

"May I see your ticket, please ma'am?"

An icy shock lurched through Joan's stomach as she turned to face the conductor.

"Is there some place private we can go to discuss this?" Joan asked, batting her eyelashes at the older man standing before her in his three-piece blue uniform and matching cap. The patch on his sleeve bore the colorful logo of the *Coast Daylight*, his silver nametag read "R. Rogers."

"No ma'am. We'll need to handle this here, if you please."

"What does the 'R' stand for?" Joan asked, standing and brushing her breasts against the conductor's arm.

"Roy," he answered, taking a step back.

"Like the cowboy?"

"Yes ma'am. Now, may I please see your ticket?"

"Roy," Joan said, placing one hand on the conductor's arm and leaning in close to his ear. "I'm sure we could work something out if you could just find us a quiet spot."

"Ma'am," Roy said, trying unsuccessfully to pull away in the narrow aisle.

"Call me Joan, dear."

"Ma'am, I'm fifty-nine years old and I got two kids in college and there's a depression on. Now if I was twenty years younger and jobs were easy to come by, I would be flattered by your attentions. But right now, I just need to see your ticket. Please."

Joan sighed and frowned, her shoulders slumping. "I haven't got one." She snapped open her purse. "How much?" Joan knew that however much it was, it was more than she had in her bag. She hoped somehow to prolong the conversation until some miracle occurred that would rescue her from this conscientious servant of the Southern Pacific.

"I'm sorry, ma'am, but all tickets on the *Coast Daylight* are advanced sales. I'm not authorized to sell you a ticket once onboard."

"Why, that's ridiculous!"

"Southern Pacific policy, ma'am."

"Miss! It's miss!"

"Yes, miss. If you'd please come with me toward the front of the train."

"For what purpose?"

"Stowaways ride to the next stop in the baggage car, ma'am…miss." The conductor gestured toward the front of the train.

Joan lifted her chin as though offended and headed toward the far end of the car, the conductor falling into step behind her. As they passed through the dining car, Joan was careful to avoid eye contact with the Temple party. Transiting the long corridor through the kitchen car, Joan thought about stumbling and faking an injury. Rogers would have to carry her forward—which, at his advanced age might kill him—or, better yet, leave her and go for help. But where could she hide on a train? Instead, she continued to move through the swaying carriages as the train climbed higher into the mountains.

After what seemed like a mile of narrow aisle-ways, they finally reached the combination baggage car-chair car just behind the locomotives and their coal tender. Reaching the door separating the seating section from the baggage compartment, the conductor pulled out a ring of keys attached to his belt by a gold chain. He unlocked the door and pushed it open, then stepped aside and motioned Joan toward the stacked trunks, large suitcases, and mail bags.

"You got her," came a voice from over the conductor's shoulder. "Nice work."

Rogers turned in confusion to see Andy Archie reach inside his coat pocket and pull out a small black leather wallet. He flipped it open to reveal a shiny gold badge and then flipped it shut again, forestalling scrutiny. "We've been tailing her for three days, all the way up from Tijuana."

"What? You mean she's a criminal?"

"It's all hush-hush, part of a much bigger investigation. I'm sorry, I'm not allowed to go into any detail, but I will make a full report." Andy reached into his pocket and pulled out a folded piece of paper and a pencil. "Your full name and your supervisor's name and title, please."

"Uh, Rogers, Roy F. Rogers. And my boss is Samuel Carden, train crew supervisor out of the L.A. office of the Southern Pacific."

"Well, Mr. Rogers, Roy, I will let him know what a good job you've done. You'll be named in my report, and I will send a copy to Mr. Carden, once I've taken out the sensitive parts, of course."

"Of course," the conductor agreed without comprehension.

"Now, Roy, if you don't mind, I'm going to have to interrogate the prisoner. You don't want to be a part of that. It may get messy."

Rogers hesitated for a moment, his mind trying with limited success to catch up with his ears. "Oh, sure." He took a step toward the door.

"And Roy?" Rogers stopped and looked at Andy. "Leave that door unlocked, won't you?"

"Yes sir!" Rogers said, exiting and pulling the door closed behind him.

Andy stood silently, staring at the door, waiting for the conductor to reappear, to have pierced the charade. But he didn't.

"You didn't tell me you were a cop."

Andy turned toward Joan and smiled. He pulled out the badge and flipped it open: *Shirley Temple Police Force* was embossed on it in black letters. "You better be glad Roy isn't very observant." He stuffed the wallet back in his pocket. "Now, did you deliver the message?"

It was Joan's turn to smile.

CHAPTER 25

Andy was relieved. With so little time to prepare for this trip, he was making plans on the fly, inventing tactics and telling lies without considering the longer-term impact these would have on his well-being. In fact, his main focus right now, his only focus, was getting Shirley Temple off the train and into the waiting arms of Juan. Only then would he be paid his remaining bounty. Only then could he make his own escape.

But before he could continue with his scheme, he had to figure out what to do with the reporter. Sure, she'd come in handy—once—but now he needed to keep her out of the way. He sat down on the corner of a trunk and pulled a pack of Luckys from his pocket.

"Want one?" he asked, offering the pack to Joan.

"Sure."

Andy struck a match and lit Joan's cigarette and then put the flame to his own. He inhaled deeply and sat for a moment staring at nothing.

"Did she read the note? Did she understand it?"

"All I know is that she got it. Whether she'll follow through with it or share it with her mother, I really can't say."

Andy flicked ash off the end of his smoke and looked at Joan. "You're going to have to stay in here. If you go wandering about, Roy Rogers out there is going to get suspicious. If he starts acting jumpy, that could tip off the bad guys and the whole game is up. I hate to leave you in here alone, but I don't see any other way."

"That's all right, dear. At least in here I won't have to be looking over my shoulder the whole time. Tell me again why you need to meet with the kid."

"As I said, it's routine for surveillance work—especially when we don't know exactly what we're looking for. I just need to know if she's seen anything unusual."

"Wouldn't you be more likely to get meaningful answers from one of the adults?"

"I absolutely would," Andy nodded. "But Zanuck's orders are to keep them in the dark. Do you know Zanuck?"

"In a sense."

"Then you know it wouldn't be prudent to ignore his orders."

"How will you keep from alarming the kid?"

"She knows me. I'll just tell her it's part of a game." *That much was true*, Andy thought, as he stood. "Do you need anything?" he asked, turning toward the door of the baggage compartment.

"Oh my, yes, quite a bit, in fact. I need a story, a nice, big, fat juicy one with villains and good guys."

Andy grinned. "And you'll get it. Let me ask a different question: Do you need anything right now?"

"Something to eat would be very nice."

Shirley Temple Is Missing

Andy bought an egg salad sandwich, a pack of peanut butter crackers and a bottle of Coke from the railroad's news agent and delivered them to Joan. He purchased a newspaper for himself, and was now sitting restlessly in his seat scanning its headlines and sneaking peeks at his watch. He couldn't seem to focus on the stories about the Italian army in Ethiopia or the next day's college football games. It was 2:30 p.m., the train approaching King City, and still another hour before he was to meet Shirley.

Shirley was excited and bored all at the same time. So far, she'd kept Andy's note a secret, but she still had to figure out how to escape from the constant supervision of her mother and Griff without arousing suspicion. Mother seemed to be enjoying her new friends, the ladies who worked for President Roosevelt. They'd jabbered all through lunch about what they were going to do in San Francisco. The only thing that sounded interesting to Shirley was Fisherman's Wharf. Maybe they'd get to see some big fish or even a whale!

Griff had waited until Shirley and the ladies had returned from lunch, then he'd gone to get something to eat. He'd be back any minute now.

By three-fifteen, Andy could wait no longer. He pulled himself up out of his seat, took his hat down from the rack above and began shuffling toward the dining car. He could only hope that his makeshift plan was about to succeed. But he wasn't going to let his red hair give him away again.

CHAPTER 26

San José

Fausto stepped out of the aviator's coveralls, folded them, and handed them back to the pilot.

"Thank you, my friend," he said, peeling off a twenty-dollar bill and sticking it in the pilot's breast pocket. "As agreed. And as agreed, no one will know of our flight?"

"No one will be the wiser," the pilot said with a nod.

Fausto turned toward the hangar. He located a wash room and bathed his face in cold water. Peering into the murky mirror above the rust-stained sink, he admired his good looks. He pulled a comb from his pocket and brought his thick, black hair back into order. He leaned over the sink and, using his hand as a cup, sucked in several mouthfuls of the refreshing water, then he dried his hands on the dirty towel and exited the wash room.

He stepped out of the hangar and into the bright sunshine, glancing around for Marcello and the car from the consulate. He had made it very clear to the consul's driver that he was on a tight schedule and that promptness was key to his mission—although, naturally, he hadn't shared exactly what that mission was. There were only four automobiles parked beside the hangar and none was a Cadillac.

Damn! Fausto thought, checking his watch. *Where is that idiot?*

Fausto looked out toward the gravel road leading to the hangar. A car was approaching at a rapid clip, a dust cloud trailing in its wake. It wasn't the car he was waiting on. He had specifically instructed Marcello to bring the Cadillac. Fausto intended his triumphal ride to be completed in style worthy of his achievement. The black Chevrolet sedan pulled up ten feet away and the dust cloud swept past it. The car door opened and a short, skinny young man with hair as dark as Fausto's stepped out. "Benvenuto a San José!" Marcello called out with a smile.

Fausto frowned and strode toward the car. "Where is the Cadillac, Topo? I told you to bring the Cadillac. I am on important business!"

Marcello clenched his jaw but managed to keep the smile on his face; Fausto knew he hated his nickname— "Mouse"—bestowed on him because of his slight build and bucked, rodent-like teeth, and used it all the time just to needle him. "Of course, of course. And I would have if it had been up to me, Fausto, but His Excellency, he needed his car this afternoon. Perhaps you'd like to discuss it with him?"

Fausto slapped the younger man on the back of the head. "Get in. We have a rendezvous to keep and you've already made us late! What's the matter with you? You can't tell time?"

"Ah, Fausto—I stopped at Spider Kelly's and had a beer with my lunch. Stop bustin' on me!"

"My apologies, Topo. I would never want official consulate business nor any of the special missions I complete for His Excellency to interfere with your nutrition. Perhaps if you would give me a list of your personal appointments, to include your meal times, I could conform to your schedule."

"You're making fun of me, aren't you, Fausto?"

"What gives you such an idea?"

CHAPTER 27

On the *Daylight*

"Mother," Shirley began, standing beside her mother's chair and laying her small hand on her forearm. "May I please go get some ice cream? The waiter at lunch said it was free."

Gertrude Temple was drowsy, the fine meal from the dining car and the gentle rocking of the train combining to lull her into deep relaxation. She had to force herself to respond. "If Griff will go with you."

"Griff's asleep."

Gertrude looked behind her to see Griff, head back, mouth open, eyes closed, a blanket draped across his lap. *She can't get lost on a train. Besides, she's still in her "Tommy" disguise.* "All right, Shirley, but come straight back here when you're finished, understand?"

"Yes ma'am!" Shirley kissed her mother on the cheek and then skipped toward the door separating the observation car from the rest of the train. "I'm going to get some ice cream!" she exclaimed to the passenger agent as he held the door for her.

Andy was seated in the middle of the dining car, checking his watch every thirty seconds and straining his eyes as though to see all the way to the end of the train. Finally, at 3:32 p.m., the far door opened and in she came. He let out a long, silent sigh. *Here we go!*

Andy stood, and Shirley saw him right away. "Hi, Sure Shot," Andy said with a smile. "I'm glad you could make it."

"Oh, it was easy," she said, smiling broadly. "I just told Mother that I wanted some of that free ice cream."

"What did you tell Griff?"

"He was asleep."

"Did you take a nap too?"

"Not me. I was too excited."

A waiter approached the table. "What may I get for you this afternoon, lady and gentleman?"

"Ice cream!" Shirley replied.

"What flavor?"

"Regular, please."

Andy grinned. "Two vanillas, please," he said. Once the waiter had retreated toward the kitchen, Andy leaned forward and said, "That's a pretty good disguise you're wearing. I bet nobody figured out you were you." Shirley smiled and started to answer but was cut off by the loudspeaker.

"Ladies and gentlemen, our next station is Salinas, largest city of the Salinas Valley and the transfer point for the Monterey Bay Area. Passengers heading to Del Monte, Monterey, Carmel, Watsonville, and Santa Cruz will find motor coaches to those destinations waiting just beyond the stations. Please remember to claim your hand baggage at the elevator as you step off the train. Passengers continuing on to points north are kindly requested to remain on the train. Thank you."

"I guess that's us, huh?" Andy said.

"Yep."

"Well, too bad in a way."

"Why?" Shirley asked.

"Well, you brought your slingshot, right?"

Shirley grinned and patted her pocket. "You bet!"

"Well, I was just hoping we could get in some practice at one of these stops."

The train began to slow, and the waiter reappeared carrying a tray with two generous servings of vanilla ice cream. He set them on the table along with linen napkins and monogrammed silver spoons. "Can I get you anything else?"

Andy smiled at Shirley and then looked up at the waiter. "Yes. How about two bottles of Coke?"

"Very good, sir," the waiter said with a smile and moved away again.

Shirley was already digging into her ice cream. At the studio, she was forbidden to eat in the cafeteria with everyone else. Mr. Zanuck didn't want her to get fat. Ice cream was a treat.

"You like Coke, right, Sure Shot?"

"Who doesn't?"

"I have an idea." The train gave a gentle lurch as it came to a stop. "We drink our Cokes and then at the next stop, we get off and use the bottles as targets. What do you say?"

"OK!" Shirley said, her eyes sparkling with mischievous delight.

CHAPTER 28

It was a long hour and a half between Salinas and San José, the next stop, the most critical stop on the trip in Andy's mind. He'd rarely engaged in so long a conversation with a six-year-old girl. They lingered over their ice cream and enjoyed their Cokes, looking at the window at the fields of crops, trying to identify different greens that made the Salinas Valley "the salad bowl of America," as one of the announcements had put it. Finally, Andy left two cents on the table to cover the deposit on the bottles and stuck one bottle in each of his coat's outer pockets.

Offering Shirley a tour of the train, he led her through the long corridor past the kitchen and into the coffee shop. He let her stand on the articulated joint between the kitchen and coffee shop cars as the train navigated a curve in the tracks, watching as the train appeared to bend under Shirley's small feet. He stopped at the rear of one car and asked the porter to show Shirley how the small baggage elevator worked.

"Could you ride in it like a real elevator?" she asked.

"Well, now, I suppose you could," the porter replied with a smile, "but I don't think your daddy would fit."

Shirley smiled and winked at Andy, but she was enjoying her adventure and didn't correct the porter's assumption.

Shortly after five o'clock, a new announcement came over through the train's speakers. "May I have your attention, please! Our next stop is San José."

As the announcement droned on, Andy leaned over to Shirley. "How about it, Sure Shot? Want to get in a little target practice at this stop? I've got two targets in my pockets and you've got the slingshot."

"Oh, yes!" Shirley's eyes brightened as a smile spread across her face. "I haven't had any time to practice in two days."

"Come on, then," Andy said, taking her by the hand and moving toward the end of the car. Other disembarking passengers were gathering up their belongings and porters were standing by to assist with bags. Andy approached one of the white-jacketed men, reaching into his pocket and leaning to whisper something in his ear. The porter's eyes shifted to Shirley and he nodded. Andy handed him a silver dollar, which the porter slipped into his pocket.

The train eased to a stop. One porter hopped quickly down the metal steps of the train and placed a step stool on the platform below the bottom step. Andy swept Shirley up, catching her by surprise.

"Oh my!" she exclaimed as he placed her on the baggage elevator between two small overnight bags.

"Duck in there tight, Sure Shot!" Andy called with a grin. Shirley giggled as the shelf on which she sat began to move.

She could see light below her and within a few seconds was staring into the smiling face of another porter. He reached up and pulled her off the shelf, setting her gently on the station's platform.

"Come on," Andy said, taking her by the hand. "I know a good spot over this way."

They blended in with the crowd, most of it moving away from the train and into the station. Fewer passengers were headed toward the *Daylight*, waiting for the off-loading passengers to clear the way before they began to board for their trips to San Francisco.

Andy led the child all the way through the station and across the adjacent street. He turned left, keeping himself between Shirley and the road and heading away from the station—and the train. They passed a cannery and a livery stable before reaching a corral enclosed by a high fence composed of four horizontal rows of boards nailed to evenly spaced posts.

"Find some good pebbles," Andy said, striding up to a post and placing a bottle on top. A block away, he heard the hiss of steam and the clanking of slack being taken out of the linkages between railroad cars. "All right. Remember what we worked on. Keep that arm straight."

Shirley closed one eye and squinted along the line of her arm. She drew back the pouch and let it fly. And missed. "Aww!"

"Try again," Andy said, bending over and picking up a small rock. "When you let go, don't jerk, just let it go nice and easy."

Shirley widened her stance and sighted along her arm. The train began to move—imperceptibly at first, and

133

Andy felt he was watching one of those cartoons where everything happened in slow motion. Shirley's shot nicked the post a couple of inches from the top.

"Almost. See how rusty you get when you don't practice?"

"I'll get it this time!" Shirley said.

"Focus. Keep your eye on the target and your arm straight."

The last car cleared the station and passed from Andy's sight. *This might actually work!* He turned then and watched Shirley's smooth release. The missile streaked toward the bottle, catching it near the bottom and causing it to wobble, then topple from the post.

"You hit it!" Andy said, throwing his hands in the air.

That's when the black Chevrolet rolled up behind them.

CHAPTER 29

"Ladies and Gentlemen, our next station stop will be San Francisco," blared the announcement on the public-address system at 5:45 p.m. "Passengers holding white baggage checks with green stripe or yellow baggage checks will find their baggage at the Yellow Taxi loading zone in the station. This is Mr. T.R. Holmes, your train passenger agent, speaking. I want to say now for myself and for the conductor and for every Southern Pacific employee on the train that we have been happy to have you with us today. We hope that your trip has been a pleasant one."

"Have you seen Shirley?" Mrs. Temple asked Missy and Grace, finding them gathering up their playing cards in the tavern car. She had Griff at her side, who was impatiently looking up and down the car, fingering the gun in his pocket.

Missy looked up, concerned. "Well, she walked by over an hour ago, headed to the dining car for some ice cream. We figured she was still there, charming the wait staff."

"Probably so," Mrs. Temple said, but there was a deep crease between her eyebrows. "She asked permission to go alone, and I figured she'd be safe. And then, well, I guess I fell asleep longer than I intended—Griff too—so we're a little worried. C'mon, Griff, let's go on to the dining car."

"We'll come with you," Missy said. Grace stowed the pack of cards in her purse and the two secretaries got to their feet and hurried through the swaying car behind the other two.

They passed through several passenger cars, keeping an eye out for a child in a cap and overalls, but no Shirley. She wasn't in the dining car either.

"Can I help you, ma'am?" the dining car supervisor asked.

"Yes, I'm looking for a…child," Mrs. Temple said. "Six years old, about four feet tall, wearing corduroy overalls and a newsboy cap."

"A little boy? Oh yes, he was here, having a dish of ice cream with his father. But they left together some time ago," the official said.

"His father?" Mrs. Temple asked.

"Well, I assumed it was his father. They seemed to know each other quite well. Let me get the waiter who served them. Russell?" he gestured to one of the servers in his immaculate white mess jacket and apron. "Didn't you serve ice cream to a man and a little boy earlier this afternoon?"

"Yessir," said Russell. "'Bout 3:30. They had some Cokes, too, and then they left after an hour or so and headed in that direction." He indicated the front of the train.

"C'mon," Griff said. "Let's keep looking."

"Attention, ladies and gentlemen. This is your passenger agent, Mr. T.R. Holmes. We have a report of a child missing on the train. Please notify the nearest official if you have seen a child, six years of age, wearing overalls and a newsboy cap, who answers to the name 'Tommy.' Thank you for your cooperation!"

After the announcement, several passengers came forward to share their sightings of a small boy and a man who had been strolling through the train. "They seemed to be having such a good time, I just assumed it was a little boy and his daddy, stretching their legs," one woman said apologetically. "He was so pretty I almost thought he was a little girl."

Then a porter confessed, rather shamefaced, to allowing a little boy to ride in the luggage elevator. "It was perfectly safe," he said, "and his father asked me to do it. I assumed they got off the train in San José, because they did not re-board."

By the time the *Coast Daylight* rolled into San Francisco, the train was in a controlled uproar. Passenger Agent Holmes had asked each witness for a detailed description of the man with the little boy, but the most anyone could recall was his plain dark suit, white shirt and a gray fedora pulled low over his eyes. Average height, average build. A bit of a limp, one passenger thought. Standing in the front chair car, next to the baggage room, Holmes reassured Mrs. Temple that no stone would be left unturned to find the child, and asked Missy and Grace to take the distraught woman back to the observation car.

Griff stayed behind and muttered something in the agent's ear. His eyes grew wide. "Well, this certainly changes the situation," he said. "We'll tear the train apart, but I also want you to accompany our railroad detectives back to the station in San José. We may be able to pick up a trail there."

Griff muttered something else.

"Don't you worry, sir," Mr. Holmes said. "We'll keep this confidential!"

Behind him, the baggage car door was open about an inch, and a green eye peered out.

CHAPTER 30

San José

Though never short on self-confidence, even Fausto was surprised at the ease with which Andy Archie had coaxed Shirley Temple into the car.

"Uh oh, Sure Shot. Looks like we missed our train," he had said to the little girl. She'd pouted for a moment, but then Andy had seen the Chevrolet and waved. Fausto had directed Marcello to stop and, sliding across the back seat, had rolled down his window.

"Any chance you're heading north?" Andy had asked. "We lost track of the time and missed our train."

"We're going as far as San Francisco. Can we offer you a lift?"

Shirley's face had brightened, and Andy had helped her climb up into the back seat. "My mother's on the train," she had explained. "She'll miss me if I'm not back onboard by the time it gets to San Francisco."

"Well, then," Fausto had said with a chuckle, "let's get moving so we can take you to your mother."

"My name is Andy and this is my pal Sh—"

"Tommy!" the little girl interjected.

"Call me Juan."

"Oh, that's a Spanish name, isn't it?" she asked.

"Si. You're very clever for someone so young. How did you miss your train?"

"We were practicing with my new slingshot. Andy got it for me. Want to see?" Shirley pulled the weapon out of her overall pocket and held it up for his inspection.

"Very elegant," Fausto said as Shirley yawned, nestling into Andy's side. The let down as the sugar from the ice cream and the Coke had left her small body, combined with the lack of her normal midday nap, were catching up with her.

By the time the car reached the outskirts of San José, its gentle vibrations had lulled the child to sleep.

"Pull over," Andy said. When Marcello looked at Fausto in the rear-view mirror, he nodded. Marcello pulled the car into an Esso station, well away from the pumps. "I've delivered the girl. That's all I signed up for. Let's settle up and I'll be on my way."

"Marcello," Fausto said, "go get something to drink." Marcello killed the engine, pulled the hand break and climbed out. Fausto reached into the pocket of his gray suit coat and pulled out a roll of twenty-dollar bills secured by a red rubber band. "Here you are, my friend. Five hundred dollars, as agreed." Andy took the roll, slipped the rubber band up over his wrist and began counting. "You don't trust me, friend?" Fausto asked, a wounded note in his voice.

"It's not that at all, friend. It's just that I don't ever intend to see you again, and so I want to take this opportunity to confirm that my trust is justified." Fausto chuckled.

Andy counted the money quickly, snapped the rubber band back in place and shoved the bills into his pocket. "Besides, if all the money wasn't there, I wasn't going to trust you with the kid." Andy leaned over the sleeping child toward the other man, close enough to smell Juan's cologne. "Make sure nothing happens to her or you *will* see me again—and that would go very badly for you. Friend."

With that, Andy positioned Shirley against the seat back and climbed out of the car. He crossed the highway and started walking back toward town.

By the time Marcello returned, Fausto had gotten a blanket from the trunk and covered the sleeping child.

"Take a left," Fausto directed once he'd resumed his seat. "I want to get off the highway. We'll take 5 North."

"That will take forty-five minutes longer," Marcello protested.

"At least," Fausto said. He was, at the moment, quite satisfied, and if it took extra time, so be it. Fausto knew that his sleeping passenger would soon be missed, if she hadn't been already, and searchers would concentrate first on major highways like 101. Fausto leaned forward, catching Marcello's eye in the mirror. "What happened to you, Topo?"

"What do you mean?"

"Your lips are purple."

"Nehi."

CHAPTER 31

Andy Archie thumbed a ride back into San José on the bed of a lettuce truck. He hopped off, waving thanks to the driver, and walked the last three blocks to the bus station. He went immediately to the men's room and entered a stall, latching the hook behind him. He took note of the brown shoes in the neighboring stall.

He took off his fedora, balancing it on the toilet paper holder, then removed his suit coat and hung it on a nail. Next, he removed his shirt and tie, rolling up the tie and sticking it in the back pocket of his pants, and draping the shirt over his coat. He took out the roll of twenties and carefully peeled off five at a time. A hundred dollars went into each shoe, another into his wallet, the fourth into the breast pocket of his coat, and the last into his front pants pocket.

Andy smiled with satisfaction. All in all, much easier and less painful than falling off a horse.

His fortune stowed, he pulled a small, flat tin of baby powder from his outer coat pocket. Working quickly, he scooped as much baby powder as he could in his hand and sifted it into his hair. He rubbed it on the back of his head and into his eyebrows. Taking another peek through the door's gap to be sure the coast was clear, Andy unhooked the door and stepped up to the sink. Using his fingers, he evened out the powder as best he could, hiding his red hair under a dusting of white.

He returned to the stall and re-hooked the door, dumped the remaining powder in the toilet, and tossed the small tin into the water tank on the wall above it. He put his shirt and coat back on. Pausing for a moment, running through a mental checklist, Andy then reached up and pulled the chain. He watched as the powder swirled down the bowl. He picked up his hat, folded it as flat as he could, and jammed it up between the tank and the wall, feeling regret for only a moment. It was his only nice hat, but at least he now had the wherewithal to buy another. Or five.

Exiting the stall, Andy took a last quick glance in the mirror. *Best I can do.*

Andy strolled casually through the waiting room of the bus station, careful to avoid eye contact with anyone. He approached the ticket counter and bought a seat on the next bus out, headed to Fresno, then sat down among the other waiting passengers. Andy glanced at his watch. *The* Coast Daylight *ought to be pulling into San Francisco right about now,* he thought. *If they haven't missed Shirley by now, they will shortly. Then all hell will break loose.*

When the bus to Fresno left in twenty minutes, Andy would be on it. From there, he'd either transfer to another train or take a bus. Once he got somewhere safe, he'd send for Iris and the boys and start over again, maybe go to Mexico and open a pub.

Andy picked up a discarded San José *Mercury* and began idly turning the pages. Suddenly, an advertisement for the film *Curly Top*, showing at a local theater, caught his eye. He stared at the ad, which showed Shirley Temple shaking a finger at her co-star, John Boles, then quickly turned the page.

CHAPTER 32

San Francisco

You wanted a story, you got one! Joan told herself. As the remaining passengers had ambled off the train at San Francisco's Third Street Station, Joan had blended in, hoping to avoid the attention of conductor Rogers or any other Southern Pacific official. As she walked through the mission revival-style arches leading from the train platforms to the spacious lobby, Joan dug around in her purse for money.

If Bottoms had really wanted to take care of me, he'd have left me with some cash. She palmed three nickels and two dimes and then looked around for a phone booth. A row of booths stood just inside the set of arches leading to the taxi stand. The area was crowded with redcaps and luggage carts trailing behind well-dressed men and women from the just-arrived *Daylight*.

Joan reached the booths, but all of them were occupied. She opened her purse again and fished out a Chesterfield. She was looking for a match when the door of a nearby booth swung open and the occupant stepped out. Joan put the smoke between her lips and moved quickly to claim the vacant phone booth.

She set her coins on the top of the phone and pulled the door closed behind her, activating the overhead light. She dropped a nickel in the round slot at the top of the phone and dialed "0."

"Operator."

"Yes, collect call from Joan Roswell to the Los Angeles *Standard*, Dixie 8757."

"Stand by, please."

Joan could hear clicking and talking over the line. While she waited, she cracked open the door of the booth, turning off the overhead light. From her concealed position inside the booth, she scanned the crowd, searching for Bottoms. Surely, he would know what was going on and that he owed her the story.

"Los Angeles *Standard*."

"Get me—"

"One moment please, caller," the operator intervened. "Will you accept a collect call from Joan Roswell?"

"Let me transfer you to the city editor, please."

Joan waited while the newspaper's switchboard routed her call to the city editor, hoping that Billy was at his desk.

"City, Bryce."

"Billy!"

"One moment, caller. Will you accept a collect call from Joan Roswell?"

There was a painful moment of silence on the line before Billy Bryce answered with a half-hearted, "Yeah."

Shirley Temple Is Missing

"Go ahead, caller."

"Billy, I've got the biggest story since the Lindbergh kidnapping! Are you ready to copy?"

"Hang on, hang on. Let me grab a pad." Joan could hear rustling on the far end of the connection. "All right, shoot."

"Headline: Shirley Temple Missing! Dateline: San Francisco—"

"What the hell are you doing in San Francisco?" Billy snapped.

"Shut up and listen! 'Twentieth Century-Fox screen star Shirley Temple is missing following the arrival in San Francisco earlier this evening of the Southern Pacific's *Coast Daylight* express train from Los Angeles. Temple, who was accompanied by her mother, Gertrude, and bodyguard John Griffith—'"

"A six-year-old has a bodyguard?"

"'—was traveling in disguise and was last seen having ice cream in the train's dining car with—'" Joan paused. If she revealed Bottoms's identity, she would forfeit the "inside story" she had been promised.

"Joan! Are you still there? Can you hear me?"

"Yes, I hear you now. Where did you lose me?"

"...in the train's dining car with..."

"'...with an unidentified man. When Miss Temple did not return to her ticketed seat in the observation car following the train's scheduled stop in San José, her mother became alarmed and alerted railroad officials.'" Joan paused.

"Got it! Go on."

"That's all I've got right now. I'm trying to get a statement from Mrs. Temple. We developed a good rapport when I visited the set yesterday. I'm sure she'll talk to me."

"How about the bodyguard? What does he say?"

"I can't find him. He's probably conferring with the railroad detectives and the local police."

"Anybody else on the story yet?"

"No, Billy. This is a scoop!"

"Sources?"

"Me, dammit! I saw Mrs. Temple talking with the railroad officials. She was very upset."

"You're the reporter, Joan, not the story. Did they actually announce that Shirley Temple was missing?"

"No, all they said was 'a small child.' But I know it was Shirley because Gertrude Temple was the one reporting it. I saw her, Billy! I even got her autograph."

"Wait a minute. You asked a six-year-old for her autograph?"

"That's not the point!"

Billy's voice became calmer, his initial excitement yielding to his skeptical prejudices. "You're right, Joan. It's not the point. The point is that you're making assumptions—reasonable though they may seem—when an experienced reporter would be gathering facts. Figure out a way to get to Mrs. Temple. And the bodyguard too. Is Mr. Temple along on the trip? You've got to get some confirmation other than what you think you saw. I'm not saying you're wrong, but what you've got right now is too thin for me to run."

"This is a story, Billy, a big one! You've got to trust me. Shirley and Gertrude were even traveling with two of President Roosevelt's secretaries."

"Well, find out what you can from them too. That gives the story a political angle. And get a quote from the railroad. How can a kid, the most famous kid in the world, get snatched off of one of their trains in broad daylight? You've got a good lead on a story that no one else is even aware of yet. Work the story, Joan. Dig up the facts to support your hypothesis. Call your publicity friend over at the studio, what's his name—Harry Brand."

"I can't."

"What d'ya mean, you can't? You're a reporter, dammit! He's the studio's publicity agent! Make him sweat a little."

"He won't accept a collect call from me."

Billy was silent for a moment. "All right. I'll call him. But just this once, Joan. I don't have time to do my job and yours too."

"Thanks, Billy. You're a sweetheart."

"Don't thank me, just bring in this story. Where can I reach you?"

"I'm in a phone booth at the station in San Francisco."

"I mean where are you staying the night?"

"Billy," Joan paused searching for the right strategy. "I jumped on the train this morning when I saw John Griffith get on. I thought maybe there'd be a story in it."

"Good instincts."

"Yes, but poor planning. I haven't got a dollar. Can you put me up somewhere?"

"That's Martin's beat," Billy said, referring to the paper's San Francisco bureau chief. "Call him and let him know you're in town. He can help you with logistics."

"But it's my story, right?"

"It's your story, Joan. Don't let it slip away from you."

"Give me Martin's number."

"What am I, a phone book? Look it up!"

Joan hung up the receiver with somewhat more force than was necessary and began thumbing through the directory, which was lying on a shelf below the phone. Unbidden thoughts were flitting through her head. Had "Bottoms" really been legitimate? Or had he duped her into helping him kidnap Shirley Temple?

CHAPTER 33

From the station master's office in San Francisco, Gertrude had called her husband and Griff had called Darryl Zanuck. Missy and Grace had sat uncomfortably on straight-back chairs, clearly able to hear Zanuck's foul language as he blasted his former bodyguard. From there, a grim-faced Griff had joined a carload of railroad security men headed to the San José station.

It was after 7 p.m. before the three women checked into the St. Francis Hotel. Sitting on her bed, a tearful Gertrude beside her, Missy put in a long-distance call to the White House and was relieved to hear the cheerful voice of the chief switchboard operator, Louise Hackmeister. She dispensed with all chit-chat. "Hacky, it's Missy. I must talk to Steve. It's quite urgent, so I need my 'telephone detective' to track him down!"

"Got it," Hacky said.

In less than a minute, press secretary Steve Early's Virginia-accented baritone sounded in her ear. "Missy, what seems to be the problem? Hacky said it was urgent."

"Oh, Steve! I'm at my wit's end!" Missy said. "I'm calling from San Francisco. This is a long story, but the high point is that I was on a train with Shirley Temple and her mother today and little Shirley has gone missing. Mrs.

Temple is afraid she's been kidnapped, but we're not sure we can trust the local police. We've heard so much about police corruption out here, and Mrs. Temple is terrified that Shirley will be hurt. Could you get in touch with J. Edgar Hoover? And, please, send a cable to the President and let him know about this. I hate to interrupt his vacation, but he'd want to know."

"I'll do it right away," Steve said. "Give me your number, Missy, I'll call you as soon as I have news."

After Missy hung up, she patted Gertrude Temple's hand. "Try not to worry, Gertrude," she said reassuringly. "The FBI always gets their man. Just look at what they did to John Dillinger and Baby Face Nelson last year."

Gertrude blanched. Too late, Missy remembered that two innocent bystanders had been wounded when Dillinger was killed, and the apprehension of Nelson had been fatal not only to the gangster but to two FBI agents.

Grace saved the moment. "Gertrude, why don't I stay with you in your room tonight?" she suggested. "We can order some room service, and play a few hands of gin to relax, if you like."

"Yes, Grace, that would be lovely," Gertrude said, rising. "And a glass of gin may help too."

"I'm sure room service can provide that," Grace said. "Thank goodness we don't have to worry about Prohibition any more. Come on."

They had barely left the room when Missy's phone rang. "Steve?" she said.

"Why, no," said a woman's voice. "Miss LeHand? It's Joan, Joan Roswell. You remember we met the other day at Fox?"

"Yes," Missy said stiffly. "What do you want?"

"Well, dear, I just happened to be on the train today, you know, the *Daylight*, with you and Griff and Mrs. Temple, and an adorable little child dressed in overalls who I think might have been Shirley. And I was just heart-broken to hear she had gone missing."

"Go on," Missy said.

"There was someone else on the train, dear," Joan said. "Someone I recognized. At first, I thought he was a bodyguard, but now I'm thinking that perhaps he had something to do with her disappearance. I wonder if I might come up to your room and have a little chat. I'm in the lobby."

The hair on Missy's neck rose as she thought of dealing with the scoop-hungry reporter, but she felt she had no choice. "Yes, please, do come up," she said. "I'm in Room 1219."

CHAPTER 34

Washington, D.C.

J. Edgar Hoover slammed down the phone on his wide, highly polished desk, staring with unseeing dark eyes about his fifth-floor office at the new Department of Justice building on Pennsylvania Avenue. *Shirley Temple! What an abomination! What a case! What an opportunity for the FBI!*

Although he was of only middling height and on the pudgy side—in contrast to the tall, physically fit young men he favored as special agents—Hoover made up for his less-than-impressive appearance with his forceful personality and formidable mind. He had a law degree, which he believed was essential to successful law enforcement—so essential that from the time he took over what had been the Justice Department's Bureau of Investigation in 1924, he preferred agents with law degrees. An ability to handle firearms had been secondary—in fact, the agents had not been allowed to carry guns for many years—which had led to the deaths of a number of agents. However, that shortcoming had been remedied. Hoover's men were now trained to fire anything from an automatic pistol to a gas-riot gun, but most especially the Thompson machine guns favored by their prey. Hoover's G-men always got their man. Or woman, as the case might be.

On the wall of Hoover's office was a map of the United States, covered with pins showing the locations of the FBI's offices. He walked over to the map, staring at San Francisco, but he didn't need to read the name neatly typed on the slip of paper affixed there by his secretary, Helen Gandy. He quickly walked to the black Bakelite intercom on his desk and pressed down a key. "Miss Gandy," he barked. "Get me Wainwright."

CHAPTER 35

Aboard the USS *Houston*

It had been a fine day for fishing off the Cocos Islands of Costa Rica. The President's bodyguard, Gus Gennerich, had landed a 148-pound sailfish, the biggest catch of the trip. FDR had landed a slightly smaller one, but all on board agreed it was the "handsomest" of the two, and a telegram had been dispatched to the Smithsonian to see if the museum would like to add the fish to the exhibits of the Museum of Natural History.

Now, gathered around a card table in the President's cabin playing poker, the men were basking in the glow of their exploits and teasing Harry Hopkins, who had gotten seasick and was throwing up over the side of the launch at the time Roosevelt landed his big catch. One of the ship's radio operators dispelled the jocular atmosphere with an urgent message from the White House.

"I've already had my dose of bad news for the month with that pompous thug Mussolini's invasion of Ethiopia," Roosevelt said as he quickly scanned the contents. "Spinach!" he exclaimed. "This is from Steve Early. Missy says that darling little Shirley Temple has been kidnapped. Steve's contacted Hoover and put him on it."

"Well, that will suit J. Edgar just fine," remarked Hopkins, taking a drag on his cigarette. "He never passes up a chance to showboat."

"He won't undermine his own investigation by blabbing to the press," FDR said grimly. "After she's found—that's another story." He scratched out a message to Steve Early, ordering the press secretary to keep him informed, and another to Hoover emphasizing the need for quick action. "Send this out posthaste," he ordered the radio operator. "Highest security."

The news had dispelled the President's holiday mood. "You know, after that terrible crime wave of bank robberies and kidnappings the past two years—Dillinger, the Barker Gang, Bonnie and Clyde—I thought we finally had things under control with our expanded Federal Bureau of Investigation," he complained to Hopkins. "Why, Hoover went on the record just six months ago, telling Congress that the crime of kidnapping has virtually ended in the United States. Now this."

The President stared down at his hand of cards. "That's all we need right now," he said quietly, "for a child who has lifted the spirits of so many Americans to turn up dead. It would be worse than the Lindbergh kidnapping." He sighed. "And poor Missy! She was so looking forward to a carefree vacation."

CHAPTER 36

Los Angeles

Darryl Zanuck slammed down the telephone and kicked the corner of his desk. To say he was unhappy that John Griffith had allowed Shirley to go missing on a train was like calling Mount Everest a mole hill. Darryl Zanuck was livid. He stormed up and down his office, swinging a polo mallet, ignoring the green and gold walls hung with African hunting trophies, even stumbling over his rhinoceros foot trash can.

Just when things were going good, really good!

Darryl Zanuck's first job in the movie business had come at age eight, as an extra in a two-reeler. In 1918, he had lied about his age, enlisted in the National Guard and wound up fighting in France. After the Great War, Zanuck had returned to Hollywood and found regular work as a screenwriter, penning scripts for dog star Rin-Tin-Tin at Warner Brothers. At the age of twenty-nine, Zanuck was head of that studio's production efforts. He might still have been there if that cheap bastard Jack Warner had lived up to their salary deal, but Jack hadn't, and Darryl had quit.

Shirley Temple Is Missing

Within days, Zanuck had started a new studio with screenwriter Joe Schenk, the brother of movie mogul Nicholas Schenk, head of Loew's Inc. *Take that, Jack!*

The new studio, Twentieth Century Pictures, had produced hit after hit and become Hollywood's darling—largely through the efforts of Darryl Zanuck. Earlier in the year, Zanuck and Schenk had purchased the bankrupt Fox Studios and formed Twentieth Century-Fox. They had inherited Fox's most valuable asset, Shirley Temple, and Zanuck had groomed her, marketed her, and protected her with an obsession rivaling her mother's. The only ingredient missing was love. He didn't love the kid—but he sure loved the money she brought into the studio.

Like Shirley, Zanuck had started as a kid and had learned the business from the bottom up. He had the scars to prove it.

Griffith is going to have scars by the time I'm finished with him.

Plucking the ever-present cigar from his gap-toothed mouth, Zanuck leaned over and thundered into his intercom, "Get me on tomorrow's first flight to San Francisco!" Only the death of Will Rogers, previously his most reliable box office star, during a flight in Alaska just two months before prevented Zanuck from leaving on the spot. If he was going to fly, it was at least going to be in the daytime so he could see where the hell he was going.

CHAPTER 37

San Francisco

Corey Wainwright, the special agent in charge of the FBI's San Francisco office, could always tell when the phone call was coming from his boss. The ring seemed different, faster, like the FBI director's machine-gun like diction. It was said that Hoover had started speaking rapidly to overcome a boyhood stutter. Now, only a few stenographers could keep up with him. When Wainwright's home phone began ringing shortly after 7:30 p.m., he recognized that ring.

"Wainwright," he said.

"We've got a serious problem," the Director said, with no preamble or pleasantries. "A little girl has gone missing," he said. "A very famous little girl. Probably the most famous little girl in the world." He paused dramatically. "Shirley Temple is missing. She was traveling on the *Coast Daylight* from L.A. today with her mother and disappeared about five o'clock, when the train stopped in San José. Her mother didn't realize she was gone right away, thought she was with someone else in their party. Of course, they turned the train upside down once they arrived in San Francisco, but no luck."

"Yes sir," Wainwright said. It was best to listen to Hoover until he ran out of word-bullets.

"The White House called me a short while ago and instructed me to go at this full throttle. In fact, I'm flying out there first thing in the morning."

Wainwright raised his eyebrows. The last time he remembered the Director breaking his neck to intervene in a case was when he insisted on personally making the collar on the notorious gangster Albert Karpis back in May. Hoover had been mortified when an unfriendly senator had asked during a hearing if he had ever made any arrests. He had to admit that he had not—until he took a charter flight to New Orleans to bring Karpis in himself.

Hoover galloped on. "I want you to put every available man in California on it, but remember, this has to be kept completely confidential, and that means no involvement from any local police, especially that notoriously corrupt police force in San Francisco. Understand?"

"Of course, sir."

"The Temples and the people at Twentieth Century-Fox are braced for a ransom message, but they haven't gotten one yet. Our hope is that we can find little Shirley before this leaks to the press."

"I'll get right on it, sir," Wainwright said. "Where is Mrs. Temple now?"

"She's staying at the St. Francis Hotel on Union Square," Hoover said. "She's not alone, fortunately. She was on the train with two of President Roosevelt's secretaries, Miss LeHand and Miss Tully. Miss LeHand is a very sharp woman and she seems to be handling things from that end. You can call her there and arrange to interview Mrs. Temple."

"I'm on the case, sir," Wainwright said, his mind churning. He'd have to call his secretary, Mary Stipley, at home, brief her, and set her to contacting the FBI's California-based agents. Meanwhile, he'd go by the hotel to speak to this Miss LeHand and Mrs. Temple.

Hoover wasn't through yet. "The FBI has a fine reputation in America," the director said. "We've brought some of the worst criminals in history to justice in the past two years, and my G-men are hailed as heroes in the War on Crime. All that will be forgotten if we can't find Shirley Temple."

Wainwright got a sinking feeling as he translated the message behind the director's words. *If* you *can't find Shirley Temple.*

CHAPTER 38

It was fully dark by the time Marcello guided the Chevrolet around the western edge of Lake Merced. The child in the back seat was still asleep and the usually talkative Fausto was staring silently out the window. Marcello turned off Highway 5 and continued past the stadium

Fausto had refused to allow a stop for dinner. "Our little guest is traveling incognito," he had explained. And now, at seven-thirty, Marcello's stomach was complaining of hunger. He turned right on Pacific, then at the end of the block, left onto Webster.

"Go around back to the garage entrance," Fausto said.

Marcello turned the car into the consulate's rear courtyard and pulled into one of the vacant stalls in the ground-level garage.

"I thought you said His Excellency was using the Cadillac?" Fausto grumbled, seeing the shiny, blue car parked in the adjacent stall.

"Si, Fausto. He must have returned early."

Fausto got out of the car. "Come, carry the child," he ordered Marcello.

Marcello opened the back door and pulled Shirley toward him, noticing that her cap had fallen off and a headful of ringlets had tumbled out. He lifted her to his shoulder. "Where to?"

"Follow me. Signora Beneventi has prepared one of the second-floor bedrooms for our guest." Fausto led Marcello to the service lift and pushed the call button. While they waited for the car to arrive, Fausto pressed the call button on the intercom mounted in the wall. Normally, Fausto would never use the service entrance, but this wasn't a typical situation.

"Yes?"

"It's Fausto. Please tell Signora Beneventi to meet me on the second floor." He replaced the cap on Shirley's head. When the car arrived, Fausto opened the door and lifted the cage up, then gestured for Marcello to step aboard.

Shirley stirred. "Where's Andy?" she asked, blinking her eyes.

"He has gone to get your mother," Fausto said soothingly. "Go back to sleep." He pulled the cage back down as Shirley's eyes closed and her head again found Marcello's shoulder. He pushed the "2" on the panel and the lift jerked and began its ascent.

Signora Beneventi, head of the consulate's housekeeping and kitchen staff, was waiting when Fausto opened the elevator door. "Good evening, Signore Trevisano. Good evening, Marcello. And who have we here?"

"Our special, but confidential, guest, signora. Kindly lead us to the room you have prepared."

Shirley Temple Is Missing

Signora Beneventi led the men and their burden down a long corridor and opened a door on the left. Inside, the room was dark except for the light from a small lamp beside the large canopied bed.

"Signora Beneventi, would you be so kind as to prepare our guest for bed—preferably without waking her?"

"Her? But she's dressed like a boy."

"A clever ruse to prevent anyone from recognizing us," Fausto explained with a smile.

After seeing the child to bed, Fausto dismissed Marcello and headed down to the consulate's basement using the back stairs. He pushed through the heavy metal door and walked along the concrete-walled corridor, past the coding room, which His Excellency never allowed him to enter, and on to a small room at the end of the hallway.

Fausto unlocked the door and flipped on the light switch. *Excellent!* he thought, looking around the room at the equipment that had been set up. *Bernardo is ready for the morning's work. Now I must go and prepare.*

CHAPTER 39

Missy eyed Joan Roswell with suspicion bordering on active dislike. "OK, Miss Roswell," she said. "Tell me what you know about the man who was with Shirley."

The reporter smiled. "First, dear, I need some assurances. My editor isn't buying my story without any sources to corroborate it, so I need your promise that you will help me get some. Me, and exclusively me."

"I'm not sure I can promise that," Missy said. "It's really up to the Temples, the studio, and, of course, the FBI."

"The FBI?" Joan tittered. "My, this is getting interesting! You're bringing in the G-men!"

"Yes," Missy said evenly. "Kidnapping is a federal offense, after all. I wouldn't be surprised if J. Edgar Hoover attended to this one personally... Cigarette?"

The two women lit up, staring at each other through their smoke like two gunslingers facing down on the main street of a western movie set. Then a knock came at the door.

Missy rose to her feet. "Who's there?" she asked.

"Corey Wainwright," said the deep voice on the other side. "FBI."

Shirley Temple Is Missing

Missy cracked the door and eyed the badge presented by the tall man in the dark suit. She let him in.

"How do you do, Mr. Wainwright," she said, taking in the man from the tip of his tan fedora to the toes of his highly polished black shoes. *Nice,* she thought. "I'm so grateful to you for coming out so quickly." She turned to Joan. "This woman may have helpful information for us, but she's not being very cooperative. Perhaps you can persuade her."

"Joan Roswell," the reporter said, standing and extending her hand to the G-man, who had removed his hat. She took in his closely cropped blonde hair and cleft chin, unconsciously sticking out her chest. "I'm with the Los Angeles *Standard.*"

Wainwright swung around to Missy. "What's the press doing here?" he demanded.

"Miss Roswell was on the train today and recognized Shirley," Missy explained. "She heard the announcement about a child's disappearance and put two and two together. She also saw something that may help us find her." Missy narrowed her blue eyes at Joan. "Unfortunately, she seems to think a scoop headline is more important than a child's life."

"You're putting words into my mouth, dear," Joan said, color rising in her cheeks. "It's just that my first duty is to our readers, to keep them informed."

"Hogwash," Wainwright said, moving closer. "Listen, lady, if you're withholding information from a federal investigation, I can arrest you right now and charge you with obstruction of justice."

Joan quickly backed down. "No need to get nasty," she said. "Let's all talk this over like reasonable people."

Missy interjected, "Agent Wainwright, why don't I bring Mrs. Temple and my assistant Grace Tully into this discussion? They're in the adjoining room."

"Good idea," the agent said, nodding.

When Missy left the room, Wainwright riveted his attention on Joan. "Spill it," he said.

"Not until I get a promise of an exclusive," she said firmly. "Tell me you'll keep this under wraps until Shirley is found—one way or another—and that I'll get an interview with Mr. Hoover."

"I can't promise that," Wainwright said. "But I *can* promise if you don't stop playing with me, I will arrest you right now and take you over to the FBI office for interrogation." He pulled a pair of handcuffs from his coat pocket and dangled them in front of Joan.

The door opened then and Missy returned with Gertrude and Grace. Wainwright quickly stuffed the handcuffs back into his pocket while Missy made the introductions. "Mrs. Temple, I am so sorry this has happened," he said. "I promise you the Bureau is doing everything possible to get Shirley back to you. We've got men on this all over the state. Director Hoover sends his assurances that we won't rest until she's safe."

"Thank you, Mr. Wainwright," Gertrude said. Then her eyes fastened on Joan; she looked familiar, but Gertrude couldn't quite place her. "Er, is this your secretary?" she asked.

"I'm Joan Roswell, Los Angeles *Standard*."

Missy stepped in before Gertrude could react. "Miss Roswell happened to be on the train today," she said, "and saw something that she believes would be helpful. She came forward voluntarily, out of the goodness of her heart, isn't that right, Miss Roswell?"

"Yes," purred Joan. "Out of the goodness of my heart."

CHAPTER 40

"I recognized a man on the train, someone I'd seen when I was at Fox the day the White House group took its tour," Joan explained to the group crowded into Missy's room. "You may have seen my by-line in the *Standard* the next day; I wrote about your visit to Fox, along with the picture the studio sent. Anyway, I had recognized Shirley on the train, and, wanting to get a story, I identified myself to the man. He told me he was on board as a sort of back-up bodyguard for Shirley. He said neither Mrs. Temple nor Mr. Griffith knew about him."

"And you believed that?" Mrs. Temple scoffed.

Joan colored. "He was very plausible," she said. "I had no reason to think he was lying. Anyway, he gave me a note to pass to Shirley, inviting her to meet him for ice cream later in the afternoon. I managed to put it in her hand when she passed my table in the tavern car."

"What did the note say?" Wainwright asked testily. "I'm sure you read it."

"Yes," Joan admitted. "It seemed harmless. He addressed her as 'Sure Shot' and told her to bring her slingshot with her, and not to tell Griff where she was going."

On the word "slingshot," there was a sharp intake of breath from Gertrude Temple. "What did this man look like?" she demanded.

"Average height and weight," Joan said. "Nothing really special, except he had bright red hair. That's how I recognized him."

"Do you know who that might be, Mrs. Temple?" Wainwright asked.

"Yes, I do," she replied excitedly. "He's one of the stunt men from *The Littlest Rebel,* though he got injured during the shooting and just seemed to be hanging around the set a lot, looking for extra work, I imagine. He taught Shirley to use a slingshot on the set. She was quite fond of him. I think his first name is Andy. Griff knows him too. He came by Shirley's cottage the day before we left and brought her a new slingshot. She was very pleased about it and insisted on bringing it with her on the trip."

"This is very helpful," Wainwright said. "What time did the note ask Shirley to meet him, Miss Roswell?"

"Three-thirty," Joan said.

"And what time did Shirley leave the observation car, Mrs. Temple?"

"Right before then," Gertrude said. "I could just kill myself for letting her go unattended. I fell asleep and didn't wake up for more than an hour. Griff too."

"I have no doubt this man is somehow involved in her kidnapping," Wainwright said. Then he leveled an eye at Joan. "That means you are, too, Miss Roswell, wittingly or unwittingly. That makes you an accessory to kidnapping."

Joan reddened as the furious stares of the women and the G-man bored into her. "Don't be ridiculous," she snapped. "I was acting in what I believed was the child's best interest!"

"Miss LeHand, could I see you in the hall for a moment?" Wainwright asked.

The two walked outside into the corridor, leaving Joan to the wolves. "I hate to put you in this position," he said, "but I wonder if you could put Miss Roswell up for the night, keep an eye on her. I don't want her fouling up the investigation by asking the wrong people questions, letting suspects know that we're on to them. If she went back on her word about publishing the story, it would blow everything wide open and cause the rats to hole up." He smiled suddenly. "I know you hadn't counted on being a warden, Miss LeHand. I'll even handcuff her to the bed if you want me to, but I think she's scared enough about her complicity that she won't try to get away."

Missy looked into the nice-looking agent's face, liking both his quiet authority and the little gap between his front teeth. "I suppose so," she said, laughing a little. "The things I do for Franklin Delano Roosevelt!"

"It will just be for the night," Wainwright promised. "I'll be back by 8 a. m. to take her off your hands."

Back inside the room, Wainwright explained the arrangements he and Missy had made and gave Joan a severe talking to. "Remember, if you should try to slip away, we'll come after you with guns blazing," he said. "The FBI doesn't care if you're a man or a woman, if you've broken the law."

"Don't worry," Joan said bitterly. "I saw what you G-men did to Ma Barker when you tracked down her gang in Florida."

Alone in the room, Joan turned to Missy. "I'm afraid I don't have any luggage, or even a change of underwear," she said. "Could I possibly borrow a nightgown, so I can rinse out my things?"

"Sure," said Missy. "But I draw the line at sharing my tooth brush."

CHAPTER 41

Los Angeles

She'll be sorry she ever set foot in this newsroom, Billy Bryce fumed as he hung up the phone. *Here I am doing her job in the middle of the night, calling Hollywood people at home when I should be home drinking Scotch and listening to Phil Harris on the radio.*

Harry Brand, to Billy's surprise and disappointment, had scoffed at Joan's tale of a kidnapping. "Why no, of course not," Brand had said. "Shirley's had a little head cold, so she's not been at the studio today, but she'd already finished filming *The Littlest Rebel* anyway. I can give you a tentative release date if you're interested."

"No, thanks," Billy had said. "So, you're telling me that Shirley Temple and her mother are home in Santa Monica right now?"

"Shirley is at home with her father, but Mrs. Temple went up to San Francisco with some friends. John Griffith traveled with her on the same train. John's nephew had been down visiting and John was taking him back to his sister who lives up there. I'm sorry to hear some kid is missing, but I guarantee you it's not Shirley Temple. Thanks for checking with me before running the story, Billy. Saved us all a lot of embarrassment—especially the *Standard*. Tell your reporter to check his facts next time."

Just what I need: a lecture on journalistic ethics from this studio flack. "Will do, Harry. Sorry to have bothered you at home. Good night." *Wait till I get my hands on her.*

CHAPTER 42

San Francisco

Joseph Gallo was glad he had not gone down in a hail of bullets, like his fellow gang members John Dillinger and Baby Face Nelson. He was glad he wasn't rotting in a jail cell on Alcatraz Island, like Al Capone and Machine Gun Kelly. Instead, he'd turned state's evidence, sung like a bird to the FBI, and been given probation. But some nights, like this one, when the roly-poly Italian known as Big Joey was back at his old job as a bouncer outside Spider Kelly's, he wished for just one more caper, one more chance to make a big score, so he could live in luxury for the rest of his life.

Not that life was bad. Spider's was the rowdiest jazz joint on Pacific Street, near San Francisco's waterfront, a block that came alive every night with the rhythms of jazz, twirling bodies on the dance floors, and the flow of all manner of alcoholic refreshment, from ale to whiskey. And Gallo just loved being in the thick of it all, watching from the end of the bar as the tide of humanity washed up to the taps and the dance floor every night, especially on cool, clear Friday nights like this one, and then watching it flow back out in the wee hours of Saturday morning, leaving the flotsam of life behind.

"Big Joey!"

Gallo turned around to see Marcello, the driver from the Italian consulate. The young man was a lover of jazz—and other things purveyed in abundance at Spider Kelly's.

"How are you, Topo?" Gallo asked, clapping Marcello on the shoulder. "How are things in the world of high diplomacy?"

It was after midnight and it was obvious Marcello had been on Pacific Street for several hours. His eyes were half-lidded, his mouth a bit slack. *Hope he isn't driving one of the consulate cars tonight,* Gallo thought.

"Other than having to take orders from a dim-witted consul, his shrew of a wife, and that peacock Fausto, not so bad," Marcello laughed. "Boy-oh-boy, did Fausto have me on a job tonight. Picked up a man and a kid at the train station in San José this evening, very secretive. If I didn't know better, I'd say Fausto is doing a little kidnapping on the side."

Gallo's ears pricked up. The Dillinger-Nelson gang had specialized in bank robbery, but kidnapping had proved most lucrative for the Barker Gang—that is, until they were wiped out by the FBI. "C'mon, Topo! Fausto's too much of a pretty boy to get his hands dirty in something like that," he said, laughing.

"Well, we pull up next to this man and a little boy who are doing, you know, slingshot practice outside the train station, and the man says, 'oh my oh my, our train just

177

pulled out of the station. Let's ask these nice men for a lift.' We take them into the car, and it's zzz-time for the kid—asleep in about two minutes. Then the man gets out and leaves the kid. When we get to the consulate, Mr. Fancy Pants has me carry the kid upstairs, which is when I discover he's a she. Head full of curls. And get this," Marcello's speech was slurred, but Gallo believed his tale. "I swear on my mother's grave, the kid is Shirley Temple."

Shirley Temple! Gallo's eyes lit up like one of Spider's pinball machines. *Well, the Lord indeed does provide.* "You're busting on me, Topo. Shirley Temple? In San Francisco? It'd be all over the papers."

"Not if nobody knows about it," Marcello said. He swayed, and Gallo reached out a steadying hand.

"Here, sit down, paisano," Gallo said, patting the stool next to his. "Let me buy you a drink."

SATURDAY, OCTOBER 12, 1935
SAN FRANCISCO

CHAPTER 43

It was the bright sunlight that finally woke Shirley. Signora Beneventi had entered her bedroom and pulled back the heavy gold brocade curtains, letting in the light.

"Good morning, signorina! And how did you sleep?"

"Good morning," Shirley said, stretching and rubbing her eyes. "Is my mother here yet?"

"No, dear. You will be taken to your mother after breakfast." There was a knock at the door and a young man entered carrying a tray. "I wasn't sure what you wanted, so Cappi here brought up a little of everything." The young man set the tray on the side of the bed and withdrew.

Shirley's eyes grew big as she surveyed her breakfast tray. "My! You must have a big kitchen," she said, taking in the baskets of fresh, fragrant bread and fancy fruit pastries, dishes of butter and jam, a bowl of fresh fruit and glasses of milk and juice. Signora Beneventi chuckled and left the room.

"How is our guest this morning?" Fausto asked sweeping into the room with a large brown paper bag in his hand. He was wearing a light gray suit with a sky-blue tie and white shirt. His tanned face set off his even white smile.

"Good morning, Juan!" Shirley said. She was smiling as she smeared jam onto a piece of buttered bread. "We're going to see my mother after breakfast."

"That's right, after breakfast and this morning's scene." Fausto walked over to the bed where Shirley sat enjoying her breakfast.

"Do you work for the studio too?"

"Yes, but only part of the time. Mr. Zanuck asked me to be your producer only for this morning." Fausto frowned and reached down to touch Shirley's hair. "What happened to your curls?"

"Mother always curls my hair before I go to sleep at night. That's when I learn my lines too. Mother repeats them for me until I know everybody's lines, not just mine."

"Hmm. I see. Perhaps I can help you with your lines this morning. There aren't very many. I'm sure you'll have no trouble with them. But I may have to get someone else to help you with your hair."

"Do I get to do any stunts? Andy's a stunt man you know. Is he in the scene too?"

"No stunts today, no. But I do have a uniform for you to wear." Fausto said. He reached into the brown bag and pulled out a short, gray military-style tunic with a belt at the waist and gold epaulettes with red flashes on the shoulders. Four rows of colorful ribbons adorned the left breast and were topped by a pair of gold wings.

"I like uniforms!" Shirley said with a grin.

Renata Palladino thought Fausto by far the most handsome, the most dashing man on her father's staff. Not only was he tall and nicely proportioned, with broad shoulders and narrow hips, but his brown eyes were lively, his dark hair luxuriously thick and his nose a copy of Il Duce's—strong and confident. Plus, he always smelled so nice. So, when Fausto knocked on her door that Saturday morning and asked her for a favor, eleven-year-old Renata was dressed and following at his heels in record time.

"What is this favor you wish me to perform, Fausto, and what will I receive in return?"

"Ah, you sound already like a diplomat, negotiating everything." Fausto stopped in the corridor and turned to Renata, leaning down to look her in the eyes. "You do this one small favor for me and I will take you out to dinner. Just the two of us, somewhere nice. Agreed?"

"Deal!" Renata said, because that's how Americans talked in the pictures. "What is it you need me to do?"

"I need hair styling assistance." Renata nearly swooned at the thought of running her fingers through Fausto's hair. "Not for me, of course," he said looking down. "Come along, and you'll see." Whatever momentary disappointment Renata felt evaporated as they entered the guest bedroom and she came face-to-face with Shirley Temple.

CHAPTER 44

At 8 a.m. on the dot, Corey Wainwright knocked on Missy's hotel room door. He identified himself and the door swung open. He smiled at the attractive secretary, who was already nicely put together in a dark blue suit and matching hat, but his smile disappeared when he didn't see Joan. "Where is your guest?" he asked, a line forming between his eyebrows. "She didn't get away, did she?"

"No, she's in the bathroom," Missy laughed. "She's been occupying it for some time, in fact. Would you mind waiting for her to come out? I want to check on Mrs. Temple and Grace, and I'd like to make a confidential call to the White House from their phone without anyone else listening in," she said, inclining her head toward the bathroom door.

"Sure, take your time," he said loudly, then he lowered his voice and moved closer to Missy's ear, noticing the pleasant perfume she wore. "Tell Mrs. Temple that two of my agents are staking out the home of the stunt man in L.A. His name is Andy Archie. His wife has no idea what he's been up to, just that he was injured on the set of *The Littlest Rebel* a few weeks ago and hadn't been bringing much money home. Then, all of a sudden, he was flush again. She said he took off yesterday afternoon in his best suit, said he had an important appointment, and she hasn't seen him since."

Missy's eyes widened, and her mouth formed a round O, that was echoed by her voice. "Oh!"

Wainwright nodded and stepped back. "Nice perfume," he said. "Is it French?"

Missy ducked her head. "Why, yes, it's my favorite, from Guerlain, L'Heure Bleue. How did you know?"

"I'm an investigator," said Wainwright. "Always looking for clues."

Missy laughed and then left the room, smiling at Wainwright over her shoulder. A few seconds later, Joan emerged from the bathroom, tugging at the zipper on her skirt. She was in a foul mood. Besides getting nowhere on the story, her panties hadn't quite dried out, and she had a run in her hose. But when she saw the nice-looking FBI agent, she put on a smile and purred, "Oh, Agent Wainwright. I seem to have gotten my zipper stuck. Would you mind?"

The agent reddened slightly, but stood behind the reporter and quickly slid the zipper up. "Doesn't seem to be stuck at all," he said.

"Well, you must have the magic touch," Joan simpered, turning around and thrusting her chest toward his. "Any break in the case?"

"Now, you know I can't tell you that, Miss Roswell," he admonished. "But perhaps Mr. Hoover will give you a briefing when he arrives." Joan's smile widened. "Off-the-record, of course."

Joan pouted, then asked, "What does a girl have to do to get a cup of coffee around here?"

Shirley Temple Is Missing

In the adjoining room, Missy shared Wainwright's news with Grace and Gertrude, who had both gotten a few hours of sleep. Gertrude, sitting on her bed, was furious to hear that Andy seemed to indeed be part of the plot. "Imagine that man befriending Shirley and then enticing her off the train!" she railed. "What kind of a monster does that?"

"A desperate one, I imagine," Missy said. "Didn't you say he had been injured? He probably lives hand-to-mouth as a stunt man, and when he doesn't work, he isn't paid. Without a paycheck, a lot of people do things they know they shouldn't. It seems someone was paying him well for his help. We just have to find out who. Can you think of anyone who would have a grudge against Shirley?"

Mrs. Temple thought a moment. "I suppose there are people who are jealous of Shirley, the parents of other child actors, for example," she said. "Jane Withers was very ugly to Shirley during the making of *Bright Eyes*, and I made sure Shirley didn't have any contact with Jane when they were off-camera. But I can't imagine Mrs. Withers doing something like this." Her eyes filled with tears. "I'm just dreading a ransom note arriving at our home and someone threatening to hurt my darling little girl."

Grace sat down beside the sobbing woman and put her arm around her. Missy sat on Gertrude's other side. "Don't be afraid, Gertrude," Missy said. "Remember what the President said in his inaugural address? 'The only thing we have to fear is fear itself?' It's really true, because when you are afraid, you can't take action. And we're taking action!"

Once Gertrude had calmed down a bit, Grace convinced her to go downstairs to the hotel coffee shop for a little breakfast. As soon as they left the room, Missy placed a call to the White House and was quickly dispatched to Steve Early's office. She gave the press secretary a rundown on the case, mentioning the stake-out at the stuntman's home, and asked him to convey the status to the President on the USS *Houston*. "I'm very impressed with the FBI's SAC here," she said. "Oh, lord, I've got the New Deal alphabet disease. That's senior agent in charge, for you civilians. Do you have any idea when Hoover is set to arrive?"

"I'll check with his secretary, Miss Gandy," Steve said. "She'll know." He sighed. "If she'll tell. That woman is more protective of her boss than you are of yours!"

"That's why they call us gatekeepers, Steve," Missy said.

CHAPTER 45

As he drove north on Third Street, Bernardo Albergotti looked out over the city's wharves and studied the superstructure of the new bridge being constructed across the bay to Oakland. Bernardo preferred to sleep in on Saturday mornings, but business was business, and when a regular client like Fausto Trevisano called, one had to answer. For once, Fausto had planned ahead.

Bernardo, one of the large number of Italian-American business owners in the city, had been given enough notice that he'd been able to complete the set-up of his camera and the testing of his lighting the previous afternoon. It had been time well spent. Initially, Bernardo had plugged too many of his power-hungry lights into the same circuit, tripping the breaker and plunging the consulate's basement into darkness. Of course, all that had been rectified now. Fausto had said he wanted to film only one short indoor scene and so Bernardo was confident that today's mission at the consulate would be completed by noon.

"You may speak of this to no one," Fausto had warned him.

"My lips are sealed," Bernardo had replied. He usually worked with at least one assistant, depending on the nature of the job, but here, too, Fausto had been adamant.

"Just you alone," he had said. "I will provide assistance."

Renata was having a wonderful morning. First Fausto had asked for her help and now she was curling Shirley Temple's hair! She couldn't wait to tell Father.

"This is an awfully nice house," Shirley said while Renata worked. "And I've only ever seen this one room!"

"Once we get your hair just right, I'll show you around. I'll take you down to the kitchen and we can make pasta with Signora Ferri, our cook."

"What's pasta?"

"Have you ever eaten spaghetti?" Renata asked.

"Sure," said Shirley.

"Well, that's one kind of pasta, but we use flour, eggs, and water to make all kinds of shapes of pasta, even farfalle—bow-tie pasta. That's my favorite. You can have some for lunch if you like."

"I'm not sure I can eat any lunch after that big breakfast," Shirley said. "But I'd sure like to make some pasta."

Renata giggled. "Fausto is going to take me to dinner," she confided. "I would invite you, but you're a little too young."

"Who's Fausto?"

"Fausto. The man who brought you here."

"I thought his name was Juan."

"Now let's see," Renata said, taking a step back and looking Shirley over. "Very nice, even if I do say so myself." She held out a hand mirror for Shirley. "What do you think?"

"Well," Shirley said, poking out her lips, "it's not as good as Mother does, but it'll do." She smiled.

"Now let's try on your costume."

"What kind of uniform is this?" Shirley asked.

"It's an Italian army uniform, like Il Duce wears." Renata held the tunic up and Shirley slid her hands through the sleeves.

"Who's Il Duce?"

"Il Duce? Why he's Mussolini, the prime minister of Italy. He's sort of like the president, only much stronger."

"Well, the President is the big boss around here!" Shirley said.

"Let me help you with the belt," Renata said coming around in front of Shirley. "It's a little loose here." She moved behind Shirley and cinched up the slack in the tunic, then took two safety pins from the dressing table and pinned it up. "How's that feel?"

"Nice and snug!" Shirley said with a laugh.

"All ready then?" Fausto said from the door.

Shirley twirled around. "How do I look?" She grinned.

"Like a Roman lioness!" Fausto said with a laugh. "Both of you come with me and we'll finish our work."

By the time Fausto had led the two girls down to the basement, Bernardo had finished dressing the small set and had checked his equipment. The final touch had been hanging the green, white, and red Italian tri-color as a backdrop. Now he was ready to film.

"Good morning, Fausto," he said as his client entered the room. "Who are these lovely ladies?" he asked just before recognition set in. Bernardo's eyes widened, and he fell silent.

"This is Renata, the daughter of His Excellency. And I am sure a filmmaker such as yourself recognizes Miss Shirley Temple."

Bernardo shook each girl's hand in turn and muttered, "Pleased to meet you," a look of confusion coloring his face.

"Renata will be your assistant. Instruct her in her duties while Shirley and I review her lines," Fausto said. He took the younger girl into the corner and knelt down to face her at eye level. "Just a few lines—and no stunts—today. Once Mr. Zanuck is satisfied with this scene, your mother will help you learn the rest of the lines. All right?"

"Okey-dokey."

"Now, there are only three lines. I'll read them to you and then you repeat them back. Once you know them, we'll film. We'll do two shots, one close up and one wide. All right?"

"All right. Renata said your name is really Fausto, not Juan."

Fausto grinned. "That's right. I used Juan as a stage name, sort of like how you have a different name in your pictures."

"Oh. I see," Shirley said with a wide smile.

"Ready?"

"Ready!"

Fausto read the first half line and Shirley repeated it. Then he went to the next and so on throughout the short script. On the third pass through, he gave full sentences. By the sixth time through, Shirley was able to repeat all the lines with minimal prompting. *Very impressive*, Fausto thought.

"I think I'm ready," Shirley declared.

Fausto turned to Bernardo and Renata. "Ready."

Renata took the marker board and chalked "shot 1, take 1" on it. Bernardo switched on the lights, checked his sound equipment, and made sure that the microphone was not hanging down into the frame. He led Shirley to a tape mark on the floor just in front of the flag, squared her shoulders and then retreated to the camera.

"Now, Renata, if you please," Bernardo nodded to his assistant.

Renata stepped in front of Shirley and held the marker board in front of her. "Shirley Temple, shot one, take one, mark!" She slapped the two portions of the board together with a loud *clack*!

"Now, Shirley, hands on your hips," Fausto said. "Stick out your chin. A little higher. That's it. Action!"

The first shot, the wide one, was completed in three takes, the close-up in just two.

"Renata," Fausto said, looking at his co-conspirator, "take Shirley upstairs and find some clothes she can wear while her own clothes are laundered. Then occupy her for a little while, won't you?"

"Of course, Fausto." She smiled and batted her eyelashes.

Once the two girls had departed, Fausto turned to the filmmaker. "How long?"

"Three, four hours. I should be back by three o'clock at the latest."

"An extra twenty dollars if you're back by two," Fausto replied.

CHAPTER 46

John Griffith looked like a defeated man when he finally arrived at the St. Francis at ten-thirty Saturday morning. He hadn't slept since his fateful nap aboard the *Daylight*, having spent the previous night journeying to San José and back with detectives from the Southern Pacific railroad. They had canvassed the vicinity around the train station, questioning witnesses, praying for a break.

What he needed now was sleep, but that was out of the question. At this point, his guilty conscience would never allow his mind to rest. Instead, he needed to contact Gertrude and share the little bit of good news he had.

"I'm John Griffith," he said to the desk manager. "I need to speak to Mrs. Temple."

"I'll ring her room, sir. You can use the telephone on the end of the counter."

Griff stepped to the end of the counter closest to the hotel's bank of elevators. When it rang once, he picked it up. "Ringing Mrs. Temple's room," the operator said.

One ring, two, then more, but no answer. Griff hung up and waved the desk manager over. "I got no answer. Is Mrs. Temple in the hotel? Has she gone out?"

"Let me check, sir." The man stepped over to the registry and flipped a page, running his finger down a column.   Then he turned toward the wall of small mailboxes behind him and ran his finger along one row until he came to 1220. It was empty. "She must still be in the hotel, sir. Her key is not in its slot. Perhaps you'd like to check in the restaurant."

"Yeah, I'll do that. If she comes down, please let her know that I'm looking for her." Griff headed across the carpeted lobby toward the hotel's dining room. Rows of white cloth-covered tables sat along the windows facing Union Square, the sunlight casting a golden glow through the room. After thirty seconds of scanning the faces at each table, Griff gave up.

He returned to the registration desk. "I'd like to go ahead and check in," he said to the same desk manager. "I had a room booked for last night, but I got detained."

"Griff!" Griffith turned to see Gertrude Temple and the two ladies from the White House hurrying toward him. Trailing several paces behind them was a man in a conservative suit followed by one other familiar face. "Thank heavens you're back! Any news?"

"Your key, sir," the desk man said, handing over Griffith's room key attached to a heavy wooden fob. Griff pocketed the key, then took Gertrude by the arm and led her and the two secretaries to one of the plush sofas positioned about the lobby.

"Can we talk?" he asked Gertrude, glancing at the others.

"Yes. This is Special Agent Wainwright from the local office of the FBI. You know Miss LeHand and Miss Tully, and this is—"

"I know Joan. We go back a ways."

Joan frowned. "Long night, dear?"

Wainwright took over. "We know the stunt man, Andy Archie, was involved. He's the one that got Shirley off the train. Some of the train's crew saw them together. Apparently, he was quite brazen."

"That's good, in a way," the reporter interrupted.

"Good?" Gertrude straightened, her eyes wide with indignation. "How can that be good?"

"I don't think he'd hurt Shirley," Joan said.

"What do you think he would do?" Missy asked.

"Demand ransom, maybe. I don't know. I never figured him for that type," Joan said.

"Well, I don't care what 'type' he is, I just want my little girl back."

"How about you, Mr. Griffith? Did you learn anything in San José?" Wainwright asked.

For the first time since the whole miserable ordeal began, Griff allowed himself a little smile. "Not much, but maybe something. A worker taking a smoke break at a cannery across from the station remembered seeing a man and a boy shooting a slingshot. A black Chevy sedan pulled up and they got in. He said his break ran from about five-ten to five-twenty."

"There are a lot of black Chevrolets in California, Mr. Griffith," Wainwright said.

"Yeah, but not very many have diplomatic tags."

"Did you get a number?"

"Unfortunately, no. But I'm guessing the list of Chevys with California diplomatic plates is fairly short."

"I'm guessing you're right," Wainwright smiled.

CHAPTER 47

Diplomacy came in many flavors, Cosimo Palladino decided as his chauffeured Cadillac turned down Webster Street heading back toward the consulate. There's the kind practiced between professional diplomats, rich with courtesy, tradition and doublespeak. And then there's the kind he'd practiced this morning, as subtle as brass knuckles and no more pleasant to apply.

As the ranking Italian diplomat in California, Cosimo had been pressed into dealing with a consequential commercial matter. As a protest against the Ethiopian campaign, local longshoremen were refusing to load two ships destined for Italy with a cargo of scrap iron. Rather than risk his political future through a direct confrontation with the longshoremen's union, San Francisco Mayor Angelo Rossi had dispatched Cosimo to meet with union chief Harry Bridges.

"We don't condone naked aggression like the kind practiced by your boss, Signore Palladino," Bridges had said over a cup of coffee in a dark waterfront tavern. "It's bad policy and lousy politics."

"I'm not here to argue politics or doctrines with you, Mr. Bridges. This is simply a matter of commerce. Two parties have engaged in a business transaction that is legitimate from any angle. One of these parties has employed your union to load goods purchased by the other. There are no politics involved."

"Of course there are. The 'goods' you're talking about are headed back to your mother country to be turned into bullets and bombs that your countrymen will use to kill uncivilized tribesmen trying to defend their homes with spears and shields. We're not going to be a part of that. We're not going to condone it."

"No one would interpret your loading of these ships as political support of the Italian government. They would rightfully and simply conclude that you were fulfilling the obligations of your labor contract, a contract that you yourself negotiated," the diplomat countered.

"Signore Palladino, we can sit her and argue all morning. We can talk until we turn blue in the face and until we drink so much coffee we have to stop to take a piss." Bridges leaned across the small, knife-scarred table. He tapped the table top with his index finger. "But we ain't gonna load them ships."

Cosimo leaned back. "Very well. I had hoped you were a man of honor who would live up to his agreements. Since that is not the case, I am compelled to bring you a message from the mayor, a message he will disavow, of course, but one which I beg you to heed."

"What's that?"

"If your men don't load the ships, the mayor will bring in men who will." Cosimo paused. "And they will have police protection, Mr. Bridges." Cosimo had pushed back his chair and stood. "Think that over, my friend."

Now, as the Cadillac pulled into the courtyard of the consulate, Cosimo was glad to be home, ready for a pleasant lunch and a quiet afternoon.

"Excellency," his secretary greeted him with as he stepped off the elevator, "remember the vice consul's appointment is scheduled for three o'clock. Signora Ferri has prepared for you a lunch plate in the kitchen. Shall I bring it up to your office?"

"No, I'll go get it myself. I need to walk around a bit."

"Very good, signore," the secretary said with a nod of his head before scurrying away.

Cosimo walked downstairs to the ground floor kitchen and pushed through the double swinging doors. "Renata!" he exclaimed with a smile, "what a nice surprise. What are you up to?" Renata was standing at the counter wearing a white apron, her face and hands dusted with flour. Beside her, a younger girl, also wearing an apron, was standing on a stool.

"Signora Ferri is teaching us to make farfalle."

"That's pasta," Shirley said, her hands white with flour.

"This is my friend, Shirley. She spent the night."

"Pleased to meet you," Cosimo said, glancing around for his cook. "Ah, Signora Ferri, you have a plate for me?"

"Si, Excellency." The heavy-set cook handed him a covered tray. "Would you like me to have someone carry this up for you?"

198

"No, I've got it. I'll let you return to your students," he said with a smile and a wink. *How much more pleasant than dealing with longshoremen.*

By a quarter to three, Cosimo had finished drafting a report to Rome concerning the shipping affair. It had taken longer than usual due to the unholy racket Renata and her little friend were making roller skating out in the corridor. He finished his report and set it in his out box. *A good thing the mayor is Italian*, he thought with a smirk. A knock on his door diverted his attention to Marcello.

"Mi scusi, Excellency," Marcello began. "Fausto asked me to set this up prior to your meeting."

Cosimo waved his subordinate into the room. From his out box, the report would go to the coding room in the basement. There the consulate code clerk would encode the message. Then it would go up to the cable room on the top floor to be transmitted to Rome. Assuming everyone was at his post, his report would greet the government's Sunday morning duty officers when they arrived for their weekend shifts.

"What is all that, Marcello?"

"A film projector and screen, signore."

Leave it to Fausto!

At two fifty-five, Fausto peered around the partially open door to Cosimo's office. The consul was on the phone, but looked up and nodded toward Fausto.

"He is quite an unreasonable fellow," Cosimo said, then paused, listening to the speaker on the other end of the line. "Perhaps, but if you buy services you've already paid for, you open Pandora's box. Who's to say that the next time they wouldn't unload our olive oil out of sympathy for California growers?"

Another pause. "Well, of course it's not as good. Not even close. I'm just making a point. At any rate, I delivered your message and left. I expect the next move is up to him. He either has his men working on Monday morning or you send in the replacements." Cosimo listened.

"I will, Angelo, and you do the same. Goodbye."

"Signore," Fausto said, gesturing toward an arm chair he had placed beside the projector. "If you please, a very short film to address the critical issue we discussed."

Cosimo moved toward the chair as the girls raced by shouting and laughing in the corridor. He was trying to recall when he'd mentioned the shipping crisis with Fausto. It didn't really fall under his area of influence. "Push that door to, please."

Fausto closed the door and then flipped off the overhead lights. He drew the curtains over the windows and, using his cigarette lighter for illumination, walked back over to the projector.

"I think you will be pleased, Excellency." Fausto turned the projector on and a blue-white light streamed through the darkness, splashing the image of a young girl onto the screen.

"It's Renata!" Cosimo said, and smiled. He looked up at Fausto beside the projector. "But why…" Renata slapped the markerboard and stepped aside revealing a chubby-cheeked younger girl with curly hair.

The child, dressed in a uniform tunic and matching skirt, thrust out her chin and placed her hands on her hips.

Just like Il Duce, Cosimo thought. Then she began to speak.

"A salute to the brave and righteous men of the Italian armed forces and their valiant leader Benito Mussolini! May their efforts be blessed by the Almighty and their successes on the field of battle bring honor and glory to the Italian Empire! The plow makes the furrow, but the sword defends it!"

She stared resolutely into the camera for another moment and then the film ran out and the screen went totally white. Fausto shut off the projector and switched on the lights.

"Would you like to see it again, Excellency?" he asked with a broad smile.

Cosimo sat dazed. "How did you do that, Fausto? When did you do that?"

"Forgive me, Excellency, but I arranged for an overnight guest here last night."

Cosimo's eyebrows shot up. He leaped from his chair and dashed to his office door, flinging it open, and sticking his head out into the hallway. Renata and her friend were rolling toward him, holding hands and giggling. *It can't be!*

With the office door firmly closed and Fausto seated in the arm chair, Cosimo leaned over with his hands on his knees and stared directly into his subordinate's eyes.

"How did you do this, Fausto? How is it that a six-year-old child spends the night in my consulate—unaccompanied—and makes a movie for you?"

"Excellency, I know you are pleased with my work," Fausto said, beaming.

"'Pleased' is not the word, Fausto."

"I borrowed the child."

"'Borrowed?'"

"Si, Excellency. I must admit it was quite a feat. I was required to employ great cunning and boldness to execute my meticulously crafted plan. I must tell you, Excellency, that the plan only worked because I was in complete control of every complicated stage of the operation."

"And accomplices, Fausto? How many others are aware of Miss Temple's presence here?"

"Only you, Excellency, and of course, me." Fausto paused. "And Marcello and Renata. And Bernardo, the filmmaker. And Signora Benvenuti." Fausto spread his hands and smiled.

"No one else?"

"No one else, Excellency!"

"How did you... separate Miss Temple from her family?"

"Ah, Excellency, perhaps it is best that you do not ask such questions."

"At this point, Fausto, perhaps it is best that I decide what is best." Cosimo straightened and walked behind his desk. "How did you apprehend the child?"

"I paid a man to get her off the train. She was traveling with her mother from Los Angeles. My man took her off the train at San José. Marcello and I picked them up and drove them here."

Cosimo stared at the younger man. "You kidnapped Shirley Temple?"

"Of course not, Excellency! I was very careful to break no laws. All I did was pick up two hitch-hikers and give them a ride."

"But one of these 'hitch-hikers' is a kidnapper, yes? And the other is his victim? Where is this man? Did he spend the night here too?"

"No, Excellency! The man does not even know my name, of course. He has no idea who put him up to his task."

"But you met with him? He can identify you?"

"I used an alias, Excellency. He has no idea who I am, and he cannot make any connection to the consulate."

"Fausto, you realize that in America, kidnapping is considered a 'federal' crime?"

"Excellency, please!"

Cosimo stared down at the floor. "I like San Francisco, Fausto. I hoped to stay here at least until Renata was ready for university." He slumped down into his leather desk chair and rested his face in his hands. "Now, I'll be lucky if they don't send me to Addis Ababa." *Mama mia!*

CHAPTER 48

Not everyone around here is a fool, Cosimo thought, reading the note his secretary had just handed him. The secretary had quickly—and discreetly—determined that Gertrude Temple was staying at the stately St. Francis Hotel on Union Square, a short drive from the consulate. *Perhaps, with a little luck, we can repair this calamity without it becoming public knowledge.*

"Ask Marcello to prepare the car. Then tell Renata to help her guest gather up her things and meet me at the elevator."

"Si, Excellency." The secretary nodded and left the office.

"There are no copies of that film, correct?" Cosimo asked Fausto, still seated in the chair in front of the consul's desk.

"No copies, Excellency."

"And of this you are certain?"

"Yes, Excellency. Bernardo was waiting for my—for your approval before producing copies."

"I am forced at this moment to rely on your word, Fausto, but I must tell you that this does not fill me with confidence. You will arrange for this Bernardo to attend me here at six o'clock this evening. You will say nothing of this to anyone, Fausto, and you are confined to the consulate until further notice. Do you understand?"

"Excellency, this film is the antidote to the child's misguided criticism of Il Duce! When audiences around the globe see this before their feature motion pictures the whole world will rally to our cause. That is the power this child has! Excellency, she is so very popular! They make dolls in her likeness. There are Shirley Temple dresses, hair bows, berets, cutout books, playing cards. With her filmed endorsement, Americans will stampede to support us."

Cosimo just stared at his subordinate. His intercom buzzed.

"The car is ready, Excellency."

"How long to the St. Francis?" Cosimo asked as he settled into the back seat of the consulate's Cadillac.

"Ten minutes, Excellency," Marcello answered from the front seat, pressing the starter. The big engine rumbled to life and Cosimo sat back and smiled at his daughter and her new friend. Shirley was back in her overalls and denim jacket, freshly laundered at the consulate. However, her newsboy cap had disappeared—a prized souvenir snatched by the laundress—as had her famous hair-do. Despite Renata's best efforts, the combination of a morning making pasta in a hot, steamy kitchen and the frenetic roller skating down the halls had left behind a matted mess.

"Now, girls, we're taking Shirley back to her mother." He looked from Renata's face to Shirley's. "It is important to us, Shirley, that you had a pleasant visit: that you had plenty to eat and that you and Renata enjoyed playing together."

"Oh, yes sir, Excellency!" Shirley responded with a smile. "I had a wonderful time. I hope Renata can come visit me sometime, if the trip is not too far."

"Yes, of course. And, Shirley, please remember that we were very kind to you when you showed up completely by surprise last night. We had no idea you would find your way to the consulate and yet when we found you there we were most hospitable. And remember, too, that we have no one at the consulate by the name of Juan."

"I know." Shirley giggled. She winked at Cosimo, leaning over Renata's lap and whispering, "That was just Fausto's stage name."

Mio Dio! "Yes, well, I'm sure your mother is going to be very happy to see you. Very happy indeed."

"Papa, can I stay and play with Shirley once she gets to her hotel?"

"That would be fun!" Shirley said, smiling.

"Perhaps another time, girls. I'm certain that Shirley's mother will wish to spend some time with her." Cosimo felt the car slowing and looked up, expecting to see Union Square and the twelve-story St. Francis Hotel. Instead, Marcello whipped the car into a narrow alley. *Clever man*, he thought, *he's found us the service entrance. Less likely to be observed.* But when Cosimo caught his driver's eye in the rear-view mirror, Marcello looked quickly away. And when the alley opened into a tiny unpaved courtyard strewn with garbage and cases of empty bottles, Cosimo knew they weren't at the St. Francis—or any other reputable spot, either.

"Marcello, where are we?"

"Change of plans, Excellency," Marcello replied, bringing the car to a halt a few feet from the rear of Spider Kelly's Saloon. The back door of the Cadillac was pulled open and a smiling Joseph Gallo peered inside.

"Well, well. What do we have here?"

CHAPTER 49

"How long to the Italian Consulate?" Griffith asked climbing into the passenger seat of Wainwright's Ford.

"In Saturday afternoon traffic, maybe eight minutes."

It had taken the FBI man and his colleagues less than an hour to determine that the automobile in question was most likely registered to either the Argentine consulate or the consulate of Italy. They had visited the closer consulate first. The consul general of Argentina had chuckled when Wainwright explained his dilemma.

"As your consulate is sovereign territory, Senõr Cepeda, I cannot enter without your invitation and I certainly can't search any of your vehicles."

"Come in. We will cooperate with you in any way we can. Kidnapping is, sadly, not unknown in our own country. A child should never be stolen away from its parents."

Cepeda had led the two men to the building's garage, members of his staff watching with concerned expressions. "Here we are, gentlemen." The consul had raised one of the twin wooden doors exposing a black Chevrolet coupe with diplomatic plates.

Wainwright and Griffith had looked at each other, then Wainwright addressed the consul. "You have been most kind, Senõr Cepeda, and most understanding. The car we seek is a sedan. I apologize for putting you to this trouble." Cepeda had shaken their hands and ushered them out a side gate and back onto the street.

"I wish you quick success, gentlemen."

Wainwright pulled to a stop before the Italian consulate's Webster Street entrance.

"Our answer could be just beyond those doors," he said, nodding toward the wooden gates that separated the building's courtyard from the street.

The two men got out of the car and buttoned their jackets as they approached the heavy wooden door bearing the escutcheon of the Italian Empire. Wainwright grasped the heavy brass knocker and hammered it with authority.

After several moments, they heard the door unlock and saw it swing open. A neatly dressed man in a dark suit peered out and said, "May I help you?"

"We'd like to see Signore Palladino on a matter of some urgency," Wainwright said.

"I'm sorry, gentlemen," the man answered with a light accent, "His Excellency is not in residence at the moment."

"Is one of the vice consuls available? Time is of the essence."

"If you will kindly wait here, I will find out." The man shut the door.

"It'd be a lot easier if we could just walk in. Don't you have probable cause, Agent Wainwright?"

Wainwright shook his head. "If I believed Shirley's life was in imminent danger, I'd go in with my pistol drawn. But that'd be my last day on the job. Mr. Hoover would have my credentials before the sun set. He believes in playing it by the book. That means the rest of us do too."

"Maybe I could just sort of walk around a little, you know," Griff said, "maybe have a smoke over by that gate."

"Don't do it, Mr. Griffith. You're with me now. Whatever you do, I'd have to account for."

The door opened again, and this time a handsome, broad-shouldered man wearing an open-collared, light blue shirt and tan slacks appeared.

"I am the vice consul, Fausto Trevisano. How can I assist you?"

"Signore Trevisano, I'm Special Agent Wainwright from the Federal Bureau of Investigation. This is my associate, Mr. Griffith." Griff noticed a flash of apprehension on the Italian's face as he looked at Wainwright's badge. "We're investigating a kidnapping and have reason to believe one of the consulate's vehicles could have been involved."

"But they should have reached the hotel over an hour ago," Fausto said, frowning.

"Who? What hotel?" Griff asked, taking a step forward. Wainwright laid a restraining hand on his arm.

"Signore Trevisano, you seem to know more about this than we do."

Fausto studied the faces standing in front of him. "This I doubt very much," he said, smiling. "One cannot live in the United States without being aware of the skill and successes of Mr. Hoover and the FBI."

"You said they should have reached the hotel. Who were you talking about?"

"His Excellency, Signore Palladino, and his daughter Renata and their house guest."

"Who is their guest?" Wainwright asked.

Fausto grinned. "I thought you knew. Miss Temple, the movie star."

"She was here?" Griff asked.

"Was, yes, but is no more. As I said, His Excellency left to take her to the hotel."

"Which hotel, Signore Trevisano?" Wainwright asked.

"The St. Francis. They would have arrived an hour ago."

Wainwright and Griff exchanged glances. "Signore Trevisano, recognizing the sovereign character of the consulate, would it be possible for us to come inside and use your telephone?"

"Certainly. Follow me." Fausto led his two guests into the broad, ground floor corridor and into a central lobby, their heels clicking on the brightly shined terrazzo floor. He showed Wainwright and Griffith to a telephone sitting on a small round table set between two red upholstered wingback chairs.

Wainwright picked up the phone. As he placed his call, Griff looked Fausto in the eye and whispered, "If anything happens to that little girl, I'll make you pay."

"Oh dear," Fausto said with a smirk, "am I supposed to be frightened? Remember, signore, that you are a guest on Italian soil. I would hate to think that you would repay our hospitality with threats. After all, we took good care of your young friend until we could determine how to reunite her with her mother. Ask her yourself when you see her."

Griff took a step toward his host. "You bet I will, mister." Behind him, Wainwright hung up the phone and turned toward Griff and Fausto.

"They're not there. Mrs. Temple says no one has arrived and no one has called. I'm afraid my call upset her again. Will you help us find them, Signore Trevisano? I'm sure your cooperation would go a long way toward repairing whatever damage has been done."

"Damage, signore? I'm not sure what you are referring to. But, yes, of course I will help you."

Wainwright pulled a notepad and pencil from his coat pocket. "You said the consul general and his daughter and Miss Temple left here at what time?"

"Shortly before four o'clock."

"By car, I suppose?"

"Yes. His Excellency left in the consulate's Cadillac."

"Can you describe it?"

"Long, black, elegant." Fausto closed his eyes. "Gray interior, very comfortable."

"Do you know the plate number?"

"No. Perhaps the consulate's driver ..." Fausto paused. "Topo!" he whispered. Then, looking back at Wainwright, he said. "The consulate's driver is Marcello Altobello. He left with His Excellency's party and he has not returned."

"Do you think he might be up to something?"

"He is not the sharpest knife in the drawer as you might say, signore. But," Fausto shrugged his shoulders, "it might be worth finding him and asking him a few questions."

"Where do we find him?" Griff asked, working hard to contain his anxiety.

"This I do not know. But Marcello is of a lower class, so I suspect he would be attracted to businesses that cater to the common classes." Fausto looked at Wainwright. "You would know these better than I."

Walking to the car, Wainwright looked thoughtful. "I served on the Italian front during the Great War and picked up a bit of the lingo," he told Griff. "When I asked the vice consul about the car, he blurted out the word 'topo.' It means mouse."

"Hmm," said Griff. "Sounds like we'll need to set a mousetrap."

CHAPTER 50

The phone call Wainwright had placed from the Italian consulate to the women at the St. Francis had sent Mrs. Temple into another tailspin. "To think Shirley was almost here!" she sobbed.

Grace and Missy exchanged worried looks. The two women had worked together so long and knew each other so well that they could communicate almost telepathically. "I tell you what, Gertrude," Grace said, "let's go back to our room and stretch out on the beds for a bit. We can turn on the radio and listen to some soft music. They're hot on the trail now. I'm sure Mr. Wainwright and Mr. Griffith will have good news for us soon."

"Thanks, Grace," Gertrude said, sniffling. "I'll call my husband and find out if he has heard anything. He's sitting at home by the phone with the FBI, waiting for a…call." She began crying harder.

After the two women departed, Missy was left again with her unwelcome roommate. "I'm going to have to ask you to step into the bathroom for a moment, Miss Roswell," Missy said, "while I place a call to the White House. And please turn on the water in the sink full force. I don't want you eavesdropping on my call."

"Honestly," Joan said, narrowing her cat's eyes. "One would think you don't trust me."

"One would be right," Missy replied evenly.

"Well, at least give me one of your Luckys so I'll have something to do," Joan said, holding out her hand. Giving an exasperated sigh, Missy handed over her pack, and waited until she heard the water running in the bathroom before she dialed the White House.

Missy filled Steve Early in on the latest developments in the case, including the apparent involvement of the Italians. The press secretary whistled. "This puts a whole new complexion on it," he said. "I'll send a telegram to the Boss right now and find out how he wants us to handle it. Why on earth would the Italian consul want to kidnap Shirley Temple?"

"I am wracking my brain trying to figure it out," Missy said. "What did you learn about Hoover? Do we have an arrival time?"

"I had to promise that old battle ax Helen Gandy a personally autographed picture from the President, but she finally told me Hoover left at 7 a.m. If he has good weather, he should arrive in Los Angeles by eight o'clock Sunday morning. Then he'll have to fly up to San Francisco."

"Good, I'll let Mrs. Temple know. I'm sure she will be grateful to have such an important man on the scene, though I have to say Agent Wainwright is very impressive," Missy said. "Thanks, Steve. Send my love to all the gang at the White House."

"Of course," Steve said. "And our love goes to you too."

In the bathroom, Joan sat down on the toilet seat and lit her cigarette. While turning on the water, she had noticed something shiny in the soap dish. It was Missy's pinky ring. Curious, she picked it up, admiring the onyx stone, and then looked inside the band.

"To MALeH from FDR, with love," it said.

"With love!" Joan smiled. Maybe she had a bargaining chip after all!

CHAPTER 51

"Would you care for a drink?" Joseph Gallo asked Cosimo Palladino as he settled into a battered leather arm chair in a room above Spider Kelly's Pacific Street establishment. Gallo, assisted by Marcello, had hustled the objecting consul and the two young girls into the back door of the bar, through its filthy kitchen and up a rickety set of stairs. Now they found themselves sequestered in a dimly lit, dusty storage room filled with boxes of empty beer bottles, broken chairs and tables, and assorted replacement parts for the pinball machines that stood in the hallway off the downstairs dance floor.

Cosimo sat facing his "host" while the girls perched on two wooden crates in front of a half-open window which looked like it had last been cleaned right before the 1906 earthquake. The window let in what little light infiltrated the room and overlooked the narrow, muddy courtyard where the consulate's car was parked.

"Thank you, no. What I would like," Cosimo said, keeping his voice low and nodding toward Shirley, "is to reunite that child with her mother."

"No can do," Gallo smiled. "That wouldn't be killing the golden goose exactly, but it would be like giving the bird away. For nothin'. We don't do nothin' for nothin', do we, Topo?"

"Nothin' for nothin'," Marcello echoed, lighting a cigarette.

Cosimo turned to his driver. "My boy, circumstances are not yet out of our hands, but be assured that they are about to exceed our ability to contain them. I appeal to your better judgment. Let's get back in the car and complete our journey and forget this unfortunate episode."

Gallo chuckled. "Nicely put, signore. Anybody ever tell you you sound like a diplomat?" Gallo pulled a thick, black cigar from his coat pocket and shoved it between his fleshy lips. "Topo, take the car up the street to Tonti's. Tell him you'll come back for it tonight." Marcello raised two fingers to his eyebrow and threw the fat man a quick salute. Within a moment, Cosimo and the girls could hear his footsteps creaking down the stairs.

"What do you propose to do with us, signore?"

"I don't propose nothin'. I'm just gonna sell you as a lot to the highest bidder." He lit his cigar and sat back, blowing a cloud of gray smoke toward the ceiling.

"I appeal to your virtue, signore. As an Italian, surely you respect the family. Surely you know that the place for this child—for both of these children—is with their parents."

Gallo leaned forward again, the buttons on his white shirt straining against his girth. "Relax, pal. Nothin' bad's gonna happen as long as you—how did you put it—use your 'better judgment.'"

Shirley Temple Is Missing

Renata nudged Shirley in the ribs. "Look," she whispered.

Shirley peered out the window and saw Marcello cross the courtyard in quick strides. He pulled open the driver's door and climbed inside. Even from the second-floor window, the Cadillac sounded powerful as its big engine rumbled to life. As Shirley leaned back, she felt a poke in her hip. She reached her hand behind her and touched her slingshot. She glanced around and then nudged Renata.

"Hand me some of those," she said quietly, looking quickly at the fat man and Renata's father before focusing on the Cadillac. Marcello was working to turn the car around in the tight confines of the courtyard. He would drive a few feet forward, then shift into reverse and turn the wheel and then repeat the steps.

Renata reached into an open pasteboard box beside her and scooped up several shiny pinballs. She held her hand out and Shirley picked up one of the heavy metal balls. She tugged the slingshot out from under her and eased toward the window. Renata looked on with wide eyes. "What are you going to do?"

"I'm going to shoot out his tires, so he can't get away! That's what the G-men always do." Shirley sighted along her straightened arm and pulled the bands back. She let the pouch go and watched as the pinball hit the mud just short of the back tire. "Too low!"

"Here," Renata said, holding out her hand. "Try again before he gets away."

Marcello had nearly completed his maneuver. One more set of turns and he'd have the big car lined up with the alley.

Shirley let fly a second shot. The pinball smacked into the round taillight, busting the red cover. "Too high!" she muttered. Renata handed her a third missile but before Shirley could fire, the back of the car disappeared into the alley.

"Nice try," Renata said, patting her friend on the arm.

CHAPTER 52

"Any great ideas?" Griff asked as he settled into the passenger seat of Wainwright's Ford.

"No." Wainwright pressed the starter and shifted the car into gear. He pulled out onto Webster and turned right on Broadway. "I'll tell you this, Mr. Griffith. Whoever's involved in this thing isn't playing with all of his face cards. It's crazy enough to kidnap America's favorite movie star, but to add a diplomat to the tally sheet? That's asking for trouble on a level they've never seen before. And we're going to give it to them."

"We going back to the hotel?"

"No. We're going to pay a call on the one guy who just might know what the hell's going on."

"Who would that be?"

"Peter P. McDonough. Pete and his brother Tom run the rackets in this city. Prostitution, bookmaking, gambling. Half the police force is on their take—one reason we want to keep the local cops out of things. They get involved and the cost of resolving the problem goes up."

"You think this McDonough knows something?"

"I don't know. I just know he's our best bet right now. We've got a lot of Italians in San Francisco.

McDonough's Irish, but he's got connections. Maybe he's heard something. Maybe he'll tell us."

"Sounds like a big maybe."

"Yeah, it is."

Ten minutes later, Wainwright pulled to a stop in front of McDonough Brothers Bail Bonds at the corner of Kearny and Clay Streets. A young tough in a cheap, blue suit was standing on the sidewalk smoking a cigarette. As Wainwright opened the car door, he looked at Griff and said, "I think it'd be better if you sat this one out." Griff started to protest, then sat back and nodded.

Wainwright got out of the car and the young man dropped his cigarette, crushed it out with his foot, and began walking toward the car. "Can't park there, pal."

Wainwright had the leather wallet holding his FBI credentials in his hand. He held it open for the young man and said, "I want to see Mr. McDonough."

"You got an appointment?"

"What do you think?" The lookout stared at Wainwright's face and then took another look at his badge.

"Who's in the car?"

"Just a friend. A civilian friend. He'll stay there."

"You packing?"

"Yep. Under my left arm."

"I'll have to take it."

"Don't even think about it. Listen, kid, I just need to ask your boss a few questions. Off the record. I'm not here to cause any trouble or embarrass anybody. Now I'm kind of in a hurry. You want to take me up or am I going to have to show myself in?"

"You J. Edgar Hoover or something?"

"Eddie!" came a voice from a second-floor window. "You forget your manners? Ask our guest to come upstairs."

"Sure, boss, sure." Eddie turned back to Wainwright. "Please follow me."

They went in the corner-facing door of the bail bond shop and around a wooden counter where a man sat reading a newspaper in between two telephones. On one wall was a calendar, the days of the month neatly X-ed out with a red pencil. On the other wall was a poster listing the numbers for both the municipal and federal courthouses, a couple of the local cab companies, the bus station and the train terminal. Wainwright followed Eddie through a set of beaded curtains at the end of the counter, past a small water cooler, and through a narrow doorway.

A flight of steps illuminated by an anemic light bulb led up to a landing off which were two doors. Eddie selected the one on the right, pushed it open and stepped to the side. He waved Wainwright ahead of him and pulled the door closed behind him.

"Special Agent Wainwright," Pete McDonough said, coming from behind his desk to shake the G-man's hand. He was a big, hearty man with intense blue eyes and a full head of white hair. Wainwright thought he'd look at home pouring tots of Jameson at any bar in Dublin. "What did I do to deserve this visit—or at least what do you think I did?" McDonough smiled and gestured toward two straight-back chairs. The two men sat facing each other. Dropping the smile, he asked, "What kind of beef you got with me?"

"No beef, Mr. McDonough. I know you're a busy man or you wouldn't be here working on a Saturday evening."

"Saturday's a big day for our business."

"Yes sir. Actually, I'm here looking for something."

"What would that be, Special Agent?"

"A favor."

McDonough's broad face slowly broke into a smile. "A favor."

"A big favor."

The smile receded, and McDonough leaned closer to Wainwright. "Tell me how I can help the FBI."

Twenty minutes later, Wainwright stepped out of the building, crossed the sidewalk, and climbed behind the wheel. He started the car and pulled away from the curb, turning back toward the west.

"You want the good news or the bad news?" he asked, looking over at Griff.

"The bad."

"He doesn't know anything."

"What's the good news?"

"He's a big Shirley Temple fan."

CHAPTER 53

Darryl Zanuck blew into the lobby of the St. Francis Hotel like one of the storms that periodically lashed the Pacific coast—and in an equally dark mood. Such a storm had delayed his flight from Los Angeles by five hours. Upon touchdown at San Francisco, he'd hopped in a cab at the airport and tipped the driver ten bucks after a quick ride to the hotel. In minutes, he was beating on the door of Room 1220.

A man's deep voice asked, "Who is it?"

"Darryl Zanuck," he said. The door swung open and he marched in, scanning the room and quickly identifying Griffith, who was seated in a chair at the desk, and Gertrude Temple, whose face appeared tired and tense. He felt some satisfaction when Griffith jumped to his feet and straightened up. Gertrude, who had been seated on one of the beds, likewise rose to her feet.

"Hi, boss. Let me introduce—" Griff began, indicating a tall man in a conservative suit, apparently the one who had opened the door. He was just re-holstering his gun.

"I'll get to you in a minute," Zanuck snapped. "Gertrude," he continued in a less confrontational tone, "I want you to know that I'm here for you and Shirley and that everything's going to be all right. I'm taking charge of this whole mess and we'll get it sorted out."

"Not so fast, Mr. ..." the other man began.

"Zanuck, Darryl Zanuck. I'm head of Twentieth Century-Fox and Shirley Temple, in addition to being a charming and delightful child, is a major asset of my studio." Zanuck turned and frowned at Griff. "It's important that everyone understands right now who's in charge here."

"We do, Mr. Zanuck," the other man said, diverting his attention. "And you're looking at him."

"Who the hell are you?"

"Special Agent Corey Wainwright, Federal Bureau of Investigation. As this is almost certainly a kidnapping, the Bureau is in charge and here in San Francisco, I am the Bureau."

Zanuck stared at the G-man, gauging his mettle, noticing the bump of a pistol under his coat and considering that perhaps discretion was the better part of valor. After all, the story for the hit movie *G-Men*, that had been released by Twentieth Century-Fox that spring, was all his. He had a healthy respect for the FBI. He re-inserted his cigar in his mouth as his mind churned ahead.

As Zanuck stood staring at Wainwright, the connecting door to the adjoining room swung open and three women crowded through. Two he couldn't identify and one he could.

His eyebrows shot up and he growled around the cigar, "What the hell are you doing here, Joan?"

CHAPTER 54

It was tight in the back seat of the Dodge coupe. Cosimo was turned sideways, his left shoulder against the back of the seat, his right rubbing against the side of the car. Renata sat in the middle, squeezed between her father and the fat man, Gallo. The driver was one of Gallo's people and had not been formally introduced.

Once Marcello had returned from stashing the car, Gallo had put the next step of his plan into motion. He'd sent downstairs for corned-beef stew and bread, beer for Cosimo, and water for the girls. "Eat up," he'd said, grinning. "Not sure what time supper will be."

After one bite, Cosimo had stopped eating. *Che schifo!* How could an Italian, especially one who appeared as well fed as Gallo, abide such disgusting slop! His culinary standards matched his morals.

"Not so hungry, Mr. Diplomat?" Gallo had said, wiping his mouth on a checkered cloth napkin. "If you're finished, come over here. You've got some work to do."

Cosimo had complied, dragging his rickety wooden chair beside Gallo's scarred, cluttered desk. Gallo had relit his cigar and handed Cosimo a sheet of plain paper. "Write what I tell you." Cosimo had removed his fountain pen from his coat pocket and unscrewed the cap.

"Mrs. Temple, care of the St. Francis Hotel," Gallo had begun. "If you wish to see your daughter again, deliver $200,000 in unmarked twenties to the Vallejo Pier at the Ferry Building at exactly three a.m. Sunday morning. No cops. No nobody. Just you and a plain black bag. Any funny stuff and you can kiss your kid goodbye." Gallo had paused and blown smoke rings toward the ceiling of the rapidly darkening room. "You got that?"

"Yes."

"Good. Read it back to me." Once he was satisfied, Gallo had pointed toward his captive. "Now sign it."

"I'll do no such thing. I'm an official of the Italian government. I'll take no part in this travesty."

Gallo exhaled a small cloud of gray smoke. He pushed himself far enough away from the desk to be able to open its center drawer. He reached into the drawer and when his hand reappeared, it was clutching a black, short-nose revolver.

Cosimo raised his chin and stared into the fat man's dark eyes. "Threaten me all you want, signore. I will not do your dirty work."

Gallo smiled. "You misunderstand, signore. It's not you I'm threatening."

Gallo's words stole Cosimo's courage and he glanced over to where the two young girls were making the best of their circumstances and managing to eat more of their food than he had of his. With a flourish, Cosimo signed the letter and handed it to Gallo.

"Let's see. Oh, you have lovely penmanship, signore. Most of the boys around here have to print their names—or sign with 'X's." Gallo had slipped the revolver into this coat pocket and pulled a white envelope from the open desk drawer. He had folded the letter, stuck it in the envelope and then licked and sealed the flap. "We understand each other now, right?"

"*Capisco.*"

"Very good. Now, here's the next step."

That had been an hour ago. Now, at seven o'clock, Cosimo, Renata, and Gallo were about to pull up at the Union Square entrance to the St. Francis Hotel. Shirley had been left at the dingy room above the saloon under the watch of Marcello. *This should have been over hours ago*, Cosimo thought as the driver eased the Dodge to the curb.

"Ready?" Gallo asked.

"Ready."

"Remember, you've got thirty seconds. Deliver the envelope to the doorman, there," Gallo nodded toward the man standing in front of the hotel's main entrance in a gray top coat and peaked cap. "Then, you get back here as fast as your skinny legs will carry you. You're not back in thirty seconds," Gallo paused and shook his head, "I don't want to think what might happen."

The car halted. On the sidewalk, a woman walked past leading a Pekingese on a leash.

"I understand, signore," Cosimo said, reaching into his pocket and pulling out his leather wallet.

"What are you doing?"

"I'll need money to tip the doorman. That's how these things work, signore."

Gallo chuckled. "Diplomats! All right, go ahead. It's your money."

Cosimo leaned the front seat forward, pulled the door handle up and climbed out. He paused on the sidewalk, said a quick prayer, straightened his coat and walked directly toward the doorman.

"Good evening, Mrs. Marshall," the doorman said to the dog walker. "How was George's walk?"

Cosimo stopped short, the seconds slipping by in his head like a countdown to disaster.

"He's been a little on the peeked side this last couple of days. I think the walk pepped him up a bit, didn't it, sweetheart?" She leaned over and patted the little beast on its head,

Hurry up! Cosimo screamed inside his head.

Now the doorman was kneeling, reaching into this pocket with one hand and rubbing the dog's ears with the other. "Here you go, pal," he said, holding out a dog biscuit. George crunched the treat, his tail wagging. A final pat on the head and the doorman stood again, bidding good night to George and his owner.

"May I help you, sir?" The doorman was still smiling as he turned his attention to Cosimo.

Cosimo thrust the message out to the man. Instead of a dollar bill, he held one of his consular calling cards on top of the envelope. "Please deliver this to Mrs. Temple immediately. Time is of the essence." Cosimo wheeled about and strode back down the sidewalk from the direction he'd come.

From the car, Gallo watched as the diplomat made his delivery and turned away. The doorman studied the envelope for a moment and then pushed open the hotel's door and disappeared from sight.

"Get ready," he said, tapping the driver on the shoulder.

Cosimo reached the car and climbed back in the back seat beside his daughter. He gave her a tight smile and a wink and reached out to take her hand.

"Go," Gallo said. The car pulled away from the curb and headed south on Powell Street. Once they'd gone two blocks, Gallo spoke again to the driver. "Anything?"

"Nothing, boss."

Gallo turned toward his guests. "Hey, if this diplomacy thing don't work out for you, maybe I hire you to be a delivery man." The fat man laughed.

CHAPTER 55

Wainwright had been working the phone from Mrs. Temple's room since his return from meeting McDonough. He was grateful that the White House women and even the nosy reporter were there to help occupy Mrs. Temple's mind and provide some emotional underpinning.

He'd sent Zanuck and Griffith downstairs to the bar. He wanted them out of the way unless and until he needed them. That had seemed to suit Zanuck just fine, Griff less so. Wainwright was glad he hadn't been the one to lose Shirley Temple on the train. He didn't intend to lose her in San Francisco, either.

He'd figured that it was only a matter of time before the kidnappers—it had to be a kidnapping—reached out with their demands and when they did, it would be Mrs. Temple who received the contact. But the waiting was nerve-wracking.

Missy came out of the bathroom with a frown on her pretty face. "Miss Roswell, did you happen to see my ring?" she asked. "I could have sworn I left it in the soap dish."

"Why, no, dear," Joan lied, her face a picture of innocence. "What does it look like?"

"It's a gold pinky ring with a black onyx face," Missy said. "Mr. Roosevelt gave it to me for Christmas one year, and it's inscribed inside 'FDR to MALeH with love.'"

"'With love!'" Joan tittered. "My, how personal!"

"Oh, he signs most everything to the ladies on his staff that way, doesn't he, Grace?"

"Yes, indeed," Grace replied, smiling. "I must have two dozen pictures and documents signed that way. He likes to pretend he's the *pater familias* and we are all his children."

Joan's face was a mask. "I'll keep an eye out for it," she said, sliding her hand into her jacket pocket. *Yes, the ring is still there.*

Wainwright was on the phone with the secretary at his office when he heard the knock on the door. "Call you back," he said quickly before hanging up. As they'd agreed earlier, Gertrude moved to answer the knock. Wainwright un-holstered his pistol and stood behind the door.

Gertrude opened the door a crack and Wainwright saw her shoulders relax. "Bellhop," she said. Wainwright kept the pistol in his hand, lowering it down by his side. Gertrude opened the door.

"Message for Mrs. Temple."

"Yes, thank you." Gertrude handed the young man a quarter and closed the door.

"May I?" Wainwright took the envelope to the room's small desk and set it down. He looked at it, noting the markings on the outside: *Mrs. Temple*, written in black ink and underlined. Gertrude and the other women crowded around as Wainwright removed a small pocket knife and sliced the envelope open from the bottom.

"Why not open it like a normal person?" Joan Roswell asked.

Wainwright tugged the folded note out. "Because it didn't come from a normal person. Sometimes our FBI lab technicians can tell a lot about where a letter came from by analyzing the glue on the envelope. If the sender licked the envelope himself, sometimes we can even get clues from his saliva."

"From his spit?" Joan grimaced.

"Sometimes. Maybe they can tell what he ate. Here we go. Nobody touch it. It's hard to get fingerprints from a piece of paper, but not unheard of." Five heads leaned over the letter that Cosimo Palladino had written, ten eyes scanned the words.

Missy finally whistled. "That's a lot of money!"

"We don't have that kind of money laying around," Gertrude said, her voice catching in a sob. Grace put her arm around her.

"Nobody does, Mrs. Temple," Wainwright said. "Usually, one has to go to a bank in a situation like this." He looked at his watch. "That's going to be a challenge at seven-twenty on a Saturday." He looked into Gertrude's eyes, which were welling with tears. "I need to go downstairs and find out where this letter came from. I also need to talk to Mr. Zanuck. I'll ask the rest of you to please stay here. Mrs. Temple, if you receive any further communications, please ask Miss LeHand or Miss Tully to let me know quick as you can."

"What am I, chopped liver?" Joan asked.

"Pretty much," Wainwright replied.

CHAPTER 56

"Two hundred thousand dollars!" Darryl Zanuck exclaimed, yanking his cigar from his mouth.

Wainwright glanced quickly around the hotel bar. "Not so loud, Mr. Zanuck, unless you want to draw a crowd and share it with the rest of the city."

"How do you expect me to lay off two hundred thousand on a Saturday night? By the time I get to my banker, he'll be three sheets to the wind. It'll take Prince Charming's kiss to wake him up before noon on Sunday!"

"That won't be quick enough. We've got less than eight hours to deliver the money, not days."

"Listen, Wainwright, my banking contacts are in Los Angeles. Even if I could get the money, how would I get it up here in time?"

A fair question, Wainwright thought. *How do you get that much, that fast and in the right place?* "Mr. Zanuck," he began, "I've got a wild idea. It's a long shot, but you're the kind of guy that could make it work." Wainwright spent the next several minutes explaining his scheme. "Like I said, it's a long shot. Willing to give it a try?"

"Just give me the address and I'm on my way."

With Zanuck and Griffith dispatched on their mission, Wainwright turned his attention back to the note, or more precisely, how the note had arrived at the hotel. "Barry, the doorman brought it to me," explained the front desk manager. "He said a man wearing a nice suit handed it to him with this card." The manager picked a business card off the shelf below the counter and handed it to Wainwright.

Cosimo Palladino
Consul General
Republic of Italy

Guess he hasn't gotten around to printing up new cards listing the Italian Empire, Wainwright thought. "Where's Barry now?"

"He's still out front, on duty."

"I'll keep this," Wainwright said, holding up the calling card before placing it in a paper evidence envelope and sliding it into his pocket. He turned and walked across the lobby, heading toward the hotel's front entrance.

He pushed through the main doors, the cool, crisp evening air carrying the scent of water from the nearby bay. "You Barry?"

"Yes sir," the doorman said, smiling. "How may I help you?"

"I understand you received a letter for Mrs. Temple. Who delivered it?"

"Yes sir. It was a little unusual," Barry chuckled. "I mean, we get messages to deliver sometimes, but not like that, of course. Not every day you see a calling card and certainly not from one of the consulates—although there are a fair number of them in the city, you know—"

"Tell me about the guy who delivered it. Did you get a good look at him?"

"Yes, briefly, but I saw his face. Nice suit. Probably forty, forty-five years old. Dark hair, balding. His card said he was Italian, right? You could say he looked it."

"Would you recognize him if I showed you his picture?"

"I'm sure I would."

"Anybody with him? Did you see where he came from?"

"Well, let's see, he walked up from the north, along the sidewalk here. I didn't see where he came from. Mrs. Marshall was walking George—that's her dog. Sweet little fellow. Really good-natured. I think he really enjoys his evening—"

"Barry," Wainwright held up his hands in a stop signal. "Did you see him get out of or into a car? What did he do after he gave you the letter?"

"Well, he turned around and went back up the sidewalk in the same direction. I didn't see where he went, though, because he said 'time is of the essence' and I knew that meant he wanted the letter delivered right away so I took it inside to the desk. By the time I came back outside, he was long gone."

"Anything else you remember about the guy?"

"Yeah, he didn't tip me." Barry leaned toward Wainwright and lowered his voice. "The Italians never do."

Wainwright thanked the doorman, gave him his business card and asked him to call if he remembered anything he thought might be useful, anything at all. Then he turned and walked up the sidewalk along which the courier had trod. He didn't expect to find anything, and he was not surprised.

CHAPTER 57

When Wainwright returned to Room 1219, he asked Missy LeHand if she would mind putting her secretarial skills to work as he planned how to exchange the ransom money for Shirley.

"Well, it's definitely a change of pace, but I'll do whatever I can," Missy said. She liked Corey Wainwright. Although she had been involved in an on-again, off-again romance with William Christian Bullitt for two years, he was posted as the U.S. ambassador to the Soviet Union, so their relationship was mostly conducted by letter. Sometimes, she thought, she liked him best when he stayed on his side of the Atlantic Ocean. During his visits home, she always found herself wondering if he was interested in her or the access she provided to the President.

In between answering phone calls from agents in the field, she had learned that Wainwright was single, had grown up in Kansas and was the oldest child in a family of five. "Why did you join the FBI?" she asked.

"Well, after the Great War and graduating from college and law school, I realized regular law work is pretty boring," he said.

Missy laughed. "That's what I told Mr. Roosevelt when he first asked me to work for him at his firm on Wall Street in 1920. I almost didn't take the job!"

Wainwright grinned. "It can be pretty dull stuff," he said. "But with the FBI, I'm using my law knowledge to make a real difference in people's lives. I'm even saving lives sometimes. I sure hope this is one of them." He smiled at the pretty secretary. "What's it like?" he asked.

"Working in the White House?" Missy said. "A lot of what I do is routine, of course. I handle all the President's personal mail, and I see that every single letter we get is answered. We receive 50,000 a week! Of course, I have a large staff to do the typing, but I do sign quite a number of the letters myself. I guess you have days like that, when it seems like all you do is shuffle papers. But then there are others that are just wild. One minute I can be in the West Wing, calming down one of the cabinet members who is in an uproar, the next writing out Franklin Jr.'s allowance check, and the next racing over to the White House to pour tea for a crowd of archaeologists. And, of course, I live in the White House, too, so I spend a lot of my off hours with the President and the First Lady."

"What about the President? What's he really like?" Wainwright asked, leaning forward, elbows on knees. It was obvious he was enjoying his rare behind-the-scenes look at the seat of power.

"Really?" Missy asked. "He's pretty much the man you hear on the radio. He's charming, funny, he truly cares about people." Her voice dropped a register, becoming even more throaty. "He has such courage," she said, looking Wainwright directly in the eye. "You can't imagine." She laughed a little. "It's a joy to work for him, but it takes a lot out of you too. His principal secretary, Louis Howe, is dying, and Marvin, his appointments secretary, suffers from tuberculosis. We're all having to take up the slack. Grace and I had really looked forward to this vacation…" She sighed. "But that's the way it goes."

"I've been noticing your charm bracelet," Wainwright said, gently reaching out and touching the gold bracelet around her wrist.

"You're very observant," Missy said, grinning.

"Part of the job," he reminded her. "My kid sister has one. I try to give her a new charm for Christmas each year." He ran his finger along the gold links. "Which one is your favorite?"

"Oh, I like them all," Missy said. "This one is kind of cute; Grace gave it to me for my birthday last month." She indicated a tiny pocket knife. "Look closer," she said, holding out her hand.

Wainwright held her hand and examined the knife between his fingers, squinting at the engraving on the charm. It read, "Let's cut up." He laughed. "I like that too." He let go of her hand and regarded Missy for a moment. "When do you have to be back?" he asked. "If we wrap this thing up tonight, maybe you can stay in San Francisco for a few days. I'd like to show you around, take you out to dinner."

Missy felt the color rising in her cheeks, but she kept the gaze of the attractive agent. "I'd like that," she said. "Oh, there goes the phone again!"

CHAPTER 58

The Boomerang Café at the corner of Columbus and Kearny Streets was a smoky, loud, jumping joint on Saturday nights. Jazz music was blasting out of a juke box in the main room while waiters in stained white aprons wove among the tables balancing trays loaded with steaks, stews, chops, potatoes, cabbage, and other heavy foods served up to please the toughened blue-collar workers of the city after a week of hard labor.

Darryl Zanuck and John Griffith stood just inside the entrance, taking in the sights and smells and sounds of men and women drinking, eating, talking, laughing, flirting. Zanuck plucked a five-dollar bill from his pocket and waved it under the nose of the closest waiter.

"Looking for Mr. McDonough."

The waiter snatched the bill from between Zanuck's fingers, nodded, and headed toward the door leading to the kitchen.

"Want me to follow him, boss?" Griff asked.

Zanuck placed a restraining hand on Griff's forearm. "We're not in Hollywood, Griff. Let's see how this plays out." Every time a waiter passed nearby, Zanuck expected him to signal them, but for the next several minutes they stood near the entrance feeling as out-of-place as Errol Flynn at a tent revival. Finally, a young man appeared from behind a set of curtains off to the right. He approached them slowly, his eyes looking them over from their heads to their toes.

"You wanted to see Mr. McDonough?" he asked over the racket in the restaurant.

"Darryl Zanuck, Twentieth Century-Fox," Zanuck said, sticking out his hand. "This is my associate, John Griffith."

The young man stared at Zanuck's hand and said, "What do you want?"

Zanuck leaned a little closer and spoke just loud enough to be heard. "We've got a business proposition to make to Mr. McDonough."

"Then make an appointment during business hours, for chrissakes. It's Saturday night. Mr. McDonough's off work." The young man started to turn away, but Zanuck grabbed him by the elbow. The young man froze, looked down at Zanuck's hand and then into his face. "You got maybe half a second to move your hand off of me before you lose it."

Zanuck dropped his hand, but held the younger man's eyes with his own. "I need to see your boss. It could be a matter of life and death. Now, are you going to take me, or do I go find him myself?" Griffith was watching, wide-eyed.

The young man exhaled and frowned. "You wait here. Both of you." He crossed the dining room again, the low cloud of smoke hanging just above the tables parting as he pushed his way through. Within a few seconds, he had disappeared back through the curtains.

"What if he doesn't come back?" Griffith asked.

"He's coming back." Zanuck continued to stare at the curtains. Thirty seconds later, the man stuck his head and shoulders through and waved them over. "See?" Zanuck smiled.

On the other side of the curtains was a smaller, darker, quieter room. Candles illuminated the wooden booths set along the far wall. An impressively stocked bar took up the wall space next to the curtain.

"This way," the young man said, heading toward the back of the restaurant. He stopped at the last booth, Zanuck and Griffith halting just behind him.

"That's fine, Eddie. Thank you." A stocky man wearing a plain blue suit, his tie loosened, a cloth napkin tucked under his chin, looked across the table at his pretty, blond companion and said, "Why don't you go freshen up, sweetheart? Give me a few moments to speak with these gentlemen."

"Sure, Pete." The young woman slid out of the booth, smiled at the two strangers and undulated across the dining room, turning every male head in the place.

"I apologize for interrupting your dinner with such a lovely young lady," Zanuck began.

McDonough waved his apology away. "Please sit down, Mr. Zanuck. Business is business, as they say, and I'm sure Eve is happy for a little break. Now, tell me: what's so important you have to get an answer on Saturday night?"

Zanuck sat down on the red velvet upholstered bench opposite McDonough, the seat still warm from Eve's bottom. Griff slid in beside him. "You know who I am?" Zanuck asked.

"Eddie said you were from the studio, Shirley Temple's studio, I take it."

"That's right. You've heard Shirley may be in the wrong hands."

"Yes, Special Agent Wainwright paid a courtesy call on me this afternoon. But I guess you know all about that." McDonough chuckled. "The FBI always gets its man, they just don't always get him by sundown."

"Since you met with Wainwright, we've received a ransom note." Zanuck saw the older man's eyes widen. "The kidnapper's demanding $200,000 in unmarked twenties by three a.m."

McDonough pulled back his sleeve and eyed his watch. "That's a lot of money to raise in a few hours. Good luck." He picked up his fork and speared a piece of steak.

"It'll take more than luck. That's why we came to see you."

"I'm not a bank, Mr. Zanuck. And I'm not a movie studio, either. I can't just print up two hundred large, like the mint. Besides, I'd have no collateral. Every dollar would be at risk."

Zanuck wanted to smile, to pound the table, to slap Griff on the back! McDonough would never have even mentioned collateral unless he was considering the deal.

"Of course, I wouldn't ask you to loan the money without some protection. As I told your man Eddie, this is business." McDonough poked out his lips and nodded. Zanuck leaned across the table. "The studio has a $795,000 policy on Shirley Temple's life. I assign part of that to you. You provide the cash. When we make the exchange, the FBI lowers the hammer on the bad guys and you get your cash back. If something happens to Shirley—"

"God forbid," Griff muttered.

"—you get reimbursed from the insurance."

"Plus interest, plus a handling charge," McDonough added.

"Sure. Three percent interest and half a point for the fee." Zanuck quickly calculated that would leave the studio a profit of nearly $550,000.

"Three and a half and one."

"Fair enough." Zanuck nodded.

McDonough chased some potato around his plate, finally scooping it up with the aid of his knife. "What if something goes wrong? What if you get the kid back—and I hope you will," he said, looking up, "but what if you don't recover the money? Now you've got no insurance claim and no way to pay me back."

"I own Shirley Temple's contract. She's the most profitable motion picture star in the world, and as long as we don't screw things up," Zanuck cut his eyes toward Griff, "she's got five, maybe six more good years ahead of her. You get a share of her contract until you recover your money, plus interest, plus your fee."

"Fifty percent."

"No. Can't do it. That number won't work for the studio. We'd be in a negative position."

"What can you do?"

"Twenty percent of net after expenses. You can have a man audit the books."

"Twenty-five and it's a deal."

Zanuck stuck his hand across the table. "Of course, I can't get the legal work done by 3 a.m."

McDonough grabbed his hand and shook. "Don't worry, Mr. Zanuck. I'll have the documents drafted and presented for your signature by midnight." McDonough wiped his lips and his hands on his napkin and then pushed his way out of the booth. "Please excuse me now. I suddenly have a lot of work to do."

CHAPTER 59

The normally unflappable Fausto had spent the last two hours worrying. His Excellency and Renata still had not returned—nor had Marcello. According to the men from the FBI, Shirley Temple hadn't arrived at her hotel either. *Such a time for His Excellency to disappear!* Fausto thought. *Just as my plan was falling into place. I will be left to personally deliver the film to Rome, to Il Duce.* It occurred to Fausto that on that point, the consul's absence might be a blessing. Il Duce would have a chance to shake his hand and congratulate Fausto on the brilliant execution of a daring plan. On the other hand, Fausto would be left to explain why his superior, the Empire's ranking representative on the west coast of America, was missing in the first place. That could be more problematic.

Fausto sat at his dressing table, staring into the mirror at his handsome eyes and face. Boldness and daring, he decided, were once again required. He stood, squared his shoulders and thrust out his chin. *I will find and rescue His Excellency and Renata. I will be twice over the hero, first for my propaganda coup with the little girl and second for my fearless apprehension of whoever has abducted the consul and his daughter. This is the destiny God wills for me!*

Shirley Temple Is Missing

Now that his call to action was clear, Fausto had to figure out his next steps. He dressed in comfortable dark slacks, a black shirt with no tie, and a gold-and-black checked sport coat. He needed to look dashing, to inspire confidence and envy, but he also needed to leave himself free to respond physically if needed.

Where to start? He knew Marcello was from the lower class, the kind who took on mindless jobs requiring little thought and no initiative. If Marcello had had a million dollars, he would still frequent the meanest establishments, such were the limits of his experience and imagination. So where might he be?

Fausto headed down the stairwell to the consulate's basement. As His Excellency's chauffeur, Marcello was provided living quarters in the building so that he might be available at all times. Fausto proceeded along the dimly lit corridor, past the coding room and his makeshift studio. Marcello's rooms were all the way to the end, ironically, underneath the garage.

Fausto twisted the knob on the wooden door. Locked. He took out his pocket-knife, opened the blade and stuck it between the door frame and the door, feeling for the bolt. He worked the blade upward until he heard a satisfying *click*, then he pushed the door open. He turned on the overhead light and the room was bathed in a weak yellow glow.

Where to start? Marcello had mentioned a bar with an odd name. Fausto looked around the room, noting where the small dresser, desk and chair, bed, upholstered chair, and night stand were placed. He would search the room, but skillfully, so that neither Marcello nor anyone else would be suspicious later.

The room was dank, windowless. It smelled of dirty clothes. The bed was unmade, girlie magazines strewn about. A short stack of plates from the kitchen, encrusted with dried food, were tipped into the small bathroom's sink.

Fausto stepped to the dresser, scanning the debris on top. There was a picture of Marcello's family back in San Gimignano; another picture, this one apparently cut out of a magazine, of Greta Garbo; an ash tray filled with pennies. On the floor, next to the wire waste basket, was a crumpled Lucky Strike pack, a matchbook tucked inside the cellophane wrapper.

Fausto was about to step into the tiny bathroom when it hit him. He bent down and picked up the empty pack, holding it into the light. On the book of matches, in gold print, were the words *Spider Kelly's Saloon, Pacific Street, San Francisco.* Fausto smiled and put the pack back in the same spot.

Plenty to go on.

CHAPTER 60

When Zanuck and Griff returned to the St. Francis, they stopped at the front desk to make some arrangements for the long evening ahead.

"I want to rent Room 1221," Zanuck said, peeling off a twenty-dollar bill. "I don't care if anyone is in there or not. If you have to move them, do it, and give them this for their trouble." The desk clerk nodded. There wasn't anyone in the room, but Mr. Zanuck didn't have to know that. "Do you happen to have a Scrabble game around this place?"

"I believe there's one in the parlor," the clerk said. "Would you like the bellhop to bring it up to Room 1221?"

"I'll meet him in Room 1219," Zanuck said, sticking his stogie back in the corner of his mouth and reminding himself again how important it is to have money. "I will also need room service, lots of it. So, send the bellhop up with some menus and a fifth of gin and plenty of ice."

When the two men returned to the rooms on the twelfth floor, they found Wainwright in Missy LeHand's room. He was sitting at a card table by the window. "How did it go?" Wainwright asked, looking up from a map as Missy let Zanuck and Griffith into the room. "Will he do it?"

Zanuck smiled. "Count on it. He approached it like a business deal—a low-risk way to make a quick profit. He'll do it."

"Nice work, Mr. Zanuck!" Wainwright said. He got up and walked to the connecting door, rapping on it and then putting his head inside. "Ladies, would you come in here?' he asked.

When Gertrude, Grace, and Joan walked into the room, he gathered them around the card table. "All of us need to understand how this thing is going to work—and what everyone's role will be," Wainwright said, pulling a chair up beside his for Mrs. Temple and taking his seat. The others ringed the table where Wainwright had spread out a map of the harbor area of the city.

"According to the ransom note, Mrs. Temple is supposed to bring the money to the Vallejo Ferry pier. That's right here on the north end of the Ferry Building. I'll have agents here, here, and here," he tapped on three corners of the building, "on the second floor above the arcade. My command post is going to be here, on the northeast side of the building closest to the pier. From there, we can watch all the routes of access. My guess is that they'll come in this way, along the Embarcadero." He traced a line from the main road to the apron leading to the pier.

"At that time of night, there shouldn't be anybody around, certainly no other vehicles, so they should be easy to spot. We'll have two more agents in each of these two positions, laying low in parked cars. We borrowed some field phones from the army out at the Presidio, so we'll be able to communicate without using radio."

"How about night watchmen?" Missy asked.

"Good question," Wainwright said, impressed. "My men will call them off about 2 a.m. The closer to the exchange, the better. We don't want them around to queer the deal, but we also don't want them shooting their mouths off. We'll keep them under wraps until our operation is complete."

He met Missy's eyes. "I need to ask you a favor, Miss LeHand," Wainright continued. "You can say 'no' if you want and no one will think any less of you."

"Ask away, Agent Wainwright," Missy said as all the other eyes in the room converged on her.

"I'd like you to stand in for Mrs. Temple." Beside him, Gertrude Temple tensed, looking up at the others.

"But I want to be there. I want to get Shirley back," Gertrude protested.

Wainwright placed a hand on her shoulder. "We're going to get her back, but I need you to stay with me. You know your daughter better than anyone and I'll need you to be able to identify her from some distance away. That way the kidnappers can't attempt to give us some other child and keep Shirley." *And that way I don't have to worry about your emotions getting the better of you at a crucial moment.*

"But I could identify her when I hand over the money!" she protested

"Yes, ma'am, but if something went wrong, you wouldn't be able to communicate with me. The bag man—lady—in this case, is going to be isolated and exposed. I need you right next to me. We'll let Miss LeHand wear your coat and your hat. In the dark, she'll pass for you.

Once the bad guys get the money, they won't care who's brought it to them. Miss LeHand, you hand over the cash. They may want to count it. That's fine. Just stand there and wait. Once they're satisfied, take Shirley by the hand and walk back down the pier toward the Ferry Building. We won't show ourselves until you and Shirley are safely away from the kidnappers."

"I'll do it," Missy said.

"Good." Wainwright nodded.

"What about the kidnappers?" Joan spoke up. "How do you plan to catch them?"

"Mr. Zanuck and Mr. Griffith are going to help with that," Wainwright said. Griffith perked up. Obviously, he was only too ready to get his hands on the people who'd stolen Shirley—and who might still cost him his job. "My best guess is that the bad guys want to make the exchange on the pier because they plan to get away by boat. Our friends at the Coast Guard are supplying us two of their patrol cutters. They'll be standing off in the bay, awaiting our signal. I'd like to assign Mr. Zanuck and Mr. Griffith to each of the boats. Lend whatever assistance the coasties require and act as a liaison for our task force."

He nodded at Grace and Joan. "Miss Tully, Miss Roswell, I'd like both of you to remain with me at the command post. I may need you to act as couriers or recorders. My request is that you stay nearby and remain flexible."

"What about weapons?" Zanuck asked.

"My agents and the Coast Guard men will be armed. But that's it." Griff didn't say anything, but no way was he going to give up his .38. "Assume that the bad guys are armed too. I don't expect it to come to that. We're going to give them the money. They're going to give us Shirley. We're going to let them think they've gotten away. Only when Shirley and Miss LeHand are out of harm's way will we lower the boom."

Wainwright looked at the faces around the table. "All right, it's nine-fifteen by my watch. My group, Miss Tully, Miss Roswell, Mrs. Temple, and the other agents, will be in position by one-fifteen. Mr. Zanuck and Mr. Griffith, you will need to be at Pier 33 at one-thirty. I've alerted the Coast Guard that you're coming. Look for a Lieutenant junior grade Alexander. Miss LeHand," Wainwright's blue eyes zeroed in on Missy, "you will remain here in the room with one of my men, Agent Trammell, until it's time for you to depart. He will drive you to this point here." Wainwright tapped the map again. "You get out of the car and walk down the center of the pier. Don't look back and don't try to find us. We'll have you under surveillance at all times. And always stay out in the open so we can see you."

Wainwright paused. Now that the hour of action was drawing closer, now that he'd laid out his plan, now that assignments had been made, he could feel an elevated level of tension, could read it in the faces around the table. "Any questions?" He looked each person in the eyes. "This is all going to work out. Now we've just got to sit tight for the next few hours."

"I've got that covered too," Zanuck said, grinning and showing his gap-toothed smile and deep dimples. As if on cue, a bellhop rapped smartly on the door. Admitted to Room 1219, he presented Zanuck with a Scrabble game and a handful of menus. He set a fifth of gin and a bucket of ice on the dresser.

"Sir, here's your key to Room 1221," he said. "Would you like me to open it for you?"

"Yeah," Zanuck said, "and while you're at it, take the booze and the ice down there and set them up."

With the Scrabble game under his arm, Zanuck handed out menus. "Dinner's on me tonight," he said. "Order whatever you like. I've taken the next room down and we can use it for eating and relaxing a bit. Now, who'd like to join me for a drink and a game of Scrabble while we wait for the food?"

Joan raised her eyebrows. "Why, Darryl," she said archly. "I always thought you were illiterate!"

CHAPTER 61

It was nearly ten o'clock by the time Fausto parked the Chevrolet and headed down Pacific Street. He walked past Spider Kelly's and all the way to the end of the block before turning around at Kearny Street and returning to the saloon. Loud music spilled out of the door, and even onto the street Fausto could hear the patrons inside celebrating Saturday night and the end of another work week.

He hadn't noticed any muscle out front as he'd strolled by. Several couples were standing near the entrance to the place. Some were chatting, cooling off after having worked up a sweat on the dance floor. Others were smoking, flirting or just giving their ears and legs a rest.

Fausto stepped through the loose group, drawing stares and smiles from a couple of the women. Inside, he took in the lay of the place: the bustling, jumping dance floor; the tables filled with late diners; the bar two-deep in customers.

Fausto scanned the room, his eyes stinging from the smoke of a hundred cigarettes and cigars. Along the long side of the dance floor, Fausto saw a man carrying two mugs of beer back toward a table. He was facing away from Fausto, but he was of the same build and height of Marcello. Fausto sidled through the Lindy hopping dancers, watching the man as he faded into the darker area off the floor. Fausto bumped into a waiter carrying a large tray filled with empty glasses and plates. The contact caused the dishes to rattle and for a moment Fausto thought the tray would fall to the floor. He reached out to help steady the tray. The waiter frowned and breathed a tired sigh, regaining his balance and resuming his difficult march to the kitchen.

The collision, mild though it had turned out, had cost Fausto sight of his prey. He stood between a pair of tables searching the faces at the tables in front of him.

"Fausto!" The call came from over his shoulder. He turned toward the sound, indistinct in the noisy saloon. A lighter flared, its glow briefly illuminating Marcello's face. The driver waved him over to the small round table where he and another, much fatter, man sat with their backs to the wall.

Marcello stood up at his approach and grabbed an empty chair from a nearby table, placing it in front of his own. "Sit down! Have a drink!" he said with a smile. Marcello waved to a nearby waiter, catching his eye and motioning him over. "Meet Joseph Gallo," Marcello said, pointing toward the fat man.

"How do you do, Signore Gallo?" Fausto asked.

"This is Fausto Trevisano," Marcello said to the fat man. "He's the vice consul in charge of culture."

"What brings you to Spider's?" Gallo asked.

"I was looking for Topo. I have some questions for him."

"How convenient." Gallo smiled. "Something to drink?" he asked as the waiter hovered beside the table.

"A Lambrusca," Fausto said, glancing up at the waiter.

Gallo chuckled, waved a fat hand and said, "Bring us three beers." The waiter hurried toward the bar. "Cigar?"

"No, thank you. As I said, I am here on business, to ask Topo some questions."

"Don't let me stop you."

"Signore Gallo, these questions are of a confidential nature. I'm sure you understand."

"I'm sure too." Gallo made no move to leave.

What's with this guy? Fausto wondered. *He can't take a hint?*

"You can speak in front of Signore Gallo, Fausto. I have no secrets from him." Marcello took a drag on his cigarette, making the end glow more brightly.

"As you wish." Fausto would not be intimidated. "I have come to find you to determine the whereabouts of His Excellency and Renata…and Renata's young friend."

"You mean Shirley Temple, the movie star that you kidnapped?" Marcello said.

"You know exactly who I mean."

"Not to worry, Fausto. They are close by and in good hands."

"I have come to relieve you of them."

Gallo spoke. "You by yourself, Fausto? You bring anybody with you? The police? The marines?" He chuckled again, his jowls and belly jiggling. He pulled a dingy handkerchief from his pocket and wiped his brow.

"At least give me the consul and Renata," Fausto said. Sometimes it was necessary to negotiate to achieve one's objective. The waiter returned and set three glasses of foaming beer on the table.

Marcello blew smoke toward the ceiling. Gallo raised his glass. "Saluti."

I'll play his game, Fausto thought, raising his glass and taking a long drink. He looked around for a napkin, then settled for wiping his mouth with the back of his hand. "Now, signores, down to business, if you please." Gallo sat like an Italian Buddha, fat, inscrutable. Marcello leaned back in his chair, cigarette dangling from the corner of his mouth. "It is my intention to leave here with His Excellency, His Excellency's daughter, and Miss Shirley Temple. Tell me how together we can make this happen." *There.* He'd laid his mission on the table, a starting point for discussions, a basis for negotiations.

"How much you got?"

"It is only myself, signore. I trust that I am dealing with honorable men who will be bound by their word."

"I thought you were dealing with me and Topo," Gallo said, laughing. Marcello joined in.

Fausto choked back his annoyance. "I appreciate a sense of humor," he said, smiling in an attempt to show that he could find common ground with these miscreants. "Now, friends, what say you? How shall we resolve this issue?"

"Like I said before: how much you got?" Gallo shifted his gaze from Fausto to Marcello, nodding to the latter. He returned his attention to the vice consul.

Marcello raised one arm and slowly placed it behind his head, but Fausto's focus was on Gallo. Clearly, he was calling the shots. Clearly, Topo was just a lackey, same as at the consulate. The fat man was the one to persuade.

"Signore Gallo," Fausto began, "I think perhaps you do not realize that I am here with a commission from Il Duce and with the authority and power of the Italian Empire. I seek only the release of my friends."

"Sure, sure. A noble mission, wouldn't you agree, Marcello?" Gallo waved his cigar in the air. "The problem is see, me and Marcello here ain't exactly noblemen. We got no titles, we got no authority, no commissions." Gallo smiled. "And unless you got two hundred-large in your pocket, we got no more time for you, mister consul of vice." He chuckled.

"Signore, you have stretched my patience to the breaking point. It is clear you do not realize with whom you are dealing!" Fausto snapped.

"No, signore," Gallo replied calmly. "You're the one who doesn't know who he's dealing with."

Before Fausto could reply, a blow to the back of his head made everything fade to black.

CHAPTER 62

Pete McDonough had been working the phones from his office above the bail bonds shop ever since Zanuck and his friend had left the restaurant. It was the middle of the month and his "clients" were grumbling. Protection money wasn't usually due for two more weeks. Coming up with an extra two hundred dollars on a Saturday night was tough for a lot of the small business owners who looked to McDonough to watch out for their interests with the cops and with city hall.

Let 'em bitch, McDonough thought, as he explained the situation to a tavern owner farther down Clay Street. *If it's in my best interest, it's in theirs too*. Of course, it was easier on the saloon-keepers and bar owners. The taverns and public drinking establishments would be flush with cash on Saturday night. For these businesses, all Pete had to do was call up the owner and let him know a bagman was making the rounds.

"I know it's an extra assessment, boyo. Believe me, it'll be worth it. Have faith in the old man, will ya?" He paused, listening to the voice on the other end. "Ah, now that's the spirit. Thanks, Tommy. I'll send one of the boys around to pick it up." McDonough hung up the phone and stretched. He was making good progress, but he still hadn't put the finger on some of his wealthier clients.

"Eddie, bring the car up. Let's go pay a call on Miss Fine. And tell Stewart I need those papers finished by the time we get back."

CHAPTER 63

In Room 1222, a cut-throat game of Scrabble was underway. When Darryl had opened up the box and laid the board on a card table, Joan had sidled up beside him and asked nonchalantly, "Care to make it interesting?"

"What do you mean?" he asked, sucking on his cigar. *She's still a gorgeous broad. And I bet she doesn't have a cent to wager.*

"Fifty bucks," she said. "Winner take all."

"Are we letting Griff and Gertrude in on it?"

"I think not," Joan said. "Deal?"

Zanuck grinned. He hadn't gotten his daily dose of amorous exercise, and Joan was pretty good in the sack.

When Griff, Gertrude, and Grace joined them in the room, Grace offered to be the officiant. "We don't have a dictionary, but I'm an excellent speller," she said. "I'll keep score too. Does that suit everyone?"

"Fine with me," Zanuck said. The others nodded. They closed their eyes and drew tiles for the highest number. Joan clapped her hands when she drew the X with its eight points. She would be followed by Zanuck, then Griff, and finally by Gertrude.

They turned the wooden tiles upside down so the letters wouldn't show and filled their display racks, studying what fortune had handed them.

Joan quickly laid out her word in the center of the board: CHEAT. "Thirteen points," Grace said.

Zanuck frowned. He had a lousy selection. Finally, he laid down TART, giving Joan a sardonic grin. "Four points," Grace said.

Griff plunked down REGRET, earning thirteen points. Gertrude, smiling slightly, spelled out TEMPLE. "Twenty points!" said Grace. "Gertrude wins round one."

They replenished their display racks. With a little smile on her lips and her eyes locked on Zanuck's, Joan spelled out CREEP. Twenty points.

Zanuck took a deep drag and spelled out MOGUL. "Ooh, I don't know how you knew how to spell that word," Joan tittered. "You must have found it in a fortune cookie." Ten points.

Griff's word was MOVIE, while Gertrude spelled GREED. Again, they replenished their tiles.

"I'm going to build on Mrs. Temple's ground work," Joan said, adding a Y to spell GREEDY. Seventeen points.

Following Joan's lead, Zanuck added an S to MOGUL, earning twenty points. Griff spelled out GUN, mumbling, "Sorry, it's all I've got." Gertrude winced and, her chin trembling a bit, spelled out GIRL.

Joan narrowed her eyes when she replenished her tiles, then, flashing a smile, laid down VAIN. It was a triple-word score of twenty-one.

"Very good," Grace said. "Mr. Zanuck?"

Smiling, he lifted a letter from his display and added it to the word GIRL. Grace stared. "I'm sorry, Mr. Zanuck, that's not a word."

"Girls isn't a word?" he asked. "Since when?"

"Well, 'girls' is a word," Grace said. "But it doesn't end in Z. According to the rules of the game, you lose your turn."

Zanuck reddened. "I'm a little dyslexic," he mumbled.

Griff studied his display and said, "I'm out. My mind just isn't cooperating. I think I'll have another drink."

"I'm out, too, Griff," Gertrude said. "You two continue, we'll just watch."

Joan and Zanuck drew new letters. Smiling brightly, Joan added a Y to CREEP. "Excellent!" said Grace. "That's thirty-four points! That brings you up to seventy-five, and, let's see, Mr. Zanuck has thirty-four."

The two players stared at each other across the board. "I'm out," Zanuck said. "I don't feel like winning tonight."

"That's all right, dear," purred Joan, looking like the proverbial cat that swallowed the canary. "I definitely feel like a winner." She laid her hand on the table, palm up.

CHAPTER 64

Dolly Fine was the city's most successful madam. Due in part to the protection she purchased each month from McDonough, as well as the relations she and her employees enjoyed with San Francisco's movers and shakers—particularly within the police department—Dolly Fine operated the city's most elegant bordellos featuring the most beautiful girls. She prided herself on managing a product line filled with variety: "A flavor for every taste," she liked to say. And she took care of her girls, too, with good living conditions and monthly visits from a physician, who also happened to be a customer. Let one of the johns get a little rough with one of her girls and the man would find himself on the business end of a police nightstick. Yep, Dolly took care of her girls—and she took care of business.

Pete McDonough knew Dolly was a shrewd woman. That's one reason he'd put her off until very late on this rapidly passing Saturday night. He wanted a little practice before he had to face Dolly.

He rang the front bell of Dolly's house on Carmel Street. He'd called ahead to let her know he was on his way. No benefit to surprising her. His request would be surprise enough.

267

The beveled glass front door swung open and golden light spilled out onto the broad front porch. "Come in, Mr. McDonough," the butler said, taking Pete's hat. "Miss Fine is in the parlor."

McDonough turned to his left, the thick maroon carpet swallowing his footsteps. He entered the parlor and there she sat, six feet tall, and every inch of it gorgeous. She was wearing a loose but revealing black velvet gown. "Want a drink, Peter?"

"Whiskey, neat."

The statuesque blonde stood and stepped around the wooden bar in the corner of the room. "I hear you're raising money for a special project."

I shoulda known better than to think I could surprise Dolly.

Pete laughed. "Who you been listening to?"

"Just folks. Sit down, you're making me tired." Dolly walked over and handed McDonough a glass of amber liquid. "I made it a double."

McDonough took a sip. "Ah, that's fine, it is. Fine indeed." He looked up at his hostess, who towered over him. "Now you sit down." He patted the spot beside him on the sofa. Dolly sat, adjusting her gown to show off both her cleavage and her long legs, and Pete enjoyed the sight and smell of her. She was some beautiful woman. And smart too.

"We've been handed a bit of a challenge, Dolly my girl. But I choose to see it as more of an opportunity. I'm confident you'll see it in the same light."

"Maybe if you'd shine a little light on it I could see it at all."

Shirley Temple Is Missing

"It seems a certain small movie star has gone missing in our fair city. Her studio wants her back but doesn't have the, shall I say, 'mechanism' in place to raise the ransom needed in the time allotted."

Dolly sat back on the sofa and crossed her long, lithe legs. "Who and how much?"

"Shirley Temple. Two hundred thousand."

She arched her brows. "What do I get?"

"Why, Dolly," McDonough feigned surprise, "what do you always get? Insulation, my girl. Insulation from the changing winds of politics. Protection from the occasional righteous campaigns to stamp out vice. Access to the administrative, judicial, and political machinery of the city. And, of course, my personal gratitude and friendship."

"You could convince a leprechaun to part with his pot o' gold." Dolly chuckled and shook her head. "But I'm not a wee little man and I'm not so easily swayed by your silver tongue. What do I get?"

"A fair share of the return on your investment. But to get anything at all," McDonough had dropped the blarney now and was all business, "I need $10,000 and I need to walk out that door in the next five minutes."

"I don't have that kind of money sitting around here."

"I know. You've got three times that kind of money sitting around here." McDonough downed the rest of his whiskey. "We're a good team, you and me. You're good at what you do and I'm good at what I do." He leaned over, his hands on his knees, his face just inches from Dolly's. "Trust me on this, Dolly. It'll work out profitably for both of us."

Dolly looked away and McDonough could tell she was weighing her options. She stood up and looked down at her guest. "You wait here," she said, tapping on McDonough's chest with her scarlet-tipped finger.

McDonough watched as Dolly sauntered from the room. From what he could see, Dolly's business was doing pretty well. Her home was in a fashionable part of the city. It was lavishly furnished. Dolly's clothes were elegant. She even had a butler working at midnight. *I shoulda asked for more.*

Stewart Garrity's eyes were red, whiskers stubbled his chin. He should have been in bed two hours ago if he expected to get Maureen and the kids to mass in the morning. But sometimes being the in-house lawyer for the McDonough Brothers meant critical projects with urgent deadlines.

Now, as he stood in front of Pete McDonough's desk, he mentally reviewed the work that his boss was reading. Pete had dictated the key figures to him in between the dozens of phone calls he'd made earlier in the evening. "We got one shot at this, Stew. Make sure it's airtight. That Hollywood bastard's got a tough reputation and if you leave just one legal loophole, Zanuck'll find a way to thread your needle."

McDonough sat behind his desk, its green-shaded lamp illuminating a circle within which he held the legal documents he would shortly present to Darryl Zanuck. He flipped over to the final page. Garrity waited. The boss was no lawyer, he didn't understand the nuances or complexities of the law, but he was smart, and he understood people and how they were governed by their emotions. Especially greed.

"Very good, Stew. You've got duplicates?"

"Yes sir," he answered, handing over a thick envelope. "All you need are signatures: yours, his, and a witness for both."

"Who can witness?"

"Anybody, just as long as they're real people."

CHAPTER 65

Marcello was stronger than he looked, which was a good thing because Fausto was heavy. Hefting the unconscious man's body up the backstairs was a one-man job simply because the stairway was so narrow. When the sweating Marcello finally reached the doorway at the top of the landing, he kicked it with the toe of his shoe. Gino, one of Gallo's assistants, unlocked it from the inside.

"What's this, Topo?"

"The illustrious Fausto Trevisano, vice consul and protector of the empire," Marcello answered, rolling his burden off his shoulders and onto the floor in the corner of the room.

Gallo closed the door behind them. "Any trouble?" he asked Gino, his eyes playing over the supine forms stretched beneath the windows on the opposite side of the room.

"No. The little one cried for her mother, but the older girl calmed her down. The old man didn't say much, just kept staring out the window muttering about being sent to Ethiopia."

Gallo nodded. "Go get the car. We've got to move them. If Galileo here could find us," he nodded toward Fausto, "so can the cops."

Shirley Temple Is Missing

"We going to the place?" Marcello asked.

"Maybe.   Just get the car and drive around back. Give me a few minutes to think."

"Whatever you say."

SUNDAY, OCTOBER 13, 1935
SAN FRANCISCO

CHAPTER 66

At ten minutes before one, Pete McDonough climbed out of the back seat of his chauffeured LaSalle in front of the St. Francis Hotel. There was no doorman after 11 p.m., so McDonough hoisted the black leather bag full of money and opened the brass-framed glass door himself.

He was tired now. It had been a long day even before the two Hollywood guys had shown up and made their proposition. Pulling all the strings to collect that much money in just a few hours had challenged even Pete McDonough. *I'm getting too old for this.*

McDonough walked up to the registration desk and laid a dollar bill on the counter. "Please call up to Mrs. Temple's room. She's expecting me."

The sleepy desk clerk folded the bill into his pants pocket and did as requested. "Room 1220, sir. You're to go right up. The elevators are to your left."

Dolly's contribution had put him over the top, but they'd all come through, all but that skinny little bastard Huffman. "It ain't due for two more weeks," he'd whined. "I can't afford a shakedown like that twice a month." *What you can't afford is to piss me off.* McDonough pulled the elevator's brass gate shut. At this hour, there was no attendant. He'd have to operate the lift himself. The car began its slow ascent, McDonough watching the numbers illuminate as he climbed past each floor.

He stepped out of the elevator on the twelfth floor, got his bearings, and headed toward Mrs. Temple's room. He hesitated for a moment, facing the door and listening. He knocked softly. Within a few seconds, he heard the safety chain unfastened and the door squeaked open. A handsome woman of about forty with dark circles under her eyes greeted him.

"Mr. McDonough?"

Pete nodded. "Mrs. Temple." He stepped into the room and the door closed, revealing the G-man, pistol in hand. "You can put that away." He turned to Gertrude and offered his hand. "Peter McDonough at your service, ma'am. Sorry we have to meet under such circumstances, but I am pleased to be of assistance. My brother Tom and I are both big fans of your little girl and we're happy to help you get her back."

Gertrude placed her hand on his shoulder, smiled through her tears, and said, "Thank you, Mr. McDonough, for all you've done. I don't know where we'd be without you."

By now, McDonough was virtually surrounded. In addition to Mrs. Temple, there were three other women, plus Wainwright the FBI man and the two Hollywood swells.

"You've got the money, Mr. McDonough?" Wainwright asked.

McDonough nodded and gave the black bag a little lift. "Want to see what two hundred grand looks like?" He moved toward a small table in a corner by the window. He set the bag on top, unfastened the latch and pulled it open. "It's all there. I checked it and had my accountant verify it. No monkey business. One hundred straps of twenties."

"How'd you do that?" Joan asked, crowding in to touch more money than she'd ever seen in her life, more than she'd ever dreamed about.

"Ignorance is bliss, darlin'."

Wainwright held out his hand. "Thanks. You may have saved the day. We still haven't turned up anything on the street. At this point, our only play is the swap; the money for Shirley."

McDonough shook his hand. "I'll leave you to your work, but first, Mr. Zanuck and I need to make everything nice and tidy." McDonough pulled the large envelope from the bag and removed the contents. "Here, sir, are two copies of our agreement. You sign, I sign, and we'll need a witness."

"I'm a notary public," Grace volunteered.

"You'll do nicely," McDonough said with a smile.

Zanuck scanned the document. He looked up, his eyes flashing. "These terms aren't what we agreed to."

"Ah, well, you see, Mr. Zanuck, raising this money was quite a bit more involved than even I had imagined, quite a bit. Saturday night and all. Late at that. I had to make some promises on my own without benefit of consultation with you. But," McDonough glanced at Mrs. Temple, "I felt sure I was doing the right thing to help bring little Shirley home."

"Your interest rate is two points higher!"

"No sir, only a point and a half more than what we agreed to, and the handling fee: unchanged."

"This says thirty percent of Shirley's contract!" Zanuck's voice had reached a new pitch, his face now crimson, the veins on his neck threatening to burst. "The studio can't do that! I can't do that! You're holding a gun to my head!"

McDonough looked at the faces around the table. "I'm not even carrying a gun, Mr. Zanuck. My intention is simply to help all of you out of a tough situation—not of my making, mind you."

"What's the thirty percent about?" Gertrude asked, her eyes darting back and forth between Zanuck and McDonough.

"If for some reason the crooks get away with the money, we need to provide some collateral for Mr. McDonough," Zanuck spat.

"But you're not going to let that happen are you, Agent Wainwright?" Gertrude said.

"No ma'am. We'll do our best to apprehend the kidnappers."

"Then I don't understand the problem, Mr. Zanuck. If it isn't going to happen, you're not really risking anything."

McDonough bit his tongue to keep from smiling. "Of course, you don't have to accept these terms, Mr. Zanuck. You can always go to your Hollywood bank to get the money."

Zanuck stared at the open bag on the table for a moment, then sighed, reached into his pocket, and pulled out his gold fountain pen.

"Right there," McDonough said, pointing to a blank above the typed name Darryl F. Zanuck.

"I got it, I got it," Zanuck growled.

Once Grace witnessed both sets of signatures, McDonough stuffed the original contract back into the envelope. "Mr. Zanuck, ladies," he said with a nod. "My best wishes for a successful transaction. Agent Wainwright, perhaps you would walk me out."

McDonough crossed the room and opened the door, stepping out into the hallway. Wainwright followed, pulling the door closed behind him.

"Thanks again for your help. I don't know how we would have managed to come up with the cash," the G-man said sincerely.

"I doubt you could have. I'm glad we could help." McDonough hesitated, gazing for a moment at the tips of his shoes before looking into Wainwright's eyes. "I'm friends with quite a few policemen in the city."

"So I've heard."

"Yes. If it would be helpful in your efforts, I would be pleased to have them augment the work of you and your colleagues. All you need do is call me. I've got kids too, y'know." McDonough offered his business card. "I've written my private line on the back. Good night, Agent Wainwright."

"Good night, Mr. McDonough. And thanks again."

The older man stepped back into the elevator and the door slid shut.

CHAPTER 67

They were already running late. Wainwright checked his watch: one-eleven. He, Grace Tully, Joan Roswell, and two of his agents, Ammons and Wells, were crammed into one of the Bureau's sedans driving northeast on Market Street toward the bay. Wainwright had been unwilling to leave before accounting for all the money and quickly reviewing everyone's responsibilities. Agent Trammell had arrived, been quickly introduced, and then left behind with Missy and the money. They'd leave the hotel at two forty-five escorted by a second FBI car.

"What do you like to do for fun?" Joan asked, jerking his mind back to the present. She was seated in the middle of the back seat, a foot on either side of the transmission hump.

"Not this, that's for sure. I'd rather be home in bed."

"Asleep?"

Hollywood dames! "At this time of night, yes!" He pointed through the front windshield. "That's our destination."

Ahead, Joan and Grace could see a tall, white clock tower illuminated by flood lights, pointing into the night sky. It rose above a long, arched arcade stretching out along the waterfront.

"Drive us around back, Joel. We'll go in the service entrance off the loading dock." The driver crossed the wide lanes of the Embarcadero, passing along the south side of the Ferry Building before turning left. The car rolled up the long side of the building, passing the docks for ferries running to Oakland, Alameda, and Larkspur, before stopping at a truck ramp.

"All right, let's go. Noise and light discipline," Wainwright said, climbing out of the car.

"What does that mean?" Joan asked, sticking a cigarette in her mouth and pulling her lighter from her purse.

Wainwright reached over and covered the lighter. "No talking and no smoking," he whispered.

Wainwright followed Wells and Ammons as they entered the darkened building through a service corridor. They followed the hallway to a stairwell and climbed to the second floor. "This way," Wells said. "Watch your step." They walked past closed doors and stacks of boxes and crates, all the way to the north end of the building.

"This thing is longer than a soundstage," Joan whispered.

Wells stepped aside, and Ammons unlocked a door off the right-hand side of the corridor. "In here," he said.

The office looked out from the northeast corner of the building with an unobstructed view of the Vallejo Pier from the point where it connected with the vehicle apron to the point where it disappeared into the darkness of the bay. Wainwright made note of the work his agents had done. In the corner sat a battered wooden desk, on top of which were three pairs of binoculars and a small green army field phone switchboard.

"How many lines we got?" Wainwright asked as Joan and Grace wandered toward the windows.

"Five. One for each observation post," Ammons replied.

"How do we talk to the Coast Guard?"

"I couldn't get a radio set up. But I got this." Ammons reached beneath the desk and pulled out what looked to be a small spotlight on a handle. "It's a signal lamp. Look, it's got this shutter device here and you toggle it to send dots and dashes, like Morse Code."

Wainwright raised his eyebrows. "Do you know Morse Code, Jim?"

"Well, not all of it. But I worked out some key signals with Lieutenant Alexander. We send S-O-S if we want the patrol boats to come charging in. We send B, that's dash-dot-dot-dot, to confirm the bad guys are in a boat. A is for attack. That's just dot-dash."

"It'll have to do. Too late for anything else at this point."

"What's that over there?" Joan asked pointing out the east-facing window at a sprinkling of lights in the distance.

"Oakland. Here," Wainwright said, handing Joan and Grace each a set of binoculars. "Have a look. But stay back from the windows. I don't want anyone out there getting a look at us." Next, Wainwright bent over the switchboard and turned the crank on the field phone. He made contact with each of his observation posts before setting the phone handset back in its bag.

Shirley Temple Is Missing

Ammons and Wells had taken positions a few feet back from the windows. Ammons's binoculars were trained down the pier, back toward the city. Wells was scanning in the other direction, out toward the bay.

"What do we do now?" Joan asked.

Wainwright glanced from his agents to her. "We wait."

CHAPTER 68

Zanuck and Griffith had been waiting for twenty minutes in front of the St. Francis before the Yellow Cab finally showed up. It was cold, but clear, a typical October night in San Francisco. Zanuck had been smoking his cigar but saying nothing. They had climbed into the back seat, Zanuck first, sliding over behind the driver.

"Pier 33," he had said.

They rode the first few blocks in silence. Finally, Griff could stand it no more. "What do you think, boss?"

Zanuck stared out the window at the vacant sidewalks as the buildings along Market Street slid silently past. "I think if we don't get Shirley back before dawn, you're going to be out of a job." He blew a cloud of gray smoke toward the roof of the cab and looked at Griff. "Me too."

Griff decided that he preferred the silence.

They drove north on the Embarcadero until they reached Pier 33. Zanuck paid the cabbie and he and Griff started walking toward the silhouettes of two boats docked farther out toward the bay. As they drew nearer, they could see men moving about on the decks and two gangplanks connecting the boats to the pier.

"Lieutenant Alexander?" Zanuck said, approaching a man wearing a visored cap, his hands jammed down into the pockets of a navy-blue pea coat.

"Mr. Zanuck? Mr. Griffith? Right on time," Alexander said, shaking hands with both passengers. "Mr. Griffith, I'm putting you on board the first boat with Chief McCoy. Mr. Zanuck, you come with me."

Griff walked up the gangway and introduced himself to the coast guardsman in charge of the seventy-five-foot-long patrol boat. He was a stocky, red-faced man with a broad smile. "Welcome aboard, sir. How about a cup of coffee?"

"Please," Griff said. He needed whatever caffeine he could get after nearly two days with nothing but his train-board nap—*and look at the trouble that had caused!*

McCoy handed him a tin mug. "Hope you like it black."

"As long as it's hot." Griff took a long draught. He looked around at the level-deck boat. It's wheel-house was just forward of mid-ship and was topped by some kind of radio aerial. Storage lockers were mounted to the stern, beneath a set of davits securing a small row boat. *A lifeboat?* He hoped not. "What kind of armaments you carry?"

"Come on, I'll show you," McCoy said and set off toward the bow. "Watch the lines there." He nodded, gesturing with his own mug of coffee. Forward of the wheelhouse on a sturdy-looking mount sat a small gun. "This is our one-pounder. Fires a 37mm round. Pretty stout little piece for these waters. And, of course, down below, we've got five Thompsons and two shot guns we'll break out once we get into position."

"What would you like me to do?" Griff asked.

"I'd like you to be one of our lookouts. I'd like you to watch for two things in particular. The FBI men have set up a post on the second floor of the Ferry Building. They've got a signal lamp up there with them. If you see that light come on, make sure I know it. The other thing we're looking for is a small boat in or around the Vallejo Pier. You see one of those, raise the alarm. Of course, any time we're on the water, especially at night, if you see another boat nearby, let me know."

"Ready, Chief?" came a voice from the pier.

"All set, sir," McCoy replied. He turned to his crewmen. "Stand by to cast off. Come below and we'll get you some gear."

By the time he returned to the deck, Griff was wearing a dough boy-style metal helmet and bulky life jacket and the patrol boat was pulling away from the end of the dock. The one thing he really wanted, McCoy hadn't issued: one of the Thompson machine guns.

Zanuck peered through the darkness, his eyes straining to identify Griffith on the other boat. It was trailing behind the lead boat and to the right as they cruised slowly through the darkness. Streetlights from the waterfront were strung out to their right. The boat's engine made a gurgling sound as they crept southward.

Lieutenant Alexander had explained his instructions to Zanuck while he outfitted him in a helmet and life vest. "We're going to lay off about five hundred yards in the bay. I've got two lookouts watching the end of the pier and two more scanning the approaches. McCoy's crew will be doing the same thing. I want you to stick close to me."

"How about a weapon? Do I get a weapon?"

"No can do, sir. Orders from Special Agent Wainwright. He says you are to observe only."

"Listen, lieutenant, this isn't my first action you know. I fought in France."

"Then you understand I have to obey my orders, right, sir?"

Zanuck pressed his lips together. "Whatever you say, lieutenant."

CHAPTER 69

"Get up," Marcello said, shaking Cosimo by the shoulder. "C'mon, wake up."

"What?" Cosimo was confused, unsure of where he was. It was dark, and he was lying on the floor, covered by a wool blanket. Then he remembered. Not only was he here, but so was Renata—and so was Shirley Temple. And "here" wasn't a good place. "What time is it?"

"Night time. Now get your bony ass up. Wake up those kids too."

The door at the other end of the room opened and then closed, the outline of a large man silhouetted against dim light from the stairwell.

"Ready, Topo?"

"Almost. What about Fausto?"

"He goes. Put him in the boot."

"He's heavy, boss."

"We can't leave him here. He knows too much, and his beauty rest is bound to end soon."

"We could just, you know…"

"In the boot, Topo."

"Yes, boss."

By now, Cosimo had the girls on their feet, though neither was wide awake.

"Where are we going? I want my mother," Shirley whimpered.

Renata put her arm around the younger girl. "It's all right. We'll have an adventure. Won't we, Papa?"

What a wonderful child! Cosimo thought. *How compassionate! How unlike her mother!* "Yes," he said, "an adventure. Let's hold hands."

Marcello was hoisting something over his shoulder. Cosimo couldn't tell what, but it appeared to be heavy.

The big man opened the door to the stairway. He reached out and killed the light, plunging the stairs into darkness. "All right, let's go. Follow right behind me and no noise."

"Where are we going? I want my mother!" Shirley repeated.

"Quiet!"

"It's all right, my dear," Cosimo whispered. "Renata and I are right here. We're going to find your mother now. Come along."

They passed in front of Marcello, obviously uncomfortable under his burden. Cosimo glanced over in the darkness and only then realized that it was a body draped over his shoulders. He squeezed Renata's hand more tightly. "Right this way, girls," he said, trying to keep a light note in his voice.

Cosimo, with the girls trailing behind, followed Gallo down the steps, gingerly placing one foot below the next and praying that he wouldn't fall. He could hear Marcello's heavy steps and heavier breathing behind them.

They reached the bottom and Gallo pushed open the door leading to the courtyard. The crisp, fresh air revitalized Cosimo and he recognized the Cadillac—his Cadillac--sitting before him and pointing toward the alley. It took a moment before he realized the diplomatic license plate had been removed and replaced. *Maybe they'll take us home.*

"Get in." Gallo grabbed Cosimo by the collar and herded him toward the car. He climbed in, followed by the two girls. Behind him, he heard the trunk open. The car sagged slightly, then the trunk slammed shut. Marcello opened the driver's door and slid onto the seat. Gallo shifted his bulk onto the back seat, next to Renata. "Let's go."

"Where are you taking us, signore?" Cosimo asked as the car began to move forward.

"To a rendezvous."

"I don't want to go to a rendezvous, I want to go see my mother," Shirley sobbed.

"Sure, kid. I'm taking you to your mother right now. If she wants you back, she knows what she has to do."

"Of course she wants me back!" Shirley snapped, her lips poked out. "Of course she does."

"Yes, of course, my dear," Cosimo tried to soothe the little girl. "Don't worry. In the meantime, let's just rest and enjoy the fresh air." He began to crank down the window.

"Stop," Gallo ordered. "Remember what I have in my pocket, signore." Cosimo stopped, cold fear stabbing into his heart.

"What have you got in your pocket?" Shirley asked, looking into Gallo's face.

Shirley Temple Is Missing

"Candy—and if you and your sister sit quiet and lady-like, I may share it with you when we get there."

"Oh, she's not my sister. This is my friend, Renata."

"You're not being quiet. You want candy, or you don't?"

Shirley smiled, then pressed her lips together and pulled an imaginary zipper across them.

Up ahead, the 240-foot tall bell tower of the Ferry Building stood in stark contrast to the night sky.

Things had quieted down after two o'clock. The angry drunks had either gone home, been thrown in the paddy, or fallen asleep on the sidewalk or in one of the alleyways. Callaghan and Boyle had resumed their patrols along Clay Street as Saturday night's drinking began to give way to Sunday morning's hangovers.

Half a block ahead, a car, a nice one at that, turned right onto Clay heading toward the bay. "Look at tha' Mikey, my boy," Callaghan said, pointing. "What do you see?"

"A rich man out too late for his own good."

"Aye, but ya cannae stop him for being rich. Look again."

Mike Boyle chuckled. "You keen-eyed devil, you. Why the rich man needs to have his car repaired, doesn't he?"

"He does at that. He does at that." Callaghan switched on the red-lensed spotlight and held it out his side window, swinging its beam back and forth. "Close the gap, Mikey."

Boyle accelerated. With no other traffic in sight, the police car was within two lengths of the Cadillac in mere moments. The Cadillac pulled over to the curb and Callaghan pulled up the handle on his door. "Sit tight. This won't take but a minute." Boyle grunted.

Callaghan approached the driver's window, looking into the back seat. If this was one of the big shots from city hall, he'd want to make sure he was suitably polite. The window rolled down. A short, swarthy-looking fellow peered out.

"Ah, good evening to you, sir," Callaghan began, placing one hand on the door frame and leaning down to look past the driver into the back seat. *A chauffeur?*

"Good evening, officer," a fat man answered from the shadowy back seat. "Is there a problem?"

"Ya have a tail light that's out. I thought ya might not know and I thought you ought to."

"Very considerate, officer, especially so late at night."

"On your way home, then?" Callaghan asked.

"Yes. I'm afraid we kept the children out rather later than we should have. Their mothers are going to have our skins." The man smiled. A thumping noise sounded from the back of the car.

Callaghan cocked his head.

"Sorry, sir," the driver said quickly. "It's that universal joint I was telling you about. I'll have to take it back to the garage on Monday."

"Well, make sure they fix it this time," the big man growled. "What if we'd had a breakdown and this kind officer wasn't around to assist us? We'd have to carry these tired children home." He turned his attention back to Callaghan. "We'll make sure we have that taillight repaired too. Anything else, officer?"

Callaghan hesitated. There was something a little off about this whole thing, but he didn't want the captain—or God forbid, the chief—hauling his carcass out of bed on Sunday because he'd harassed some big shot taking his little girl home to ma. *Not worth it, boyo.*

"No sir. Have a pleasant evening and a safe drive home." He tipped his cap, then stepped back and returned to the radio car. "Wake up, Boyle!" he snapped, getting back into the car. "Three hours to go."

CHAPTER 70

"Ready when you are, Miss LeHand," Agent Trammell said, looking at his watch. It was now two-thirty. He'd spent the last hour and a half fighting to remain awake as he waited for the assigned departure time.

"Be right with you," Missy said. She was standing in the bathroom, looking into the mirror and pinning on Gertrude's slouch hat. She already had donned Gertrude's dark blue coat with its wide mink collar. She was a bit slimmer than Gertrude, but her form had been filled out by a piece of equipment Trammell had brought that gave her pause: a bullet-proof vest. Her eyes had widened when he presented it to her. "Standard equipment for FBI agents," he had explained. "It's just a precaution, you understand. Oh, and be sure to wear your gloves. We want only the bad guys' fingerprints on the handle of the ransom bag."

Trammell picked up the phone, dialed three numbers and said, "We're on the way." He removed the pistol from his shoulder holster, seated the magazine and chambered a round, then set the weapon on safe. He picked up the money bag and opened the door. "Time to go, Steve," he said to the agent waiting in the corridor. Steve folded his copy of the San Francisco *Examiner* and stuck it in the outside pocket of his overcoat.

Shirley Temple Is Missing

Trammell nodded at Missy and she walked out into the hallway. They followed Steve to the elevator and rode to the lobby together. Upon exiting the hotel, Steve climbed into the passenger seat of a dark blue Ford coupe waiting at the curb.

Trammell opened the rear door of a Plymouth sedan and stepped back as Missy climbed in. He placed the money bag on the seat beside her and got in the front beside the driver.

"Let's go," Trammell said. The driver flashed his lights and the lead car pulled away.

Trammell couldn't remember the last time he had been on a city street without seeing other traffic hustling along, but now their little caravan was the only visible life in the city. Within a couple of minutes, he could make out the Ferry Building ahead. The lead car turned left onto the Embarcadero and continued north, past the last turnoff for the ferry piers. It would travel another block, according to plan, then double back and take up a position from which it could chase any vehicle attempting to escape with the ransom.

In the backseat, Missy was fidgeting. Despite the cold air, there was a light sheen of perspiration on her forehead.

Agent Trammell turned around. "We don't want to be seen by anybody on the pier, so we're going to stop about three-quarters of the way down the front side of the building. We'll let you out there. You walk straight ahead and once you clear the side of the building, you'll see the pier. Just follow the signs for the Vallejo Ferry." Missy nodded and tried to smile.

"Don't worry, Miss LeHand. We'll have you in sight the whole time. Remember your distress signal?"

"Take off my hat."

"Right." Trammell smiled. "You'll be fine."

The car braked to a stop. Trammell got out and opened the door for Missy, reached in and got the bag. Missy swung her legs out and stood, straightening the overcoat.

"Good luck," Trammell said, handing her the bag.

"Turn the car around," Gallo said. "I want it facing the street, so we can make a quick getaway. And don't drop a wheel over the edge, either!" Gallo laughed. Once the car's back end was facing the bay, Gallo opened the rear door. "Topo." He nodded toward the driver who opened his door and got out. A dull thumping came from the trunk. "The rest of you sit tight." Gallo hefted his bulky frame out of the car and slammed the door behind him.

Gallo gestured Marcello over. The smaller man turned up the collar on his overcoat. "See that ladder?" Gallo pointed toward the end of the pier. Marcello nodded. "Go make sure Little Frankie's got a boat waiting for us at the bottom. And listen out for any noises."

Gallo leaned against the side of the car and faced the other end of the pier.

"I see something," Zanuck said, looking toward the pier through the binoculars. Beneath his feet he could feel the hum of the idling engine.

"Me too. A car. At least one man got out," Lieutenant Alexander said.

"No, no. Down below. On the water."

"Swenson!" Alexander said.

"Aye sir."

"Use your flashlight and signal McCoy: small boat base of pier. Use a blanket to shield your light. I don't want anyone on land to see it."

"Aye sir!"

"Think that's them?" Zanuck asked, lowering the binoculars.

"Who else would it be?"

Missy rounded the corner of the Ferry Building and began walking into a cool breeze. She felt better under the clear, starry sky. She was more tired than she realized; the last thirty-six hours were as stressful as the most hectic days at the White House. Still, the breeze was waking her up. The bag of money got heavier with every step, and the pier was long, stretching away into the blackness, beyond the reach of streetlights. *I guess I'm hungry. After this is over, I'm going to sleep for twenty-four hours. And then I'm going to have a good meal with Corey Wainwright,* she promised herself.

"There she is," Wainwright said, looking down from his second-story perch. "Check with the other posts. Make sure they got her in sight and that they keep her in sight."

"Want me to roll the blocking cars?" Wells asked.

"Not yet. I want the kidnappers to make the next move."

Gallo heard Marcello's footfalls on the ladder behind him, felt him approaching from his rear.

"Boat's there, boss," Marcello whispered.

Gallo checked the luminous dial of his watch. Two fifty-eight.

How long is this pier? Feels like I've been walking ten minutes. Missy's arm was tired, so she shifted the bag to her left hand. Her perspiration had turned into a full-bodied sweat. She wanted to take the hat off, to cool down, but she knew that would bring the FBI agents running and put Shirley and the whole operation at risk.

One step at a time.

"Boss," mumbled Marcello.

"Huh?"

"Down the pier."

Gallo had been resting on the front fender. Now he stood, squinting along the pier where a lone figure was walking slowly toward them. She—Gallo assumed it was Mrs. Temple—had cleared the edge of the Ferry Building. He guessed she was about a hundred yards away.

"We'll let her get about thirty feet away and then stop her," Gallo said, keeping his voice low.

"Can you see her?" Wainwright asked.

"Just barely," Wells replied. "She's beyond the reach of the last street lights."

"All posts are on standby. Post two has lost sight of her. That means we're the only ones who can still see her."

Shirley Temple Is Missing

A shape began to emerge from the darkness. When she turned her head to the side, Missy could discern the outline of a car. *This is it. Oh, Jesus, Mary, Joseph, and all the angels, protect me and that precious child.*

CHAPTER 71

"Good evening, Mrs. Temple," Gallo said when the woman got within thirty feet of the car.

Missy froze. "Good evening." She fought to keep from shaking.

"You've brought my money?"

"Yes. Two hundred thousand dollars in twenties."

"Unmarked twenties, Mrs. Temple?"

"Yes, of course. I meant to say that."

"I'd like you to bring the bag forward five paces." Missy complied. "That's it. Now set it down right there."

Missy held on to the bag. "I need to see Shirley before I set the bag down." She was trying to breathe deeply, to corral her fear, to do her job.

"I'm calling the shots, Mrs. Temple. Set the bag down and back away."

A calmness came over Missy. *This is no different than dealing with Vice President Nance or Bernard Baruch or any of the other two hundred-fifty men who want to get in to see the President every day. I just need to be firm, but polite.*

"I need to see Shirley before I put the bag down." Missy waited, breathless.

Shirley Temple Is Missing

Gallo gestured toward Marcello. "Get the kid and bring her here." Marcello went to the back door and pulled Shirley out by the collar. He walked her around to the front of the car, standing just to the left of Gallo.

Gallo looked down, reached out, and put his hand on Shirley's shoulder.

"Mother? I want to go home now," the little girl said.

"Now, Mrs. Temple, a good faith gesture on my part. And the last one. Put the bag down and step back."

Missy was satisfied that the child in front of her was Shirley. No child—except maybe Shirley Temple herself—could sound so convincingly fearful and upset. She placed the bag on the pier and stepped back.

"Farther."

She backed up two more steps. A short man, the one who had gotten the child out of the car, walked over to the bag and picked it up. He carried it back to the car and Missy lost sight of him.

Several moments passed. Missy began to shake again. "Send Shirley over."

Shirley started to walk forward, but Gallo tightened his grip on her collar. "Not yet."

"Mother? You don't sound like my mother."

"OK, boss," Marcello said from behind the car.

Gallo knelt down to look Shirley in the eye. "Can you count to twenty?"

"Of course I can! But I won't do it until you give me a piece of candy like you promised."

Gallo reached into his pocket. "You won't take a cigar instead, will you?"

She made a face. "I don't smoke."

"Here," Gallo sighed with relief, pulling a stick of Wrigley's from his pocket. "Best I can do. Now count to twenty and then walk slowly over to your mother."

"I don't think that's really my mother."

"Count to twenty and then walk slowly over to whoever you think that is."

Gallo stood and climbed down the ladder to the waiting boat. Three men were standing by to help him down. Marcello climbed down quickly, lowering the bag to Gallo's outstretched hands.

Missy heard Shirley counting. When she reached fifteen, the throaty rumble of a boat motor drowned out the rest of the count. Then things began to happen fast.

"They're gone, Papa!" Renata cried, staring out the back window of the Cadillac. Cosimo crawled out of the back seat and dove behind the wheel. He pressed the starter and the car came to life. He'd been in the dark for far too long, so he reached out and pulled the headlights knob. Suddenly the end of the pier was bathed in yellow light.

The whine of the boat racing away and the sudden illumination of the headlights startled Missy. She stumbled backwards, unable to separate the sound of the fast-moving boat from the blinding lights, and fell to the pier.

Shirley rushed forward and leaned over. "You're not my mother! You're Miss LeHand! What are you doing here?"

The bright lights and the supine form out on the end of the pier jolted Wainwright into action. "Signal the boats: Attack!"

Ammons lifted the signal lamp and flashed a dot-dash out toward the bay.

"Keep sending until acknowledged! Blocking cars move into position. Don't let that car off the pier!"

Wells cranked the field phone and began issuing orders.

"I'm going down there!" Wainwright shouted, pulling his pistol and dashing toward the door.

By the time Wainwright reached the stairway, both Alexander's and McCoy's patrol boats were converging on the speed boat, their spotlights dancing across the water as they struggled to cut off the vessel's escape.

"Mr. Griffith!" McCoy shouted above the roar of his boat's engine, "grab that megaphone and stand by to relay my instructions."

Griff turned around to the corner of the wheelhouse and grabbed a two-foot-long open-ended cone. "Get out there by the one-pounder and tell that motor boat to heave to. And hang on to something! I wouldn't want to lose you overboard on your first cruise!"

Without closing the door, Cosimo shifted the car into gear and let out the clutch quickly, causing it to jerk forward.

"Papa!" Renata cried, "don't run over them!"

Cosimo stopped the car a few feet from where the woman lay on the pier and climbed out. "Help me,

Renata!" He trotted over to where Shirley was bent over the woman. "Is this your mother?"

"No, but she's my friend and I think something's wrong!"

Missy's eyes were sweeping back and forth across the three faces in front of her, only one of which she recognized. She tried to get up, but she was so tired that her body wouldn't respond.

"Miss? Can you hear me?" the man was saying. His voice sounded like it was coming from deep within a well.

"Miss LeHand, are you all right?" Shirley asked.

Shirley. You remember Shirley. What a darling child. What's she doing out here? What am I doing out here? Where is this? "I'll take you to your mother," Missy mumbled.

"That's what they all say!" Shirley pouted and placed her hands on her hips.

"Help, children! Help me get her into the car!" the man said.

Missy watched them pick her up—it was mostly the man with a little help from the other girl. Shirley was holding her hand. They crammed her into the passenger seat in front, where she slid down so far she couldn't even see out of the car. Then the car was moving, picking up speed.

The last thing she recalled was the screech of the tires and the smell of burning rubber as the car came skidding to a halt and she slid all the way down into the floor.

Shirley Temple Is Missing

Cosimo had gotten the woman into the car and shoved the girls into the back seat. He was no doctor, but he knew the way to Saint Francis Hospital on Bush Street. He could be there in five minutes. He slammed the car into third gear and felt the powerful V-8 engine respond. *Maybe I'll be there in three minutes.* He smiled.

That's when he saw the man step onto the pier and aim a pistol right at his nose.

CHAPTER 72

"A shot across the bow!" Lieutenant Alexander shouted to his forward gun crew.

When the spotlights from the two Coast Guard patrol vessels had speared the kidnappers' boat, it had turned south, racing past the towers being built to support the new bridge to Oakland. Like a linebacker preventing a runner from turning the corner and reaching the open field, Alexander had immediately ordered his helmsman to steer a course that would prevent the small boat from breaking out into the bay. Alexander had signaled McCoy's boat to stay on the motor boat's tail. Using the shoreline as an additional accomplice, the Coast Guard boats had effectively boxed in the kidnappers. His crewmen were ready for action, armed with Thompson submachine guns and shot guns. Now all they had to do was run the kidnappers down.

"Ready, sir!" the gun chief shouted over the noise of the engine and the slapping of water against the hull.

"Fire!"

With the sharp *pom!* of its discharge, the gun belched a bright flash, the smoke ripped away by the onrushing wind. Alexander watched as the projectile sailed over the small boat, sending up a splash of gray water.

Alexander turned to Zanuck. "That should get their attention!"

Still the small boat raced on, Alexander's and McCoy's larger, more powerful vessels easily keeping pace with it, holding their positions.

"Let's squeeze 'em," Alexander said, turning to his helmsman. "Take a course to cut him off and make him either veer toward the shore or stop."

"Aye, aye, sir."

"Signalman! Use the blinker and send: stop your engines and heave to."

"Aye sir."

"You think they can read Morse Code?" Zanuck shouted above the wind.

"Not likely," Alexander replied, "but I want to give them every chance before we start shooting." Already, the patrol boat was narrowing the gap to its target. McCoy's boat was closing from the rear. Alexander turned to watch his prey.

Small, bright flashes winked from the smaller boat.

"They're firing at us, sir!" the helmsman cried.

"Return fire! Return fire! Gun crew," Alexander hollered, "target their stern. Fire when ready!"

The staccato hammering of the Thompsons assaulted Zanuck's ears. Within seconds the forward gun fired, spitting another round toward the motor boat. The round splashed into the boat's wake. Now flashes were visible from McCoy's patrol boat as well.

The next round from the one-pounder found its target. Chunks of debris flew into the air as it exploded against the stern of the smaller boat. Black smoke began to boil out of its damaged engine compartment and the boat began to lose speed. Alexander ordered the patrol boat to reduce speed and to cross the bow of the now-crippled escape boat.

"Hand me that horn," Alexander said. He took the megaphone from one of his crewman and stepped forward of the wheelhouse. He judged that the kidnappers' boat was about seventy yards away. He put the megaphone to his mouth and shouted, "Throw your weapons overboard and put your hands in the air!" He could make out at least four figures outlined against the orange glow now coming from the stern of the motor boat. Alexander couldn't tell what they were doing, but so far, no hands were in the air.

"Baker! Put a few rounds just above their waterline. Try not to hit anybody."

"Yes sir." A crewman stepped to the rail of the patrol boat, pulled the charging handle on his Thompson, and fired two short bursts, the rounds skipping across the water and smacking into the hull of the now-drifting boat. Alexander smiled as two sets of hands went up.

"Skipper, down by the stern," Baker said, pointing to the back end of the boat, which was settling into the water.

"Launch the dinghy, Chief. Weapons at the ready. Don't take any chances."

The boats were closer now, separated by no more than forty yards. "Let me have one of your weapons. I'm pretty handy in a fight," Zanuck said, coming up beside Alexander.

"No way. Those are dangerous men on that boat, Mr. Zanuck."

Shirley Temple Is Missing

"It's not the men I'm worried about," Zanuck muttered.

CHAPTER 73

"Get out of the car with your hands up!" Wainwright shouted. He was standing in the glare of the car's headlights, his .45 held straight out and leveled at where he thought the driver's head would be. *Not the most tactically sound position.* He'd reacted when he saw Missy LeHand being put into the car, and saw the car begin to move along the pier. He hadn't had time to think things through, to come up with a plan. He could hear footsteps clattering on the pier behind him. He could only hope that they belonged to his other agents.

The driver's door creaked open. Despite the bright lights in his face, Wainwright could see movement as a figure stepped from the car. And its hands were in the air.

"Don't shoot! I am Cosimo Palladino, consul general of the Republic of Italy. There is a sick woman in the car. She needs a doctor."

"Step forward where I can see you!" Wainwright kept his pistol trained on the driver.

"Coming up behind you!" Wainwright recognized the voice of Agent Trammell.

"You! On the ground with your hands spread way out," Wainwright said to the driver. The man knelt and then stretched out on the ground. Wainwright turned to Trammell. "Search him. I'll check the car."

He stepped around the driver, now spread-eagled on the pavement, and thrust his pistol into the car. Slumped on the front floorboard was Missy LeHand, unconscious. Huddled in the back seat were two wide-eyed young girls. One of them looked awfully familiar.

Yellow flames were licking at the wooden decking of the boat, the heavy marine varnish fueling the fire.

Joseph Gallo gripped the black bag in one hand, a .45 caliber pistol in his other, an unlit cigar clamped between his teeth. Off to his left, he could see a small row boat being lowered into the water next to one of the boats that had been shooting at him. He knew he had to make a quick decision.

"Frankie! How deep's the water here?"

"Shirley! Shirley!" Gertrude Temple had kicked off her heels and was padding along the pier as fast as she could run. She reached the idling car where one of the FBI agents was helping a man to his feet. *Had he been in the car?*

Agent Wainwright was leaning across the driver's seat, his legs sticking out of the door.

"Mother!"

The back door swung open and Shirley appeared from behind it. Shirley ran toward her and Gertrude dropped to her knees. *I'm ruining a pair of stockings, what a ridiculous thought.* And now she was holding Shirley, squeezing her like a teddy bear, her mind flooded with happiness and relief.

She held her daughter tightly for several moments, only vaguely aware that another child was standing behind Shirley. She pushed Shirley back to arms' length. "Let me look at you!"

"Oh, Mother, I missed you so much!"

"I missed you too, my precious. But now we're back together and we'll always stay together, right?" Gertrude smiled as a tear slipped down her cheek.

"Right! Always and forever."

Wainwright appeared from behind Gertrude. "Shirley, this is Special Agent Wainwright of the FBI. He helped us find you."

Wainwright knelt down. "Pleased to meet you, Shirley."

"Pleased to meet you too. Did you get your man? The FBI always gets its man, you know."

Wainwright's smile faded. "Well, we will, but first we need to get Miss LeHand to the hospital. Agent Trammell is going to drive her."

"Should we go with her?" Gertrude asked.

"We'll send Miss Tully. The rest of us need to stay here and figure out just what's been going on over the last two days."

Agents Wainwright and Trammell had stretched Missy out on the wide back seat of the Cadillac, her head cradled in Grace Tully's lap. Trammell had then jumped behind the wheel and headed toward the hospital.

"Will she be all right?" Gertrude asked, watching the car speed away.

"I hope so. She wasn't shot or anything like that. Miss Tully said she has a history of heart trouble, so I thought it best to get her headed to the hospital as quickly as possible," Wainwright said. "Anything from the Coast Guard?" he asked Agent Wells, who had arrived followed by Joan Roswell.

"Nothing. We lost sight of the speed boat pretty quickly."

"Well, let's hope the Coast Guard didn't." Wainwright looked at the faces around him, an interesting mixture of young, old, famous, modest, men, women, Italians and Americans. "Now, ladies and gentlemen, how did we all end up on this pier in the middle of the night?"

CHAPTER 74

Every time he asked permission, the answer was "No." So, Darryl Zanuck wasn't going to ask, he was just going to do. He backed away from Lieutenant Alexander, whose attention was focused on directing the efforts of the two patrol boats. Using their signal lamps, Alexander and McCoy could communicate over the water, literally over the heads of the men in the small boat, with little risk of their messages being understood by the kidnappers.

Zanuck eased away, the light from the fire on the motor boat providing just enough illumination that he wasn't constantly tripping over a line or a cable or some other piece of equipment on the deck. He stepped carefully over to the side of the patrol boat where four members of the crew were launching a dinghy. He watched as the first two men climbed in. The two on deck handed down their weapons.

"Want me to hold that line while you get in?" Zanuck asked one of the crewmen.

"Thanks, mister," the coastie said, surrendering the rope holding the dinghy close to the patrol boat. He and the other crewman stepped aboard. "I'll take it now," he said, turning and reaching back toward Zanuck.

Shirley Temple Is Missing

"That's all right," Zanuck said, hopping aboard with the agility of an acrobat. "Let's go." The coast guardsman shrugged and sat down at his oar. "All right, boys," he said as he and his crew mates began to row. "Henry," he called to a man in the prow, "keep those S-O-Bs covered. And watch out for Chief McCoy's boat."

The men on the motorboat had moved toward its bow, putting some small separation between themselves and the spreading flames. From what Zanuck could tell, none of the men were still carrying weapons. He could make out the silhouettes of four men, two of average build, one smaller, and one very fat. The fat man was standing behind the others, holding something, although it didn't appear to be a weapon, in his hand.

"Throw down your weapons. Put your hands up in the air! Way up!" the coastie in the bow shouted as the dinghy got closer. Zanuck could see three sets of hands reaching up toward the darkness. Then he saw movement. The fat figure had tossed something into the water. It bobbed once and then disappeared beneath the surface of the bay.

Zanuck ripped off his tin helmet and his life jacket. "Hey! What are you doing?" the boat chief asked.

No time to seek permission. Zanuck dove over the side of the dinghy, causing it to rock violently, nearly tipping it over. He plunged beneath the dark water, the only light coming from the fire above. Ahead, he could just make out a shadow sinking deeper.

Zanuck reached for the dark object—*It has to be the bag!*—but he wasn't close enough to touch it. It continued to drop through the water. He was afraid that if he surfaced for air, he might not be able to find the bag again, but he was out of breath, his lungs burning. *All those cigars!*

His head broke the surface and he sucked in lungs-full of the cold night air. A spotlight came to rest on his position.

"Mr. Zanuck!" he heard Alexander shout his name. He breathed deeply and dove back under the water. As best he could, he swam straight down. Even with the light from the searchlights, the water in the bay was dark. *Too dark.* He spun in a complete circle. *Is that it?* He swam toward the shape. It seemed to be suspended in the water, just hanging there. *Just a little farther!* Zanuck's lungs began to scream. He began to exhale as he clawed his way toward the surface.

Zanuck broke through the water, right on the edge of a circle of light. Within seconds, both searchlights had zeroed in on his head as he gasped for air. He was about to dive again when something grabbed him by the collar and he was jerked out of the water and over the side of a dinghy.

"Are you crazy?" Alexander snapped, bending over to stare him in the face. "This is no time or place for swimming. We could have lost you down there."

Zanuck worked to catch his breath. "You don't understand, lieutenant. I have to go back in the water. I need some kind of waterproof flashlight and a good, sharp knife."

"What the hell for?"

"There's something down there I need."

Five minutes later, Zanuck was shivering in the bottom of a dinghy, a wool blanket draped over his shoulders, explaining the urgency of his mission. "That's why I have to go back in the water!"

Lieutenant Alexander let out a long whistle. "I understand."

"So, get me a flashlight and a knife, will ya?" Zanuck struggled to his feet, shivering, his recent exertion in the cold water causing his leg and arm muscles to ache.

Alexander put a hand on his shoulder and pushed him back down. "Not so fast. You're a civilian, Mr. Zanuck—"

"I'm an army veteran!"

"—a civilian in the midst of a federal law enforcement operation. You're here as an observer only and, as such, I'm responsible for your safety. If you even attempt to get back in that water, I'll have you in handcuffs along with that jolly band of pirates over there." He tipped his head toward the patrol boat where the four kidnappers were sitting on the deck with their backs to each other in a rough circle. Alexander turned toward McCoy's boat. "Hey, Chief! Get Compton suited up. We have a need for his particular talents."

Petty Officer Compton was under water for less than ten minutes when he surfaced with a black bag in his hands. He pushed the bag along ahead of him as he swam back toward the dinghy.

"This what you're after, sir?" Compton asked, after he'd pulled his diving mask off his face.

"That's it!" Zanuck said with a smile. He and Alexander reached out their hands and hauled the diver into the boat. "They tied it to one of the boat's anchors and tossed it over," Compton said. "Lucky you saw where it went in. Nobody would ever find it again after a couple of days. Even with that anchor, the tides would have moved it around."

"Want to have a look? Make sure it's all there?" Alexander asked.

Zanuck nodded. He borrowed Compton's knife to cut the knot that had bound the bag to the anchor. He opened the bag and looked inside as water drained from its seams.

"Looks like it's all there. I'll let the feds count it. Good work, Compton! You too, lieutenant."

CHAPTER 75

"And so, I put the girls into the car and we set out for Mrs. Temple's hotel." Cosimo was recounting the last twelve hours to Wainwright in the makeshift command post at the Ferry Building. One of the other agents had come up with doughnuts and coffee, milk for the girls. While he awaited word from the Coast Guard, Wainwright would focus on those who had been in the car. He had pressed Joan into service as his scribe to take down a statement, and she was rapidly writing in her notepad.

"What happened next?"

'My driver, Marcello Altobello, delivered us someplace else. It seemed to be some type of tavern as it was very noisy with loud music and much carrying on. He took us up a back stairway to a room upstairs—a filthy room. They held us there until we left to come here. That's where he made me write the ransom letter."

"Who, your driver?"

"No, the fat man. He was always in charge. He threatened the children and held Renata at gunpoint while I delivered the letter to the hotel. That's why I slipped the doorman my calling card. I wanted to send a signal that I was being forced to do this."

"Did the fat man give his name?"

"Not to me, but Marcello knew him. That much was clear to me."

"Could you identify the fat man if you saw his picture?"

"Almost certainly, Agent Wainwright. And I can tell you one other thing, much as it pains me: he was Italian."

"I'm grateful for your assistance, Mr. Palladino. Please forgive me for drawing on you. I didn't know at that moment whether you were one of the kidnappers."

"Of course. It's been a most confusing few hours for all of us. Imagine, sticking one's head out the door to find one's daughter roller-skating down the hall with Shirley Temple! And then to discover that she had been an overnight guest!"

"Do you know where I can find your Mr. Trevisano? He seems to be in this pretty deeply."

"I fear this is true. He will most likely be either at the consulate or at his apartment. My office can furnish his address, but…"

The consul's brow was wrinkled, his lips drawn into a pout. "Mr. Palladino?" Wainwright prompted.

"This is awkward, of course, especially at a moment like this, but I am compelled to inform you that Signore Trevisano, as a consular official, enjoys diplomatic immunity."

Joan gasped, but Wainwright only shrugged. "That's not really my concern, sir. My job is to figure out what happened: who did what to whom, when, and how. I'll turn that over to the U.S. Attorney's office. If by then we've found Mr. Trevisano and he's still in the country, then the attorneys can sort it all out."

CHAPTER 76

"We had some ice cream and then he said, 'Let's get off and have some target practice." Shirley was recalling her story of the train ride, of getting off at San José, and getting picked up by the men in the car. "The man in the car said his name was Juan, but it wasn't. And he's not Spanish, he's Italian, like Renata and her father."

"Do you know why he took you to Renata's house?

"It's not really her house. She just lives there. It's really the consulate. It's like the Italian's capitol in California."

"Oh, I see." Wainwright smiled. "Do you know why Juan—or Fausto, that's his real name—took you to the consulate?"

"He said Mr. Zanuck wanted me to shoot a new scene."

Wainwright and Gertrude exchanged glances. "What kind of scene?"

"Well, it was something about the Italian army and a plow. My costume was a real Italian uniform."

"Did you see the film after it was shot?"

"No. Renata and I were too busy. Signora Ferri taught us how to make pasta and then we roller skated."

She sighed. "We were having a wonderful time before we had to leave."

"So, the last time you saw Andy was after you got in the car outside the train station?"

"Yes. I fell asleep and when I woke up he was gone."

"And the last time you saw Juan, or Fausto, that was at the consulate yesterday afternoon?"

"I guess so. What day is this anyway?"

"It's very early on Sunday morning, dear," Gertrude said. "When little girls and their mothers should already be in bed!"

The door to the office opened and Agent Trammell walked in with Grace Tully.

"How's Miss LeHand?" Wainwright asked, standing.

"The doc said she'd be all right," Trammell said. "Something about the rhythm of her heart getting out of whack. Too much excitement. They're keeping her overnight for observation."

"Drive me back over there, will you? I want to get a statement from her while things are still fresh in her mind." *And I want to make sure she's all right.*

"Agent Wainwright," Agent Ammons called from his post by the windows. "Coast Guard coming in to the pier."

By the time they reached the ground floor of the Ferry Building, the two Coast Guard patrol boats had moored.

Wainwright looked at Trammell. "Fingers crossed. Let's hope they got 'em."

The two agents headed toward the boats where crew members were setting out gangways.

"Any luck, Lieutenant Alexander?" Wainwright called.

"Quite a bit. You ready to take custody of these deadbeats?" Alexander asked with a toss of his head toward the stern where the kidnappers sat under guard.

"And this too?" Darryl Zanuck asked, holding up a black bag and flashing a gap-toothed grin.

Wainwright pulled all his agents in from their posts and issued new instructions. One detachment, under the supervision of Agent Wells, would take the four prisoners to holding cells downtown in the federal courthouse.

Agent Ammons would arrange transportation back to the hotel for the Temples, Grace, Zanuck, Griff, and Joan Roswell. He'd also get the consul and his daughter back to the consulate—but not in the Cadillac, which Wainwright intended to thoroughly search before relinquishing it to its owners.

Wainwright, with Trammell driving the Cadillac, headed toward the hospital. "I could get used to this," Wainwright said, leaning back in the passenger's wide, comfortable seat.

"Don't bother. I doubt even Mr. Hoover gets to ride around in this kind of style," Trammell replied with a smile.

Once they reached the hospital, Trammell parked the car along the front curb. "I don't think you're supposed to park here," Wainwright said.

"You go on in. Let me worry about the car. Besides, who cares if it gets ticketed? Diplomatic immunity." Trammell winked.

At the receiving desk, Wainwright flashed his FBI credentials and was immediately shown to Miss LeHand's room.

CHAPTER 77

After two nights with almost no sleep, Grace, Joan, Griff, and Gertrude could think of little else but falling into their respective beds when they reached the St. Francis.

There was a bit of shuffling, with Grace moving her things into Room 1219, which she was to have shared with Missy, leaving a bed empty for Shirley in her mother's room.

"Good night, kid," Griff said to Shirley, ruffling her hair. "I sure am glad to see you again." He headed to his own room.

In Room 1220, Gertrude placed a call to her husband, who had been nervously sitting by the phone in their Santa Monica home, and put Shirley on the line. While getting their night clothes ready, she watched fondly as Shirley shared some of her exciting experiences with her "best pal."

"And I made a new friend, Renata," she said. "We learned to make farfalle—that's pasta—and I want her to come spend the night with me some time." Shirley listened to her father's reply, a smile on her face, and flashed her famous dimples. "OK, I love you too, Daddy. See you soon!"

Shirley Temple Is Missing

As Gertrude helped her into her pajamas, a sleepy Shirley asked, "Mother, do we have to roll my hair tonight?"

"No, baby," Gertrude said. "Get some sleep. This is one time you don't have to sparkle for anyone." She sat by Shirley's bed, stroking her head until the child's even breathing indicated she was sleeping.

In Room 1219, Grace put on a warm flannel nightgown and was asleep as soon as her head hit the pillow, not even saying goodnight to her new roommate.

It took Joan a bit longer to get ready for bed. After wearing the same clothing for more than two days, she gratefully donned the silk nightgown Missy had loaned her, but carefully hung up her blouse and suit, patting the pocket of the jacket to be sure Missy's purloined ring was still there. She rinsed out her one pair of underpants and her stockings in the sink, and then she used Grace's toothbrush—after first running it under a steady stream of hot water.

Joan was almost ready to slip into bed when she heard a soft knock at the door. She opened it, keeping the security chain in place, and put one green eye to the gap. It was Zanuck, a grin on his face and the Scrabble game under his arm. He was also waving a bottle of champagne.

"How 'bout a re-match?" he said. "Double or nothing. I'm feeling lucky tonight."

Joan grinned back. "Oh, hell, why not?" she said, and, slipping out the door, followed him down the hall.

CHAPTER 78

Missy was almost asleep in her hospital bed when she heard the light tap on her door. "Come in," she said softly, dragging her eyes open.

"Miss LeHand?" It was Corey Wainwright. She put a hand to her disheveled hair; her usual neat roll had come completely undone, and her silver-streaked dark hair was spread out on the pillow.

"Oh, my, I look a fright," she said.

"You look fine," he said, sitting down in a chair beside her bed. "How do you feel?"

"Better," she said. "Just tired. I feel like I could sleep for a week." She laughed a little bit. "President Roosevelt said he hoped I'd get a good rest on this vacation, but I don't imagine he thought I'd be getting it in the hospital. How is Shirley?"

"She's probably fast asleep now, in her mother's room at the St. Francis," Wainwright said. He reached out and took Missy's hand, toying with the charm bracelet that was still clasped around her wrist. "That was a very brave thing you did, Missy, risking your life to reunite that little girl with her mother. If I had known you had a bum heart, I never would have asked it of you."

"I had rheumatic fever when I was a kid, and the heart problem comes and goes," Missy said. "One thing I've learned from working for Franklin Roosevelt is you never limit yourself. We're all capable of doing much more than we think we can." She smiled. "That's the first time you've called me Missy."

They stared at each for a moment, then Wainwright stood up.

"Well, it's 4:40 a.m.," he said. "You need some sleep and I've got to get back to the Federal Building and see how the interrogations are going. I'll be back tomorrow afternoon to take your statement."

He walked to the door. "Good night, Missy," he said.

But Missy was already asleep.

The visit with Missy, and knowing that she was going to be all right, was like a tonic for Wainwright—a badly needed one. He'd been going non-stop since Friday evening, his energy nearly spent. But now, he was ready to jump into another round of interrogations, ready to finish unravelling this complicated tapestry of crime set into motion by Andy Archie. *If only we could locate Trevisano.*

Wainwright pushed his way through the double doors of the hospital and walked down the steps toward the Cadillac. *At least it wasn't towed.* That's when he noticed that Trammell was not alone. Leaning against the car next to his fellow agent, smoking a cigarette, was a tall, dark-haired man wearing a garish black-and-gold checked sports jacket.

Trammell smiled when his colleague stepped off the curb and came around to the side of the car. "Special Agent Wainwright, meet Fausto Trevisano."

"Mr. Trevisano, we've been wanting to talk to you, ask a few questions. Hop in and we'll give you a lift back to our office."

"Grazie." Trevisano flipped his cigarette to the curb and climbed into the backseat.

"Where did he come from?" Wainwright asked.

Trammell laughed. "I was just standing here smoking my cigarette and I heard this pounding from inside the trunk. I popped it open and out he springs like a jack-in-the-box. Claims some mug whacked him on the back of his head and the next thing he knows he's locked in the trunk."

"How long's he been in there?"

"He didn't know. Talk about a gift-wrapped package!"

I'm more like a manager than an agent, Corey Wainwright thought as he shuttled between interrogation rooms. His agents were working in separate interview rooms collecting statements from Joseph Gallo, Marcello Altobello, and their accomplices.

Wainwright opened a door off the corridor and walked into a square room furnished with only a metal table and two simple wooden chairs. Fausto Trevisano sat on one side of the table, smoking a cigarette and facing Agent Trammell.

"How's it going?" Wainwright asked.

Trammell looked up. "Mr. Trevisano has been very entertaining."

"All I have done has been for the glory of the Italian Empire and its leader, Benito Mussolini," Fausto declared, exhaling a smoky cloud. Unshaven and rumpled, Fausto was the only person in the room who had recently slept, and Wainwright, surprisingly, found himself envious. "Do not forget, signores, had I not flushed the true criminals out into the open where you could apprehend them, we would not be sitting here as comrades to celebrate our triumph."

Wainwright shot a quick glance at Trammell, who was trying hard not to laugh. "We're not comrades, Mr. Trevisano," Wainwright said, leaning on the corner of the table and staring into the Italian's eyes. "We don't steal little girls away from their families and hold them hostage."

"Nor did I, Agent Wainwright. I picked the child up on the road and brought her safely to the city where she said her mother would be. In my care, she came to no harm, was provided for, and entertained. She was being returned to her mother when this unfortunate business occurred."

"Save it!" A knock on the door interrupted the conversation. Wainwright opened it and took a folded sheet of paper from Agent Wells. He closed the door and leaned against it, opened the note and read.

"Good news?" Trammell asked.

"I wouldn't exactly say that. Hoover's flight lands at ten-forty-five."

CHAPTER 79

Around 10 a.m., after managing a short nap on his office couch, Wainwright decided to swing by the St. Francis Hotel to let Grace know Missy was recovering, and to fill her in on the interrogations so she could seek direction from the White House on handling the sticky diplomatic situation.

Before he'd left for the St. Francis, Wainwright had shaved in the men's room and slipped on one of the spare shirts he kept in his office. He'd also stopped by the shoeshine stand in the large, echoing lobby of the building. There hadn't been a boy there to shine his shoes, but that hadn't stopped Wainwright from opening the drawers where the supplies were kept and giving his shoes a quick buffing. Hoover would notice.

Grace was alone in Room 1219, looking refreshed after some sleep and a room service breakfast. She told the FBI agent that Joan had been gone when she awoke. "I assume she went downstairs for breakfast," Grace said. "She didn't leave a note."

Wainwright frowned. "I certainly hope that's the case, Miss Tully," he said. "She may not be able to resist filing this story with her editor. It would give her a front-page by-line and a guaranteed job. Did you check the closet to see if her clothes were there?"

"Oh, I didn't think of that," Grace said. Opening the door, she was puzzled to find Joan's suit and blouse on wooden hangers, her black pumps on the floor. "Wherever can she be?"

"Well, she can't have gone far without her clothes," Wainwright said. He glanced at the other bed in the room. *Doesn't look slept in.* "Let me brief you on what we've learned so far. We'll need to get some direction from the White House, and I'm going to ask you to handle that. I'm on my way to the airport to meet Mr. Hoover's plane, and I know he will be hungry for publicity. But the diplomatic angle concerns me with things with Italy in such a flux."

Following Wainwright's departure, Grace placed a call to the White House, and Hacky, the resourceful switchboard operator, located Steve Early at home. Grace conveyed the details Wainwright had given her, including the involvement of the Italian vice consul in Shirley Temple's kidnapping.

"Whew!" Steve said. "Stories like that make me wish I was still working for the Associated Press! Instead, I think we'll be struggling to keep a lid on this. OK, I'm going to set up a ship-to-shore call with the President as soon as I can reach him. I know he'll have definite ideas about what to do."

"If you can't reach him, perhaps you can talk to Secretary Hull or Sumner Welles over at the State Department," Grace suggested.

Early laughed. "To hell with them, Grace. You know the Boss is the only 'State Department' that matters. Say, where is Missy? I thought she was handling this."

"Oh, Steve, I forgot to tell you! She delivered the ransom money to the kidnappers!" Grace said.

Steve let out an appreciative whistle.

"But it was too much for her in the end," Grace continued. "She had one of her heart spells and fainted. They took her to the hospital, but she's fine. They're just keeping her for observation."

"Well, I'll be sure the President knows about her heroism," Steve said. "I don't know what we'd do without Missy."

CHAPTER 80

The TWA DC-2 rolled to a stop outside the airline's main hangar at San Francisco's Air Terminal. An unexpected silence descended as the big radial engines shut down. A small group was waiting in the morning sunshine to welcome the newly arrived passengers.

Wainwright had commandeered a car and driver—not the consulate's Cadillac, but a conveyance more in keeping with the low-profile presence the Director expected of the Bureau's field offices. He fidgeted as he waited for the aircraft's rear door to open.

He had met Edgar Hoover, the director of the Federal Bureau of Investigation, on a couple of occasions, but those had revolved around training sessions at the Bureau's headquarters in Washington. This was the first time he'd hosted the Director at his field office, the first time the Director had made a personal visit to intervene in an investigation Wainwright was managing.

The aircraft door opened and a set of three steps was lowered. Hoover was the first man off. He was carrying a briefcase and an overcoat, a brown felt fedora sitting atop his head. He was stocky and well-dressed, with the determined mien of a man used to getting his way.

Wainwright raised his hand, catching Hoover's eye. The Director gave a curt nod and headed directly toward the agent.

"Welcome to San Francisco. How was your flight?"

"Noisy and bumpy, but a lot quicker than the train," Hoover said as the pair turned and walked toward the parking lot. Hoover checked his watch. "If I'd taken the train, I'd just be getting to Chicago."

"Do we need to get your luggage?"

"No, they'll send it on to the hotel. The St. Francis, right?"

"Yes sir."

"Tell me what you've got."

"Well, the main thing is that we got Shirley back safe and sound early this morning. She's back in her mother's arms at the hotel."

Hoover stopped and turned to the agent. "That's good work, Agent Wainwright. Very good work! Has the press been informed?"

"No sir."

"Even better." Hoover smiled.

Wainwright introduced the Director to their driver and then settled into the back seat beside his boss. Once the car started rolling back toward the city, Wainwright began to recount what had transpired since Hoover's Friday night call. As they rode through Brisbane, Wainwright related the sequence of events that had led to not only the recovery of the little girl, but the recovery of the ransom money and the arrest of four suspects.

"How did Mrs. Temple raise the money so quickly?"

"I assigned that task to Mr. Zanuck."

"Darryl Zanuck's here?" Hoover asked, surprise in his voice.

"Yes sir. He flew up Saturday from L.A. Of course, he claimed he couldn't get the money fast enough to meet the instructions in the ransom note so I had to make a suggestion."

Hoover raised his eyebrows. "Go on."

Wainwright confessed that he'd sent the studio mogul to see McDonough and that the bail bondsman had come through, albeit with some last-second caveats.

"Snake!" Hoover spat. "He runs the rackets in the whole city. He could have come up with twice that much if he wanted to. If the good people of San Francisco had the city government they deserved, riff-raff like McDonough would have been jailed for life years ago."

"The most curious part of the whole investigation is who I almost shot last night—this morning—as he was driving the getaway car."

"McDonough?" Hoover asked hopefully.

"No sir. Cosimo Palladino, the consul general of Italy."

Hoover started. "He was involved?"

"Yes sir, but as a victim." Wainwright laid out the details of the kidnapping within the kidnapping.

"I've never heard of one like this. Not even with Ma Barker's gang. And the suspects, they're Italians too?"

"Yes sir. We have two sets of suspects: Andy Archie and Trevisano in the first group, and Gallo,

Altobello, Frankie Lombardi and Joey Genovese in the second. Archie's on the lam. We've got bulletins out for him. Gallo and his group are at the Federal Building. You can see them if you want."

"And this Trevisano character?"

"He's a character all right. He's also at the office, but he's not in custody. According to Mr. Palladino, he's got immunity. I've sent a cable to the State Department asking for confirmation, but I don't have any reason to doubt the consul."

"Sensational. That's the only word I can think of." Hoover shook his head. "I want a full briefing for the press Monday morning on the steps of the Federal Building. That'll give me time to go through all your witness statements, meet the Temples, and the rest of your team. I'm already acquainted with Miss LeHand and Miss Tully, and Mr. Zanuck too. I want this case to make a big splash. It'll be good for the Bureau's reputation. Who's the press liaison in your office?"

"There's not one. We've never really had to deal with the press. Usually by the time they get wind of something the U.S. Attorney's office is driving things. There may be somebody who can help, though. Joan Roswell, a reporter from the L.A. *Standard*, was on the train with the Temples. She got mixed up in this somehow. We've had to keep her close to prevent her from spilling everything to her editor. She's expecting an exclusive or something. I figured you'd know the best way to handle her."

"You figured right." Hoover smiled.

CHAPTER 81

Washington, D.C.

When Steve Early and President Roosevelt connected by ship-to-shore radio, the press secretary outlined the convoluted story of Shirley Temple's kidnapping to the Boss, who listened intently from the radio room of the USS *Houston*.

At the conclusion, Roosevelt had one word: "Wow."

"Wow is right, sir," Early replied. "But what do we do about this? You know Hoover, he's probably setting up a press conference right now to brag on the quick action of his men in San Francisco—as he has every right to do—but we've got to consider the world situation."

"I agree," the President said. He paused, and Early heard the flick of a lighter and the quick inhale as the Boss started smoking a fresh Camel. When he resumed talking, Roosevelt seemed to be thinking aloud, turning the moving parts over in his mind. "We're officially neutral when it comes to European affairs, but we all know the rise of fascism in Italy and Germany is a threat to democratic nations everywhere. We can't even comment on the Italian invasion of Ethiopia, reprehensible as it is. Italy was our ally in the Great War, and, with Britain and France, we are very anxious to preserve that coalition against the Germans, should another war arise. If we let the press know an Italian official has kidnapped America's sweetheart in this crazy plot and the country reacts with anger against Italy and Italians, it could be enough to drive Mussolini straight into Hitler's arms."

"Yes sir," Early said, impressed as always by the President's grasp of international affairs.

FDR continued, "Let Hoover know I've put a black-out on this story. No mention of the kidnapping of Shirley Temple or the FBI's role in recovering her. I'll follow up with a telegram to Hoover, just to be sure he understands. Let Secretary Hull know over at the State Department. Give him a complete briefing this afternoon."

"Will do, sir. Anything else?"

"Oh, yes, how is Missy? Did she get in on the excitement?"

"Did she ever!" Steve outlined Missy's involvement and how she wound up in the hospital. "But they say she'll make a complete recovery," he said. "She just needs some rest."

"Poor Missy!" the President said. "Steve, send her a dozen roses—pink, if you can get them, that's her favorite color—and sign the card the usual way, 'With love, FDR.'"

"Got it," Steve said. "How's the fishing?"

"It's grand!" said the President.

CHAPTER 82

"This way, sir," Wainwright said as he led Hoover along the concrete corridor in the cellar of the Federal Building. Mindful of the Director's aggressive personality, Wainwright kept up a quick pace until he reached the cell holding the fat man who Cosimo Palladino had identified as the lead kidnapper.

Gallo was stretched out on the cell's metal bed smoking a cigarette and staring out the window. He turned his head at the sound of footsteps.

"This is Joseph Gallo, a.k.a. Big Joey and Joey Nickels. Former associate of John Dillinger and Lester Joseph Gillis," Wainwright said, coming to a stop in front of the barred cell.

"Gillis!" Hoover snorted at the real name of the man known far and wide as Baby Face Nelson. "It seems your choice of associates hasn't improved, Mr. Gallo."

Gallo swung his legs off the bed and sat up. A smile spread across his jowls as he recognized his visitor. "If it isn't the head G-man himself! You should be thanking me, Mr. Hoover. I've managed to make your boys out here look pretty good."

"We don't need help from hooligans like you."

"You got here a little too late to take credit for the arrest. Your boy there beat you to it." Gallo smiled and flicked an ash to the floor.

"We don't need foreign reprobates like you fouling our cities, Mr. Gallo. I intend to see you prosecuted to the fullest extent of the law and put away for the rest of your days." Hoover glanced around at the small cubicle holding his prisoner. "Better get used to the accommodations. And clean up that mess on the floor. We don't have maid service." A thin grin animated Hoover's face as he turned and strode back down the corridor.

Director Hoover had decided that Joan Roswell, in exchange for exclusive access to the most sensational crime of the year, would serve as his liaison for Monday morning's press conference. He set Agent Ammons to the task of rounding her up.

Wainwright pulled Ammons aside and mumbled something in his ear about Joan going missing from the room she was supposed to be in with Miss Tully. "She can't have gone far," he said. "She left her clothes in the closet."

CHAPTER 83

Ammons took the elevator to the twelfth floor at the St. Francis and headed down the hall to the rooms of the Temple party. He hated to start knocking on the doors, being all too aware that the previous two days had been filled with anxiety, stress, and too little rest. But even more than knocking on doors, he hated going back to Agent Wainwright—and Director Hoover—and admitting that he couldn't find Roswell. That, as they said around the office, could turn into a "career decision."

A quick check with Miss Tully in Room 1219 revealed Joan had not returned. *I'll start with Mr. Griffith's room,* Ammons decided, consulting the list of room numbers and names in his note pad. There, Ammons heard movement inside as soon as he rapped on the door. He heard the safety chain slide and then a bleary-eyed John Griffith was peering through the crack of the slightly-open door.

"What time is it?" Griffith's voice was gravelly and thick.

"About eleven-fifteen. I'm sorry to bother you. I'm trying to find Miss Roswell."

Griff snorted. "She sure is hell isn't in here! I haven't seen her since we got back to the hotel."

"Sorry. Go back to sleep."

"I think I will," Griffith said and closed the door. Ammons made a check mark next to 1218.

He decided to skip the Temples' room for now, thinking it unlikely Joan would be in there. Ammons moved down the hall to the next room on his list, 1221. He knocked and waited a few moments, then knocked again. The door opened and a tousle-headed Darryl Zanuck, wrapped in a sheet, looked out through squinting eyes.

"What?" he snapped.

"I'm sorry to bo—"

"What do you want?"

"I'm looking for Miss Roswell. Director Hoover—"

"Joan!" Zanuck barked over his shoulder. He turned away from the door, leaving it just slightly open, and stumbled back toward the double bed. Ammons peered inside the room, seeing the naked back of a woman as she sat on the side of the bed pulling on one of the hotel's robes. She stood, her blond hair in disarray, and made her way to the door.

"Good morning, Agent Ammons," Joan Roswell said. Even without make-up, even with her face creased by sleep, Ammons thought her a real beauty.

"Sorry to disturb you, Miss Roswell, but Director Hoover sends his compliments and asks if you could join him for lunch at noon."

Joan hesitated, as if deciding whether to accept the invitation, then said, "Tell him I'll meet him at twelve-thirty, dear."

CHAPTER 84

"Kidnapping, extortion, conspiracy, obstruction of justice, assault on a federal officer—that's just a preliminary list of federal charges," Wainwright said, his eyes running down the sheet of paper in his hand.

Hoover sat behind the desk in an unoccupied office, making notes on a legal pad. "Good, very good. We're going to load these boys up and we're not going to let the lawyers cut any deals. All these foreigners are going to understand that you don't kidnap children in the United States of America if you want to have a long and happy life."

There was a knock on the office door and Agent Ammons stuck his head inside. "Miss Roswell, sir."

"Send her in." Hoover stood, straightened his tie and put on his friendliest smile. "So, you're the famous Joan Roswell I've heard so much about," he said, stepping toward the door to meet his guest. She was a beautiful woman, even if she did look a little tired—but who wouldn't after the ordeal of the last couple of days? "Edgar Hoover," he said, offering his hand. "How about a sandwich and a cup of coffee?"

"If you don't have anything stronger," Joan replied with a laugh. Hoover guided her to an armchair in front of the desk.

"Agent Ammons, please bring us some lunch and some coffee." The agent retreated, pulling the door closed.

"Let me start by thanking you for the cooperation you've given the bureau, Miss Roswell. On the one hand, you helped us quickly break open this case. On the other, against your professional impulses, I'm sure, you helped us keep it out of the papers while Wainwright and his men solved the case. I think Agent Wainwright here would agree that the lack of interference from the press is one reason we were able to run the bad guys to ground so quickly—and reunite a little girl with her family."

"My, you've quite the way with words, Mr. Hoover," Joan purred, digging through her purse and pulling out a pen and note pad. "May I quote you?"

Hoover chuckled. "Not just yet. I've got a more attractive deal to offer."

"I like attractive deals. Especially ones that include a good story." Joan smiled, her green eyes holding contact with Hoover's.

"You've been in on this story from the beginning. I'd like for you to be its official chronicler."

"Is this a job offer?"

"Not exactly. It's an opportunity for you to tell the inside story of the most sensational, most successful FBI operation since Dillinger. You've got a famous movie star, America's favorite, kidnapped off a moving train right under the nose of her private security. You've got the

White House involved, foreign governments, nefarious crooks, organized crime—"

"They seemed rather disorganized to me."

"—dedicated agents of the FBI, heroism by civilians and law enforcement, why you've even got a sea battle! And you can have the 'inside scoop,' as you press people like to say. You can be an eyewitness to history and the lens through which that history is shared with the rest of the country. What do you say?"

Joan tittered. "Where do I sign?"

Hoover clapped his hands together. "Terrific! You'll have access to our records, first opportunity to interview witnesses and even the criminals once they've been arraigned. It's your story. I trust you to tell it fairly and that in that fair telling the Bureau's reputation will be burnished."

Ammons knocked on the door and entered with a tray holding three white ceramic mugs and an aluminum pot.

"Thanks. Set it right there," Hoover pointed to the corner of the desk. "I'll ask one thing in return, Miss Roswell: that you help me coordinate a press conference tomorrow morning. I want all the San Francisco papers and the *Mercury* from San José too. That's where the kidnapping started. If the L.A. papers can get reporters here, all the better. The wire services, of course, and radio—I want the networks to cover this. With Shirley Temple as the victim, this has worldwide appeal. Maybe we even get the BBC."

"But I get to break the story?"

"Agreed. You can release your story in time for your newspaper's deadline; it's the *Standard*, correct?"

"That's right."

"Your preliminary story can run in the *Standard's* Monday morning edition. What do you say?"

"I need a typewriter and a telephone."

Hoover had summoned Ammons back into the office and given him instructions to supply Joan with a desk, a telephone, and whatever supplies she needed. Joan shook his hand again and followed Ammons out of the office.

"What do you think?" Wainwright asked as the door closed.

Without answering, Hoover stepped behind the desk and picked up the telephone. "Get me Clyde Tolson at headquarters." After a two-minute wait, Hoover's assistant came on the line. "Clyde? Edgar. Everything's resolved out here. The victim is back with her family and the perpetrators are in custody. Wainwright's team did an outstanding job, even got all the money back. Listen, I need you to rush a little research job. Get me everything you can find on Joan Roswell. R-O-S-W-E-L-L. She's a reporter for the Los Angeles *Standard*. Used to be an actress at Twentieth Century. She's going to do some publicity work for us and I want some insurance that it gets done right. And Clyde, enjoy the rest of your Sunday afternoon."

"Mr. Wainwright?" asked his secretary. "There's a call for you from Grace Tully. She says it's urgent."

"Excuse me, sir," Wainwright said to the Director. Hoover impatiently waved him away.

"This is Agent Wainwright," he said when he picked up the phone in his office.

"Oh, thank goodness. This is Grace Tully. I heard from Steve Early just now. He had a long talk with the President and the President has issued a news black-out on the kidnapping of Shirley Temple." Grace quickly related the reasons for the President's decision. "I'm so sorry, Agent Wainwright. You and the FBI did such a wonderful job recovering Shirley, and I wish you could shout it from the rooftops. But that's politics."

"I guess so," Wainwright said. He sighed. "Wish me luck. I've got to go break the news to the Director."

"Good luck," Grace said.

CHAPTER 85

Darryl Zanuck and John Griffith got out of the car at the corner of Clay and Kearny Streets, smiled at each other, and walked in the front door of McDonough Brothers Bail Bonds carrying a brown briefcase.

"I'd like to see Pete," Zanuck said, a pleased smile still plastered on his face. He handed his card to the indifferent young man behind the counter. *This should be fun.*

"I'll see if he's in."

Probably one of the brothers' customers.

After a brief wait, the young man returned. "Right this way." Zanuck and Griffith followed their guide up a flight of creaky, wooden steps to the top of a landing. There, the young man knocked once, opened the paneled door and stepped aside.

"Mr. Zanuck," McDonough said, smiling, already on his feet. "This is a pleasant surprise."

More so for me than for you, pal. Zanuck shook hands. "You remember my associate, Griff."

"Sure, I do. Have a seat. What can I get you to drink?"

Griffith shot a quizzical look at his boss. "What are you drinking on a Sunday afternoon?" Zanuck asked.

McDonough walked over to the sideboard against his office wall. "Whiskey?" he asked, holding up a bottle of amber liquid.

"Make it three, then," Zanuck said.

Their host poured three glasses and handed one each to Zanuck and Griffith. "Have a seat, gentlemen, and tell me what brings you out on such a pleasant afternoon."

"We're here to settle up," Zanuck said with a smile as he settled into one of the matching straight backed chairs in front of McDonough's desk.

"Already?"

Griffith placed the briefcase on the desk, the latches turned to face McDonough, then sat down next to his boss.

"I'm not sure I understand."

"We were able to recover the ransom money early this morning," Zanuck explained.

"But surely the FBI boys will need to retain the funds as evidence, at least for a few weeks."

"You know, Pete, that's what I thought too, but it turns out they were willing to accept a notarized log of all the bills' serial numbers along with some photographs as evidence. So," Zanuck spread his hands apart, "we're paying you back in full. All of the money you raised, for which we are most grateful, we now return to you in accordance with the agreement we signed earlier this morning." Zanuck stood. "What time is it, Griff?"

"One-fifteen, boss."

Zanuck reached into his pants pocket and pulled out one ten and one five-dollar bill. "By my calculations, the interest on $200,000 for twelve hours at five percent comes to just under $14." He laid the bills on McDonough's desk, reached across and shook the stunned man's hand. "Pleasure doing business with you."

"But..." McDonough began as Zanuck turned toward the door.

"It's all right," Zanuck said, glancing over his shoulder as Griff stood to follow him. "Keep the change. Oh, and some of it may be a little damp." He pulled open the door and was halfway down the stairs when he heard McDonough shout.

"Can I at least get an autographed picture?"

CHAPTER 86

Hoover was fuming, his face flushed, his dark eyes burning with intensity as he paced back and forth in front of Wainwright's desk. "This fouls up everything! Everything!" the Director spat, addressing no one in particular. "The biggest coup in Bureau history and, and…" He stopped pacing and stared out the window. "We could have lived off the glow from this case for two years," he said softly.

"We could leak it. I know some of the local reporters," Wainwright said.

"We'll do no such thing!" Hoover said, spinning around to face his subordinate. "My orders come from the President himself. As much as I detest politics, I have to concede that the President has a better grasp of the international situation than I do. At least at this moment."

Hoover stalked over to the office door, yanking it open. "Get Miss Roswell in here!"

Joan was talking even before she walked through the door. "Here's an outline of the flow of the press conference. One for you," she said handing a sheet of paper to Hoover, "and one for you," handing a carbon copy to Wainwright. "The podium will be on the fifth step from the bottom, allowing you to see the faces of all the reporters and photographers standing below you. We'll have the microphones on the fourth step, so they won't obstruct your faces. NBC and CBS will cover it live. Still waiting to hear back from Mutual."

"There's been a change of plans," Hoover said, frowning.

Joan stopped short and looked up from her notes. "If you're worried about rain, I've already checked with the weather service. No rain until early afternoon. Now if you're planning to change venues, I need to know right now. The radio people will have to get new phone lines run."

"Stop." Hoover held up his hand. "The story's been changed."

Joan looked from Hoover to Wainwright, searching for understanding.

"The White House squashed the story," Wainwright said. "We can't mention Shirley Temple and the Italians because the British and the French and our own State Department are walking on eggshells trying to keep from embarrassing Mussolini. They want to keep his government from allying with the Germans."

"No Shirley Temple, no tie-in to the Italian government and all we have is a local story—a routine one at that," the Director sighed. He looked at Joan with his piercing eyes. "Cancel the press conference."

The room fell silent. Joan's eyes darted between the two men. "You do that and every newspaper reporter in town will think you're covering something up. It'll be like throwing meat to the dogs. They'll look at it as a challenge and they won't stop until they've embarrassed the Italians, the Bureau, and, more to the point, you."

"All right then, hold the press conference. Wainwright," Hoover said, "you'll give the briefing. I'll be on a plane heading east."

"That would also be a mistake," Joan said quickly. "I've already announced your presence. If you don't show up, you'll have the same problem as if you cancel."

"What the devil can I say? I can't drag the President into this. I can't beg the press for sensitivity to the international situation. Without Shirley and the Italian angle, it's essentially a local crime."

"Maybe not," Wainwright said, looking from his boss to the reporter. "We can still charge Gallo and his accomplices with automobile theft—"

"We need federal charges!" Hoover snapped.

"Parole violation. He's on parole from federal convictions. That gives us jurisdiction."

Hoover frowned. "You want me to stand in front of the networks and say we called them all out to discuss a parole violation?"

Joan smiled and began to titter.

"What's so funny, Miss Roswell?"

"The President wants to protect the Italians' image, right? Help him."

Hoover and Wainwright traded confused glances. "What do you have in mind?" the Director asked.

"Who got kidnapped?"

"Shirley Temple."

"Who else?"

Wainwright saw it first. "The Italian consul and his daughter."

"Right," Joan nodded. "And by whom?"

Hoover spoke slowly, thoughtfully. "By disgruntled Italian nationals seeking to damage the historically strong ties that exist between the United States and the Republic of Italy."

"Now you've got national news worthy of a press conference, dear."

"Nice work, Miss Roswell," Wainwright said, surprised by the reporter's insight and quick thinking. He glanced at his boss. A scowl had settled on Hoover's face.

"I'm afraid, Miss Roswell, that the President's gag order applies to you just as it does to us."

"We had an agreement, Mr. Hoover. I've kept my end of it."

"I, regretfully, am unable to keep mine." Hoover looked down at the toes of his polished shoes.

"You can't gag me, Mr. Hoover. Freedom of the press and all that."

"Wainwright? Could you give us a little privacy?" the Director asked.

"Of course, sir," Wainwright said, rising from his chair and quickly exiting the room.

Hoover perched on the front of the desk and picked up a thin folder. "I can't silence you, Miss Roswell. I can only appeal to your sense of patriotism and your good judgment. I've already explained why the President believes silence is in the best interests of our country. He believes it serves the cause of peace, that keeping Italy out of league with Hitler reduces the risk of a European war."

"What has that got to do with America's best interests? We're not Europeans."

Hoover opened the folder. "I've learned some interesting things about you since our conversation this morning. You have quite a track record."

Joan felt the fine hairs on her neck prickling. "I don't have a criminal record at all, Mr. Hoover."

Hoover smiled, looking up from the folder. "Everybody has a record. Some people have a lot of unpaid debts, for example. Some are two months behind on their rent."

"My finances are nobody's business and certainly not criminal issues."

"Bounced checks," Hoover continued looking down at his notes, "unpaid traffic tickets. That's really small stuff. Uh oh, here's something. Consorting with married men." He looked up again. "You understand what I mean when I say 'consorting?' Several names listed here, Miss Roswell."

"All in the past."

Hoover poked out his lips and shook his head. "Not according to Agent Ammons, although technically eleven o'clock this morning is in the past, isn't it?" Hoover stood, looking down at Joan's reddening face. "I wouldn't enjoy leaking any of this information, Miss Roswell." He leaned over so that his face was close to hers. "But I will do what I have to do to protect our country from all enemies, foreign and domestic. Don't doubt me on this."

Suddenly, his mood changed. "But I think we can come to an understanding that would be helpful to you as well as the country—and the Bureau."

"Go ahead," Joan said.

"As you can tell from the file we've been able to compile on you—on a Sunday at that—I am privy to all sorts of interesting information. In fact, my secretary, Miss Gandy, guards a file cabinet in my outer office just full of interesting information about prominent people, many of them in show business. We could do some horse-trading, you and I."

"What do you want in trade?" Joan said, trying to conceal her physical loathing of the portly director. *Surely not that!*

"The War on Crime that we waged against the gangs—Dillinger, Baby Face Nelson, the Barkers—is largely over," Hoover said. "But we have a serious problem in this country with communism. That evil doctrine threatens the happiness of the community, the safety of every individual, and the continuance of every home and fireside. Communists would destroy the peace of this country and thrust it into a condition of anarchy and lawlessness and immorality that passes imagination. Miss Roswell, it won't surprise you to learn that there are many communists in Hollywood. The ability of these masters of deceit to use movies to further their nefarious agenda is a direct threat to our American democracy, and I won't rest until they are rooted out."

He locked eyes with Joan. "I imagine you are in position to hear things I'd like to know about."

Joan nodded. "I could give you a list of names right now. Of course, if I were to get some big scoops that earned me a permanent job at the *Standard*, I'd be in position to find out a lot more."

Shirley Temple Is Missing

Hoover smiled. Joan smiled back.

"Miss Roswell," Mr. Hoover said, "I think this is the beginning of a partnership that will benefit our great country—as well as you and me."

CHAPTER 87

Darryl Zanuck stuffed his dirty clothing in the small bag he'd carried with him on the airplane. He was glad to be heading back to Los Angeles and glad to be taking the train. He'd endured a stressful two days since receiving Griff's gut-wrenching phone call Friday evening, but things had turned out OK. He'd even gotten in a little recreational therapy this morning. He smiled to himself.

There was a knock on the door. "It's open!" he called out.

Griff stuck his head in. "Need help with anything, boss? Gertrude and Shirley are already downstairs. The car's waiting to take us all to the station."

"No, thanks. I've just got this grip and this portfolio." Zanuck picked up his things and followed Griff into the corridor.

"I want to apologize again, boss," Griff began as the elevator began its descent.

"I'm glad we were able to get tickets on the overnight train. We can keep our little asset confined this time!" Zanuck cut his eyes toward Griff. Then he laughed and slapped the bodyguard on the shoulder. "Everything turned out all right. But let's make sure we don't go through this again, agreed?"

"Yes sir!"

The elevator settled, and the operator opened the gate. The two men stepped off and Zanuck turned toward the front desk.

"The car's this way, boss," Griff said, stopping to wait for Zanuck.

"I want to drop this in the mail at the desk." Zanuck held up a large envelope.

"What is it."

"It's an autographed picture of me. I'm sending it to Pete McDonough."

"Boss, when he asked for an autographed picture," Griff said, "I think he meant one of Shirley."

Zanuck grinned and said, "Yeah, I know."

CHAPTER 88

Late that afternoon, Agent Wainwright drove over to San Francisco Memorial with Grace Tully to pick up Missy LeHand. An orderly pushed her in a wheelchair across the polished lobby floor to the waiting sedan. Missy was pale but smiling, holding a vase full of delicate pink roses. "F.D. sent them," she explained to Grace once she was settled into the backseat. "Isn't he the sweetest man?"

Wainwright saw them to Room 1219, unable to stop himself from yawning as they rode up in the elevator. Outside the room, he said to Missy, "I'd love to take you to dinner tonight, but I'm afraid I'd fall asleep in my chair. How about tomorrow night? I hope you and Grace plan to be at the Director's press conference in the morning. We could make some plans after that."

Missy laughed. "I could use another forty winks myself," she said. "Yes, I'm sure Grace will want to go. But, unfortunately, our plane leaves at four for Los Angeles. We're taking the Super Chief back east tomorrow morning."

Wainwright's face fell.

"We could have lunch, though... Corey," Missy said, blushing a little.

Shirley Temple Is Missing

"It's a date," the agent said. He leaned in and gave Missy a kiss on her forehead. "Get some sleep."

In their room, Grace filled in Missy on the President's press black-out regarding Shirley Temple, and they decided to write some bland letters to friends to make it sound as though they had an ordinary weekend in San Francisco. Missy wrote to Bill Bullitt, her long-distance boyfriend. "We have had such a gay time I have only been able to drop into bed when I got to my room," she wrote. *Well, at least the last part is true.* Grace sent postcards to her mother and her sister, Paula, in Washington. "A swell trip! See you soon!"

About 6 p.m., a bellhop delivered a large box of chocolates to Room 1219. The card read, "Missy and Grace, I can't thank you enough. Please come visit us next time you are in California. Gertrude Temple." Underneath it, Shirley had carefully printed, "Thank you very much. Love, your friend, Shirley Temple."

"Now that's something to add to my scrapbook," Missy said. "What a sweet child."

"Her mother was a lovely roommate this weekend too," Grace said. "Even with all the pressure she was under, she was always kind and courteous."

"I wish I could say the same thing about *my* roommate," Missy said. "How'd she behave last night? She still has one of my nightgowns! And I suspect her of stealing my pinky ring."

Grace grinned. "To be honest, I don't think she stayed in this room last night. When I woke up this morning, she was gone, and the bed hadn't been used. But her clothes were still in the closet."

Missy raised her eyebrows and the two friends burst into gales of laughter. They were still wiping the tears from their eyes when they heard a knock at the door.

"Speak of the she-devil," Grace said, opening the door for Joan Roswell.

"Hello, dear," Joan said. "I just came to check on Miss LeHand, and let her know I found her ring." She reached into her pocket and produced the onyx pinky, placing it into Missy's hand.

"Oh, thank you," Missy said, arching an eyebrow. "Wherever did you find it?"

"In the bathroom," Joan said. She gave Missy a sly smile. "That's quite an inscription in that ring, FDR 'with love.'"

Missy bristled. "Oh, don't be making something big out of that. The President writes 'with love' on just about everything he gives to the staff, doesn't he, Grace?"

"He surely does!" Grace said indignantly.

Joan purred, "Well, I can understand that, but I don't know that the average American would. Nice flowers," she said, nodding at the roses. "Did the President send those too?"

"What do you want?" Missy asked.

Joan seated herself in the desk chair and crossed her legs. "I want access," she said. "I want to be the first woman reporter to attend one of the President's press conferences."

Missy sputtered. "You know I can't do that! It's a long-standing tradition that only male reporters attend.

Now, I can get you into Mrs. Roosevelt's press conferences without any trouble at all."

"You don't understand, dear," Joan said. "I'm trying to break through a barrier here. I'm not interested in being one of a flock of old hens clucking around the First Lady."

Missy and Grace exchanged long looks. Finally, Missy said, "I'll see what I can do. And kindly return my nightgown!"

MONDAY, OCTOBER 14, 1935
SAN FRANCISCO

CHAPTER 89

The press conference took place on the front steps of the Federal Building at ten o'clock on Monday morning. Joan Roswell handed out a typed agenda to twenty-five members of the press, including correspondents from three radio networks and four wire services.

At ten-oh-two, Hoover, trailed by Wainwright, walked out of the front door and down the steps to the microphones. Following the agenda, Hoover spoke first. He described the ordeal of Cosimo Palladino and his daughter in heavily edited detail. By previous agreement among all parties, neither the consul nor Renata were present. Next, Wainwright detailed the charges pending against Joseph Gallo and his accomplices, explaining the federal laws, among them conspiracy, which had been violated. "Following their arraignment and trials, these men will be remanded to the custody of the U.S. Immigration Service for deportation proceedings."

"Are there any questions?" Joan asked from behind the microphones once Wainwright had finished.

"Oliver Kaplan from the *Chronicle*, Mr. Hoover. Why are you here?"

"I am here to demonstrate the resolve of the United States government to respond vigorously and effectively when the safety of diplomats serving in this country is jeopardized. Let this case be a warning to any foreign anarchists: the United States of America will defend not only our borders and our government, but also our friends from around the world who have come here to help maintain good international relations, relations like those which have long existed between America and our Great War ally, Italy."

There were a few more questions, all of which Hoover smoothly fielded, but soon, the radio men were taking down their equipment and the newspaper reporters began to drift away.

Joan Roswell shook hands with Hoover and Wainwright. "Next time you're in Los Angeles, give me a call." She smiled.

"I may just do that," Hoover smiled back.

"What bone did you throw her?" Wainwright asked as the two men watched the beautiful blonde woman climb into a taxi.

"Not much in the scheme of things. My thanks, of course, and a first-class train ticket back to L.A. I understand Miss LeHand offered some behind-the-scenes access to the President. I didn't get involved but that probably tipped the scales." Hoover paused as the cab pulled away from the curb. "I did give her a Hollywood story."

"Really?"

Hoover pulled a folded copy of the *Examiner's* front page from his coat pocket. Next to a headline proclaiming, "Press Conference Today; Hoover to Detail

Investigation," was a smaller article. "Here," Hoover pointed.

> ### CRAWFORD, TONE WED
> **By Joan Roswell, Special to the AP—Englewood, New Jersey**—*Confidential sources report that actress Joan Crawford and actor Franchot Tone were secretly wed at the home of Englewood Mayor Herbert Jenkins on Friday evening. Crawford, the former Mrs. Douglas Fairbanks, Jr., is currently starring in MGM's* I Live My Life. *Tone returns to the silver screen in next month's MGM production of* Mutiny on the Bounty *starring alongside Clark Gable and Charles Laughton.*
> *The happy couple is honeymooning at an undisclosed, fashionable New York state hotel. Representatives from the studios declined to comment. This is Crawford's second marriage and Tone's first.*

"You amaze me, sir," Wainwright said with a chuckle. "How'd you know about that?"

"In our business, information is currency. Want to keep someone from telling a secret? You better have another secret to trade. Never forget that."

"Do you know at what 'fashionable' hotel the 'happy couple' is staying?"

"Of course. But if you give everything away, the press will get lazy." Hoover chuckled. "I'll bet the newly-weds don't stay 'happy' for long."

After Hoover re-entered the Federal Building, Wainwright walked down the steps to Missy and Grace, who had watched the press conference from a discreet distance. "How about lunch, ladies?" he asked. "You've hardly gotten to see the city. We can take a cable car down to Fisherman's Wharf. There's a great little place that just opened, serves the freshest seafood in the city. We can get a bite there and walk around a bit, look at the seals."

"Oh, you two go," Grace said. "I've still got packing to do at the hotel."

"Are you sure?" Missy said.

"Go on!" Grace urged her. "I'll be fine."

Missy and Corey had a lovely afternoon. They rode a bright green cable car down the Powell-Mason line to Taylor Street, where they ate clam chowder and sourdough bread at the Fisherman's Grotto. It had recently been opened by an Italian family from Sicily, the Geraldis. "There are plenty of good, hard-working Italian families in San Francisco," Corey said. "I don't want you to get the wrong idea because of Topo and Big Joey." Suddenly, he began to laugh.

"What's so funny?" Missy asked, smiling at the handsome agent.

"I learned something funny about Marcello Altobello yesterday," Corey said. "His nickname is 'Topo.' It means mouse in Italian."

"Well, that's one mouse that won't escape the trap," Missy said. "Now the FBI can say it always gets its man— even if the man is a mouse!"

They watched the seals in the harbor, and looked across the bay to the forbidding new prison at Alcatraz

Island. "I wonder if any of our new 'friends' will wind up there?" Missy wondered.

"Maybe for a short while," Corey said. "But most will be deported back to Italy. I'm sure Mussolini will be glad to have some new recruits for his army of occupation in Ethiopia."

"Where will it all end?" Missy asked. "I thought the Great War was going to be the 'war to end all wars.'"

"I did too," Corey said. "After this weekend, I'm sure not anxious to go back to Italy."

At two-thirty, they reluctantly turned their steps back toward the trolley stop and returned to the St. Francis. Grace was waiting in the lobby with their luggage and, with the help of a bell hop, Wainwright loaded it into the trunk of his car. Then he delivered the ladies to the airport.

"Write me some time," Missy said as they said good-bye. Grace stood discreetly several yards away. "And if you're ever in Washington, come over to the White House. I'll introduce you to the Big Boss, as Shirley calls him."

"I'll suggest Mr. Hoover hold a conference of all his SACs very soon," Wainwright said. "Good-bye, Missy."

Missy stood on tip-toe and kissed his cheek. "Good-bye, Corey," she said. "Thanks for everything."

EPILOGUE

Rome, Italy

Fausto Trevisano followed the secretary along the wide marble arcade. He had worn his tailored dark wool suit, his pocket handkerchief, folded just so, complementing his white shirt. His shoes had been polished and buffed until he could see his face smiling up at him.

He had been preparing for this day ever since His Excellency the consul had told him he was to report to Rome. His excitement had grown with each passing day, peaking as he had boarded the train for Chicago. He'd enjoyed a weekend in America's Windy City, marveling at the tall buildings, the elegant shops along Michigan Avenue, and the dark, menacing waters of the lake. Once he had resumed his trip, his excitement began to build again.

He had read a lot on the voyage, sitting, when the weather permitted, on a blanket-covered deck chair, enjoying the cold ocean air, the expanse of endless blue water. Gibraltar had taken his breath away as his ship had steamed through its straits and into *mare nostrum.*

Following his half-day train ride from Naples to Rome, Fausto had checked into a fine hotel on Via Veneto and prepared for this morning's visit. Now, as he trailed behind the aide, he felt his chest swell with pride in his service for the empire, for Il Duce. *What great assignment awaits? To what capital shall I be posted? Is it too much to hope for an ambassadorship? Then I too will be known as "Excellency."*

His guide opened a door on the right and stepped inside. Fausto followed. Several young women wearing the uniform of the women's army auxiliary were seated behind desks, their nimble fingers dancing across typewriter keys, the resulting noise sounding like a battlefield filled with machine guns.

The guide knocked on yet another door, hesitated a moment and pushed it open. He stood to the side and waved Fausto through. Fausto came to a halt in front of a desk behind which sat a handsome, though balding man, of approximately forty-five. His remaining hair was dark and very short, a pencil-thin mustache rested above his unsmiling lips.

The man, uniformed as a major in the army, sat back in his chair, a cigarette glowing between his fingers. He said nothing, simply staring at Fausto for a long moment.

"Fausto Trevisano, at your service," Fausto said when the silence finally made him uncomfortable.

"Your reputation precedes you, Signore Trevisano," the major said. He continued to stare, and Fausto wondered if perhaps his fly was unbuttoned.

"I am pleased to hear this," Fausto said, flashing a smile more confident than he actually felt.

The major finally looked down at the papers on his desk. "Il Duce has need for someone with your special blend of skills. Someone who understands the logistics of complex operations and has the heart of the lion. Someone who inspires all who know him."

Fausto nodded his head. "I stand ready and able to report to the embassy of Il Duce's choice."

"There are no obstacles to your immediate assignment? No errands or chores you must complete before your new posting begins? No family visits, nothing like that?"

"Nothing at all. I stand before you and await Il Duce's command."

"Excellent." The major leaned over and began to fill in a form on his desk. "I am writing today's date on these travel orders. Carry them along with one suitcase." The major handed the documents to Fausto.

"Will the rest of my luggage be shipped separately?" Fausto asked as he scanned his orders. "Ah, there appears to be a mistake," Fausto said, smiling, the first beads of sweat beginning to pop out on his forehead. "These are military travel orders."

"I am not in the diplomatic corps, I am in the army. Just as you now are, *Caporale* Trevisano." The major stood and pressed a button on his desk. The guide reappeared at the door. "Take Caporale Trevisano to the quartermaster and have them fill his requisition for equatorial gear." He switched his attention back to Fausto. "You'll find our standard uniforms are much too hot for Ethiopia."

Washington, D.C.

The mail clerk at the White House gave Missy two packages a few weeks before Christmas, both marked personal. The first bore the return address of the Federal Bureau of Investigation and came from J. Edgar Hoover. "I am happy to send you Courtney Ryley Cooper's new book *Ten Thousand Enemies*," read the letter. "Naturally, because of the subject matter treated upon in this book, it has meant a great deal to me, and I trust that you will find some things of interest in reading it. Unfortunately, one of the most interesting cases, as you well know, will likely never be included in a volume such as this. Thank you for your assistance and discretion in this matter."

Missy smiled a bit grimly and picked up the next package, a much smaller one with a San Francisco postmark. Inside it was a white jewelry box, which she opened. On a bed of cotton lay a gold charm, shaped like a tiny mousetrap, and baited with a heart. She delicately lifted it out of the box and turned it over, reaching for her glasses so she could read the inscription. It said simply, "4:40 A.M." This made her smile in a different way, and a little color appeared in her cheeks as she gently laid the little charm back in its box.

Her intercom squawked. "Yes, F.D.?" she said.

"Come in here a moment, would you, Missy?"

The President was alone in the Oval Office, reading a newspaper. "Say, Missy," he said, "I see that Shirley Temple's new movie *The Littlest Rebel* is being released at Christmas. Why don't you see about getting a copy and we'll watch it during the holidays when my grandchildren visit. Sistie and Buzzie should love it."

"Of course, F.D.," Missy said. She got a mischievous grin on her face. "You aren't planning to show them that special feature, are you?"

The President roared with laughter, almost as loudly as when she had sneaked the short scene of Shirley Temple in her Italian army uniform into his projector a few weeks before. He'd said it was the best imitation of the Italian dictator he'd ever seen, and suggested copies be anonymously sent to movie houses all over America.

"You got that autographed picture off to little Shirley, didn't you?" he asked.

"Yes, she should have it by now," Missy said. "Is there anything I can do to help you prepare for your press conference?"

"No," the President sighed. "The mangy mongrels will be in here in about ten minutes, snapping and baying and snarling."

"Call me if you need me to restrain them," she laughed. "I'll be at my desk."

"Is your 'special guest' here yet?" the President asked, raising his eyebrows.

"She just checked in at the south gate," Missy said. "Thanks, F.D."

When Missy stepped back into her office, the "special guest" had arrived.

"Hello, dear," purred Joan Roswell. She was sporting a stylish new fox fur neckpiece, complete with head and paws, draped around the shoulders of her hunter green wool suit. Missy greeted her with a simple, "Hello, Joan." *Probably caught the poor beast with her bare hands and skinned it with her teeth.*

"I had the most interesting chat with Mr. Hoover this morning," Joan said as she lit a cigarette. "He's given me all sorts of useful leads to follow up in Hollywood, and he's even promised me a personal tour of Alcatraz Prison next time he's on the west coast. He might even get me an exclusive interview with Prisoner 433. You know, Al Capone? Now, where should I sit to do my eavesdropping on the news conference?"

"I'll crack the door," Missy said, giving her an icy, blue-eyed stare. "You should be able to hear everything from where you are sitting. I'll only allow you to do this once. The President is very strict about his male-only press conferences. And, remember, Joan, this is our quid pro quo."

Joan exhaled her smoke, and looked at Missy blankly. "I'm sorry, dear," she said. "I don't speak French."

El Sauzal, Mexico

Corey Wainwright removed his Panama hat and wiped the headband with his handkerchief. It was already over eighty degrees on a June day in 1936, and the clock had yet to strike ten in the morning. He loosened his tie. *The hell with the dress code. It's too damn hot!* Fans on the ceiling of the train station were turning lazily, doing little to alleviate the stuffiness as travelers milled about. Most of them seemed to be waiting to board the train for its return journey to Tijuana and San Diego.

After today, he would close the case on the Temple kidnapping. Then he'd seal the file, bury it in a box with a couple of dozen other closed investigations and send it to the federal records storage facility in Oakland. And that would be the end of it—the end of the most extraordinary investigation of his career—an investigation he was under orders never to discuss privately or publicly.

Wainwright exited the station into the hot, bright morning sun. He was grateful for the hat and the sunglasses Missy had recommended. The President had fished the waters off the peninsula last year and had shared with his secretary how bright the sun had seemed, reflecting off the sandy ground and the marshmallow-white clouds. In fact, against the deep blue of the sky everything below appeared light, from the loose-fitting, rough cotton clothing worn by the men and women to the whitewashed buildings.

Wainwright stopped in a cantina at the corner of Calle Primera and paid a nickel for a Coca-Cola. *Once this is over, I'll have something stronger.* He stood in the shaded corner of the open-air room and looked at his written directions. *No point getting there too early.*

Wainwright finished his Coke and carried the bottle back up to the bar. He tipped his hat and stepped back out into the sun. *Hotter already.* He walked east, past a general store with both cars and horses parked out front, then turned southeast and headed along the beach road. By

378

the time the road ran out, he could see his destination ahead. "Connor's Irish Pub" the hand-painted sign read.

The sand was deeper here, spilling into his shoes. He thought about taking them off but figured the sand would burn his un-calloused feet. He pushed through the low dunes and stepped onto a wooden porch, pleased for the roof which for the moment at least was blocking the sun. He removed his hat again and mopped his neck and his brow with the handkerchief.

The pub was little more than three walls nailed together from rough-hewn lumber around a cracked and pitted concrete floor. The two side walls each ran about half the length of the roof, leaving most of the tables and chairs covered, but still with unobstructed views of the beach and the surf. The bar sat along the structure's long back wall. There were already two patrons seated there with their backs to the sea.

Wainwright took a seat near the edge of the floor closest to the waves. The rhythmic splashing of the waves against the shoreline was soothing after the jerking, screeching sounds of the train. Here was peace and quiet, a slower pace. *A man could do some serious thinking here.*

The table looked like it had met every knife blade in Baja at some point over the last thirty years. He thought about adding his own initials and the date. *I won't be here that long.* He set his hat on the wooden chair next to him and leaned back.

A light-complexioned woman wearing a loose cotton blouse and colorful, full skirt stepped from behind the bar and walked toward him. "*Que vas a tener?*" she said when she reached Wainwright's table.

"You don't look Mexican," he said with a smile.

"Neither do you. You're a wee bit overdressed too. You want a drink?"

"I heard you could get a cold Guiness here."

"You're in luck; the refrigerator's working today. Be right back."

A pretty woman. Must be the real thing to follow a man to the middle of nowhere.

When the woman returned, she set a frosty glass of dark liquid on the table along with a bowl of fried tortillas. "Let me know when you need a refill," she said. "My name is Iris."

"Thanks. Say, is Connor here? I'd like to meet him; find out how he came to be all the way down here."

"He's in back tending to accounts. I'll send him out." She smiled and headed back toward the bar.

The cold stout was a refreshing sensation on the back of his throat. Wainwright looked out at the blue waters and enjoyed the gentle breeze blowing in. *It's really not bad in the shade.*

"I'm Connor," the red-headed man said, extending his hand. Wainwright stood.

"Pleased to meet you. I'm down from San Francisco, wanted to say hello. Join me?" Wainwright nodded toward the table.

"Sure. Don't get that many visitors all the way down here." He sat in the chair opposite Wainwright and gestured toward Iris at the bar.

"I know it's a little early in the day," Wainwright said with a chuckle.

"Well," Connor smiled, "never too early for a friendly drink. It's when you're drinking alone that you have to be careful. San Francisco, huh? Never been there."

Iris set another glass on the table, winked at Connor, and retreated to the bar.

"I guess we're even," Wainwright said, still friendly. "I've never been to El Sauzal before."

"What brings you down south?"

"Just tying up some loose ends on a business deal."

Connor took a sip of Guiness. "What kind of business you in, Mister—?"

"The name's Wainwright, Corey Wainwright. I'm in law enforcement." He reached into his pocket, pulled out a small black wallet and flipped it open to reveal his FBI badge.

Connor froze for a moment, his eyes widening as they looked down at the badge. "No kidding," he managed to say.

"No kidding." Wainwright closed the wallet and placed it back in his pocket.

Connor took another drink, set his glass down and looked Wainwright in the eyes. "I don't guess that badge does you a lot of good in Mexico, does it?"

Wainwright smiled. "It seems to have gotten your attention, which is why I'm here, Mr. Archie."

"The name's Connor."

"You're a lucky man, Mr. Archie. You committed a federal crime and you got away with a lot of loot and your reputation more or less intact."

"I think you've got me confused—"

"We both know I haven't. But you can relax. I'm not here to arrest you—as much as I'd like to. I'm here to convey a message from J. Edgar Hoover, the Director of the Federal Bureau of Investigation. That name sound familiar?" Wainwright didn't wait for a response. "Because of your role in a certain kidnapping scheme, you're *persona non grata* in the United States, Mr. Archie."

Connor cleared his throat. "I don't know what that means."

"It means 'I hope you like tortillas, pal, because if you ever set foot north of the border I'll arrest you before you can say Sure Shot and Iris over there will have to manage this joint on her own.'"

Wainwright kept his eyes on Connor's as he reached over for his hat. He stood, put it on and walked over to the bar. "Thanks for the beer, Iris," he said, handing her a silver dollar. "It was nice to talk to you."

Iris smiled as the stranger walked across the plank porch and back onto the sand. At the edge of the pub, her husband sat staring out to sea.

HISTORICAL BACKGROUND FOR THIS BOOK

SHIRLEY TEMPLE IS MISSING is a work of fiction, though some of its characters were real people—used fictitiously, of course. In fact, Shirley and Missy LeHand had at least one meeting, similar to the one described on the Twentieth Century-Fox lot, when Shirley posed for a picture in her hoop-skirted *Littlest Rebel* dress with Missy and some other studio guests. However, the meeting did not result in a train ride on the *Daylight*. (In fact, the *Daylight* did not have its maiden run until 1937.)

Shirley was never kidnapped, though the studio did receive some extortion threats, and Twentieth Century-Fox did indeed take out a $795,000 insurance policy on her life. She was that important an asset to his studio. Zanuck assigned his own bodyguard, John Griffith, to protect his little star.

Of the Washington crowd, J. Edgar Hoover served as director of the Federal Bureau of Investigation for more than fifty years. Grace Tully, Steve Early, and Marvin McIntyre worked together in the West Wing of the White House, and Grace and Missy were such close friends they often spent their vacations together.

Most of the other characters in the book are fictional. Alas for Missy, the imaginary characters include

383

Corey Wainwright. The devious reporter Joan Roswell migrated into this book from Kelly Durham's Pacific Pictures Series, set in the 1940s, after Joan had become a successful syndicated gossip columnist who made studio heads quake in their shoes.

Finally, Shirley Temple was indeed a terror with her sling-shot, which she used on the backside of Eleanor Roosevelt during a visit to Hyde Park in 1938. She got a well-deserved spanking from her mother.

If your curiosity about Shirley, Missy, J. Edgar Hoover and their times is piqued by our mystery, we recommend the following books:

- *Child Star: An Autobiography* by Shirley Temple Black. New York: McGraw-Hill Publishing, 1988.
- *The Little Girl Who Fought the Great Depression: Shirley Temple and 1930s America* by John F. Kasson. New York: W.W. Norton & Company, 2014.
- *The Gatekeeper: Missy LeHand, FDR and the Untold Story of the Partnership that Defined a Presidency* by Kathryn Smith. New York: Touchstone, 2016.
- *Ten Thousand Public Enemies* by Courtney Ryley Cooper, with foreword by J. Edgar Hoover. Boston: Little, Brown, and Company, 1935.

Shirley Temple Is Missing

- *Public Enemies: America's Greatest Crime Wave and the Birth of the FBI, 1933-34* by Bryan Burrough. New York: The Penguin Press, 2004.

ABOUT THE AUTHORS

Kelly Durham and Kathryn Smith attended D.W. Daniel High School near Clemson, South Carolina together, but didn't become friends until more than forty years later when Kathryn began editing some of Kelly's novels. This is their first collaboration.

Kelly lives in Clemson with his wife, Yvonne. They are the parents of Mary Kate, Addison and Callie, and also provide for their dog, George Marshall. A graduate of Clemson University, Kelly served four years in the U.S. Army with assignments in Arizona and Germany before returning to Clemson and entering private business. Kelly is also the author of THE WAR WIDOW, BERLIN CALLING, WADE'S WAR, THE RELUCTANT COPILOT, THE MOVIE STAR AND ME, HOLLYWOOD STARLET, TEMPORARY ALLIANCE and UNFORESEEN COMPLICATIONS. Visit his website, www.kellydurham.com, or contact him at kelly@kellydurham.com.

Kathryn lives in Anderson, South Carolina with her husband, Leo. They are the parents of two grown children and the grandparents of four small children. A graduate of the University of Georgia, Kathryn worked as a daily newspaper reporter and editor before entering nonprofit management work in Anderson. She is the author of the only biography of Marguerite LeHand, THE GATEKEEPER: MISSY LEHAND, FDR AND THE UNTOLD STORY OF THE PARTNERSHIP THAT DEFINED A PRESIDENCY (Touchstone, 2016) as well as A NECESSARY WAR, a collection of interviews with World War II veterans. Kathryn speaks widely on Missy LeHand, sometimes impersonating her in period costume. Visit her website, www.kathrynsmithwords.com, and the Missy LeHand page on Facebook.

ABOUT THE COVER ARTIST

Jed Bugini-Smith, a native of South Carolina and a high school mate of the authors, moved to Italy after a long and successful career as a senior creative leader in marketing. Today, Jed focuses his talents on personal expression and embraces writing, painting, and photography with equal passion. His blog, ItalyWise.com, which has developed a loyal following, chronicles his transition to becoming an American expat in Italy. Jed shares insights and advice about managing a multitude of logistics, as well as writing about navigating a host of mental and emotional challenges that come with making such a monumental life change.

An accomplished painter, Jed is a Signature Member of the prestigious National Watercolor Society.

Don't Miss the Next Missy LeHand Mystery!

The President's Birthday Ball Affair

Birthday Balls are being held around the country on January 30, 1936, President Roosevelt's 54th birthday, to raise money for polio patients. Missy LeHand volunteers to head up the money-counting detail at Washington's elegant Shoreham Hotel, where the glamorous film star Ginger Rogers is the special guest. But when Missy and Ginger try to take the money to the bank's night deposit, they are waylaid by armed men and the money is stolen.

Who is behind this crime, that not only deprives polio patients of desperately needed funds, but also is politically embarrassing to FDR? Once again, Missy and Corey Wainwright, who is visiting Washington for an FBI special agents' conference, team up to solve the crime. And once again, wily reporter Joan Roswell is pulling out all the stops to get a scoop!

Made in the USA
Columbia, SC
05 February 2018